UNHALLOWED GROUND

**Center Point
Large Print**

Also by Heather Graham
and available from Center Point Large Print

A Magical Christmas
Suspicious
The Island
The Dead Room
The Death Dealer
Nightwalker

UNHALLOWED GROUND

HEATHER GRAHAM

CENTER POINT PUBLISHING
THORNDIKE, MAINE

This Center Point Large Print edition
is published in the year 2009 by arrangement with
Harlequin Books S.A.

The text of this Large Print edition is unabridged.
In other aspects, this book may vary
from the original edition.
Printed in the United States of America.
Set in 16-point Times New Roman type.

ISBN: 978-1-60285-585-4

Library of Congress Cataloging-in-Publication Data

Graham, Heather.
  Unhallowed ground / Heather Graham. -- Large print ed.
    p. cm.
  ISBN 978-1-60285-585-4 (library binding : alk. paper)
  1. Private investigators--Fiction. 2. Dwellings--Conservation and restoration--Fiction.
  3. Florida--Fiction. 4. Ghosts--Fiction. 5. Murder--Investigation--Fiction.
  6. Large type books. I. Title.

PS3557.R198U54 2009
813'.54--dc22

2009027903

To the city of St. Augustine,
and especially to Derek and Pablo-the-cat
and our road trip.
To the carriage and tour companies—
and everyone who's fascinated by the unique
legends of our nation's oldest European-founded
city.
It's a remarkable place to visit.
Thanks, also, to the Inn on Charlotte,
Victoria House, and Casa de Suenos (where they
welcomed Pablo as well as the rest of us!)

Prologue

Then, during the War of Northern Aggression

St. Augustine, in northern Florida, was beautiful, especially by night. It was the image of everything graceful and lovely in the Deep South and, when seen by the gentle glow of the moon, as serene a place as one might ever hope to see. Spanish moss dripped from old oaks like the sweep of a gentle lace blanket, and a low ground fog swirled in a faint breeze that seemed to carry with it the whisper of a moan. The silver mist curled around the mournful beauty of the cemetery, caressing the cheeks of stone angels and cherubs standing atop newly dug graves, as well as those that had been there for centuries.

The moon that night had a haze promising rain the following day. The misty halo around the full orb cast an eerie glow over the earth, turning the cemetery into a magical vision with its praying virgins, weeping guardians and majestic display of marble statuary, all bathed in the pale and eerie light.

Two women came with a lantern, one with purpose, and one carefully picking her way around the gravestones and funerary art.

"This way," Martha Tyler said, lifting her lantern higher.

"How much farther?" Susan Madison asked nervously as the moon slipped behind a cloud and the shadows deepened.

Martha paused to stare back at her, contempt in her eyes. "If you are afraid, there is no reason to go any farther at all."

Well, of course, I'm afraid, Susan longed to shout. She hadn't been afraid before; it had all seemed like a lark, and why not? Life was a mess right now, and maybe Martha did have some kind of wonderful power to make everything better.

But now she *was* afraid. The beauty was gone from the night.

Only death seemed to remain.

Yes, she was afraid. She was walking in a shadowy graveyard by night, hearing nothing but the rustle of the leaves and the moan of the wind in the branches, and she was a fool ever to have thought that this would be an adventure.

She had convinced herself that she had to play this game, had to skirt the edge of social and moral insanity. The news in her life was always terrible, all about the war, death, advancing armies, defeats.

There was no guarantee that Thomas Smithfield would be alive in a matter of months, much less have anything left of his home, finances or wits. A love ritual might well be useless.

"We're here now, anyway," Martha said.

"We're here? Where is here?" Susan demanded, looking around. They had passed the MacTavish mausoleum, the giant sculpted dogs that guarded the eighteenth-century entrance to the section containing the graves of children, and even the oldest and most chipped and broken stones in the cemetery. They were standing by a small broken wall, where trees grew tall and broad, breaking through the stones of the dead, and the moss dripped almost to the ground. The earth itself didn't seem as if it belonged in any place created by man at all. It was more like a pit of churned dirt and broken pottery.

"Right here," Martha said, pointing. Her voice dropped to a whisper, so soft that Susan could barely hear it. "We're outside hallowed ground here. This wall—or what's left of it—marks the boundary beyond which they buried the indigents and the . . . the unhallowed."

Susan felt a sudden chill. It was summer, and even the nights could be sweltering here in the humid lowlands, with only the occasional breeze off the ocean to alleviate the wet heat. But tonight she was suddenly cold with a bone-deep sensation that came from far more than just the temperature.

Of course she was cold, she told herself. Martha was frightening her. That whisper she was using, the cemetery itself, bathed once again in the unearthly glow of shimmering moonlight filtered through haze and fog.

"You still have it? You didn't drop the sacrifice?"

Susan told herself that the ominous tone was all

part of Martha's act, but even so, she shuddered as she reassured herself that she still had the little vial of blood, wrapped so tightly in her hand that she had practically forgotten she was carrying it.

"Yes."

"You killed the creature yourself?" Martha asked.

"Yes."

Martha approved her answer with a solemn nod as she took the vial of blood from her. "Now the black drink."

Martha held up a small bottle filled with an inky liquid.

Susan stared at her.

"It's herbs, child, just herbs. But they create magic."

Susan wanted to refuse.

What was the matter with her? she wondered. All her friends had gone to Martha for potions and palm readings. Martha did have a talent for knowing what was going to happen. Not only could she foretell the future, but sometimes she could also actually make things happen. And always she was an amazing show-woman.

This was an adventure, Susan told herself, and maybe—just maybe—the potion would work.

Martha was standing in front of her, smiling, looking as gentle as a kitten, as well-meaning as a doting grandmother. She pressed the small bottle into Susan's hand and helped her lift it to her lips.

The concoction was sweet, not bad tasting, but it carried an aftermath of fire that sent slivers of steel running through her blood.

Suddenly crimson darkness descended, making a stygian pit of the cemetery, a fiery globe of the moon.

"I don't want to do this anymore," Susan said. Her voice sounded like a whimper, appalling her. "I'm sorry, I just want to leave."

Martha laughed, but the sound was husky and taunting, frightening her further. "Such a terrified little girl. We're here now, you've had the black drink, the worst is over. It's time."

The darkness lifted, and once again Susan found herself standing in the moonlight in the old cemetery she had walked through dozens of times before. There was nothing dark or terrifying or eerie about it; it was just a field of the dead.

And still, she wished she had never come.

But she didn't want to run away and leave Martha to tell the tale of her cowardice. It would be mortifying if everyone knew what a silly coward she had been. The things that were said about her already were bad enough.

But what were her choices.

Stay and dig up a grave? Or run out of the cemetery alone? Tamper with the dead, or flee through a haunted world of shadow and decomposition, with no companion other than her own thundering heart?

"In seconds, my pet, you will be on the road to all that your heart desires. A passion and a tempest unlike anything even you have imagined. You came to me for help. You wanted magic. You've come this far, don't stop now. Not before you secure all that you hope for on behalf of your babe and for your own life. It's time," Martha said. She sprinkled the blood across the disturbed earth of an antique grave, then lifted her arms to the night sky, the very image of a Druid priestess in a field of ancient stones or one of the voodoo queens of Jamaica, from where she had come long ago. She was not a colored woman, but neither was she white. She had no definitive color, really. She was a pasty shade, like the moon behind the haze, and her eyes were a strange and watery blue.

She didn't give Susan a chance to respond. She began to chant, her face lifted toward the sky, her arms still upraised. The words were unintelligible, a mix of English, French, Spanish and something more ancient. As Susan watched her, she felt herself becoming almost hypnotized by the magic lilt of the words. It was as if her limbs grew leaden, and any desire to be anywhere else left her. The tombstones and vaults, cherubs and angels, even the great guardian dogs, began to appear as natural a setting as the cozy parlor of her home, welcoming her.

The low-lying fog, caught in the amber glow of the moon, seemed to dance around her, wrapping her in an exciting warmth, fanning an ember deep inside her. She watched, she waited, she heard the music of the words and felt strength in the growing heaviness of her form. When she could move, she told herself, she would do so with passion and vitality. She would be vibrant and alive, filled with magic herself.

But even as the sense of well-being warmed her like a cup of cocoa on a cold night, something else was growing, as well. An inner voice warning her that she needed to shake off the leaden sensation. That she needed to run.

Because the ground was moving, erupting as if from a force deep inside, shifting the old stones that lay askew nearby. A shower of dust rose as something solid and large emerged from the ground, like a tree growing at a fantastic rate. Particles of dirt and dust and marble were caught in the faint glow of the tainted moon, gleaming like the snowflakes she had read about in books.

That inner voice screamed at her to run, but it was too late.

She saw what had risen, and a scream rose in her throat, but she couldn't move, and no sound issued from her lips. She could still see Martha, standing there now with a satisfied smile, and she knew that she was no more to the woman than a rung in a ladder, a stepping stone toward power over the darkness. She saw it all so clearly now.

13

And then she saw what was rising from the ground.

Saw that all Martha's promises had been no more than a ruse to get her there.

The horror approached her, malignant, evil, and she was paralyzed. She knew that whatever had been in the black drink was paralyzing her, saw everything so clearly now that it was too late—oh, God, far too late—to know and see and understand, to know that this had nothing to do with wonder and fantasy and magic.

She saw and felt the essence of evil, heard the rasp of its fetid breath, smelled flesh and blood and bone and the pungence of the earth as her fate stepped closer and closer still, drawing pleasure from her terror and her newfound knowledge . . .

She had not come to make a sacrifice.

She had come to *be* the sacrifice.

1

Now

The area near the nature preserve was overgrown. Salt flats and marsh met Matanzas Bay and the Intracoastal, and the water went from shallow to deep, from sloping sand to a sudden drop-off leading to a misty and strange world of fish, tangled plant growth and, despite the best efforts of local and federal lawmakers, de facto garbage dumps.

Caleb Anderson had been drawn to a shopping cart down at about twenty feet, then on to a tire rim beneath a tangle of seaweed at thirty-five, but neither one turned out to be hiding what they were looking for.

The problem was, the authorities were searching blindly. A girl named Winona Hart had disappeared. She had been at a party, but none of her underage drunken friends—half of them potheads to boot—seemed to know when she had left, where she had gone, or with whom.

He looked at his compass, then up through the filter of light to the cable from the police cruiser serving as their dive boat. In his mind, if anything was going to be found, it was going to be closer to the shore. Unless, of course, she'd been kidnapped by a boater and dumped somewhere beyond the bay and out in the Atlantic. If that was the case, their chances of finding her were almost nonexistent. The ocean was huge. True, if caught in a current or an undertow, a body might wash up on land. And if they came up with a suspect who regularly followed a certain route, even a weighted body might somehow be discovered.

But at the moment they were searching blindly. Still, he hadn't wanted to miss the opportunity to be in on the search, not when he had promised he would do everything humanly possible to find Jennie Lawson. Admittedly, this grim attempt was not to find Jennie but a local teen who had now been missing for nearly forty-eight hours, a case that might or might not be connected to Jennie's. No one knew if Jennie Lawson had actually made it to the beach in St. Augustine, her intended destination. They only knew that she had landed in Jacksonville, gotten off the plane and picked up a rental car. Neither she nor the car had been seen since.

He didn't have much hope of finding Jennie alive. Her mother had told him that she knew Jennie was gone, because her daughter had come to her in a dream the night before her disappearance was reported and said goodbye. Caleb wasn't sure what to believe, because Mr. Lawson seemed to think that Mrs. Lawson had lost her mind when their daughter had disappeared, and he had, in fact, made a motion behind his wife's back to indicate as much.

Caleb had heard of stranger things than ghostly midnight visits, however, so he had simply smiled and vowed to Jennie's mother that he would do everything he could to find out the truth, even if he couldn't return her daughter to her. That had comforted her. Closure was something people needed. Perhaps it was too painful to live with eternal hope.

So Caleb was also looking for Jennie, or any sign of her, even if he was officially on the trail of another young woman for whom many were still holding out hope. But this dive was important for other reasons, too; it was giving him a chance to get to know the local authorities and the local expert on the surrounding waters.

As he moved toward the marshy shore, he couldn't see more than a few feet in front of him, but he was accustomed to such conditions. His dive light illuminated the surrounding area as he searched, and he was methodical in covering his assigned section of the bay. He had seen the grid, and he meant to search his assigned area thoroughly, leaving no possibility that anything had been overlooked. As an out-of-stater, he was the odd man out here. If he did anything to make the other men—and the one woman—on the local forensic dive team resent his presence, he would end up ostracized, and that would be a real problem in his search for Jennie. For that reason, getting along with the police lieutenant in charge of the case, Tim Jamison, and Will Perkins, the dive master, was crucial. Caleb was there mainly as a courtesy. He worked for a private agency, Harrison Investigations. The cases they took generally had an unusual twist, something inexplicable, even supernatural, that required their very specific professional services, but in this instance it was Adam Harrison's personal friendship with Jennie Lawson's father that had brought Caleb here.

He noted a glitter of light, just this side of the drop-off. He focused his dive light, and headed toward the glint, knowing full well that it might be just another shopping basket.

But as he neared the object in the water, he knew that this was no shopping cart.

It was far too large, for one thing. The full size of it became clear as he drew closer. It was an automobile.

All too often, people intentionally discarded cars in the water. Sometimes they were just junkers and nothing more.

Sometimes they held human remains.

And as he approached the Chevy mired in the mucky, seaweed-laden sand, he saw that this car was not empty. A solid kick with his flippers brought him to the driver-side window.

A face stared out at him, the mouth widened in a giant *O*, as if in a desperate quest for breath.

The eyes . . .

Did not exist. Already, the creatures of the deep had started to feed.

"Maybe Osceola *was* a hero, but they still tricked him and caught him and cut his head off. They chopped it right off!" a young boy said. He was about ten, cute and normal-looking in a T-shirt that had clearly just been purchased at the local alligator farm, jeans and sneakers. But he spoke with a relish that unsettled Sarah McKinley. Caroline Roth, seated at the computer and running the audiovisual end of the Heritage House presentation, let out a soft laugh, stared at Sarah, then grinned wickedly and shrugged.

"No," Sarah said firmly, and smoothed down the skirt of her period outfit. She was a good storyteller and knew how to handle a large—and diverse—group like the one in the lecture hall that day, which was a mix of kids and adults, tourists and locals, couples, groups and singles. They were into the tail end of summer, so she was getting classes from schools that started early and teachers from schools that started late. There was a Harley event down in Daytona that week, so she was getting a lot of bikers, too.

One man in the crowd, though, seemed to stand out. He was tall, but not inordinately so, maybe six-three. He was dressed as casually as the next tourist in blue jeans and a polo shirt, but he didn't look like the usual tourist. He wore sunglasses throughout her lecture—not an odd thing, lots of people didn't take them off when they came in. He was built as if he were in the service and worked out heavily on a daily basis, or as if he were an athlete. He was tanned and rugged, the way a man who spent his day sailing might be, tawny-haired and attractive. What was odd about him, though, was that he was alone. He seemed the type who should be with a beautiful woman, one who was as lithe and athletic as he was himself.

"Decapitated!" another kid called out.

Sarah's attention was drawn back to her lecture. She had been talking about Osceola, the most famous leader of the Seminole people, who had galvanized friend and foe alike when he had struck a knife into a treaty that would have been a death knell for his people. Like so many others, he had been imprisoned at the Castillo de San Marcos, the coquina shell bastion built by the Spanish that was the most imposing architectural feature of the city.

Leave it to a kid to dwell on the most gruesome fact he could think of—not to mention that he had it wrong.

"History records lots of terrible things that were done, but that wasn't one of them," she said.

"Hey, I heard he was decapitated, too," a grown man interrupted.

Sarah took a deep breath. She couldn't really blame the guy—who had a sunburn identifying him as out-of-state—when even Florida school-children often had the story wrong. "Osceola was a great leader, and respected even by his enemies. The treachery that led to his capture was deplorable, and despite the Indian wars raging across the country at the time, people despised General Jesup for the way he treated Osceola, who came in peace, with his safety guaranteed, and was taken anyway. But he wasn't decapitated by the U.S. Army. He was held for a while at Fort Marion, originally known as the Castillo de San Marcos, but he died of malaria up at Fort Moultrie, in South Carolina. He was attended by a shaman from his own clan, and an American doctor, a man named Frederick Wheedon, who did have his head removed and embalmed, but only after he was already dead. And," she said, unable to resist, "legend has it that Dr. Wheedon used the head to punish his children. If they behaved badly, he would leave the head on their bedposts at night. In fact, he bequeathed the head to his son-in-law— just in case his grandchildren misbehaved. His son-in-law passed it on to a man named Valentine Mott, another doctor, who kept it in a pathology museum, but the museum burned down, and the head was lost."

She had gained the silent stares of everyone in the room, of every age, and she offered them a broad smile. "You can learn a lot about Osceola and Florida's Native Americans over at Fort

Marion, and we have wonderful books on Osceola and the history of the area in our bookstore. Remember, St. Augustine is over four hundred years old." She grinned at the boy who had first brought up the subject of decapitation. "All kinds of gruesome things have happened here."

She announced that her speech was over and was given a nice round of applause, and a number of people thanked her as they walked out of the lecture hall. A few lingered to examine the artifacts in the cases that lined the walls, but she noticed that the tall stranger who had drawn her attention wasn't among them.

Caroline, rising and stretching, started laughing as soon as the last of the four o'clock lecture group walked out of the room. "A few of those kids are going to wake up in the night imagining a head on their bedpost."

"Yeah?" Sarah asked. "I don't think that many kids have bedposts anymore."

"I'm sure lots of them are staying at local B and Bs. And lots of those beds have bedposts," Caroline reminded her.

"Well, what's a story without something scary?" Sarah asked, sinking into one of the front row seats. "And I didn't make anything up." She looked at Caroline and sighed. "Now you're going to give me a speech on being nice to tourists and downplaying our more gruesome history, right?"

Caroline shook her head. "No, not today, I'm

not." She frowned suddenly, distracted. "Do you think we know him from somewhere?"

"Him who?" Sarah asked.

Caroline looked at her and laughed again. "Him who was studly and cool. Oh, come on. You couldn't possibly have missed him."

"Yeah, I saw him," Sarah said. Caroline could only be talking about the man she had noted earlier in the crowd. "But what about him?"

"I felt like I knew him, or *should* know him, from somewhere."

"He was good-looking—"

Caroline stared at her hard.

"Okay, I admit he looked a little bit familiar, but maybe he's just so gorgeous he reminds me of a movie star or something."

Caroline shrugged. "I don't know, I just had a feeling about him. . . . It's like he looks like someone we once knew, only . . . different. I wonder if he signed in? I'll go look. And as for you scaring tourists, have some patience with the kids, huh? It's no wonder they're sounding a little gruesome. Have you seen this?"

She picked up the local newspaper, which had been lying next to her computer.

"Seen what?" Sarah asked. "I didn't read the paper today—I left right after I woke up and came here." She winced. "It's all that hammering, you know?"

"Oh, how's that going?" Caroline asked.

"Loudly."

Which was the understatement of the year, Sarah thought. She loved the historic property she had bought after her recent return to town, but it was badly in need of not just refurbishing but reinforcement, as well. The previous owner, Mrs. Douglas, had tried to salvage it before the days of community awareness, when it might have been torn down but she hadn't had the funds to do all the necessary work. When Mrs. Douglas turned eighty, she had decided she was never going to get to it, so she decided to sell and offered the house to Sarah first, because Mrs. Douglas had been friends with Sarah's maternal grandmother. Given the house's history, the price had been amazing, another special deal because she had been so close with Sarah's grandmother, and also because Sarah's grandmother's grandmother had been born a Grant, and the property was known as the Grant House. As far as Sarah knew, her mother's side of the family had actually come from Savannah, but since the name—whether the connection was real or imaginary—had helped her to acquire the property, she was willing to go with it.

"I've wanted to live in that house for as long as I can remember," Sarah said.

"I remember, and I always thought you were crazy. Old Mrs. Douglas never did anything with it, and we've been watching it crumble all these years," Caroline said. "Remember when Pete

Albright went in that Halloween? How we made up the most horrifying stories and then dared him to go in? Some head of the football team! He came out white as a ghost, saying he'd quit being quarterback before he'd sleep in the place all night. He said he heard ghosts in the walls and could feel them trying to touch him. He was absolutely terrified."

"Of course he was. We were just terrible. We told him all those old tales about the woman who sold potions and voodooed people to death. And we told him it was full of corpses—which it had been, of course, since it was a mortuary for years."

Caroline wrinkled her nose. She was a petite blonde, cute and winsome, even when she made a face. She'd dated Pete Albright back in the day.

"We were horrible. But he could be pretty macho, so I kind of think he deserved it. And as for you, well, you're just crazy for living there. That house is spooky."

"I've slept in the house, and it's just fine. And I applaud Mrs. Douglas. She couldn't begin to afford to fix it up, but she kept it from the wrecking ball. I say good for her." Sarah shrugged. "Although I do wish she'd fixed at least a few things."

Caroline smiled. "Hey, you wanted history. Not me—not to live with, anyway. Don't get me wrong, I like history fine or I wouldn't be working here," she was quick to say. Not that she really had much choice. The Heritage House was a private museum, owned and operated by her parents. They had come to St. Augustine the year before she was born, embracing everything about the city and quickly making it their home. They were delighted to boast that St. Augustine was the oldest continually inhabited European-based community in the country, founded by the Spaniards in 1565, long before the English stepped foot in Jamestown and even longer before the *Mayflower* sailed across the sea. They were history buffs, and they hadn't started up their business to get rich; they simply loved what they did. Caroline's father, Harry, wrote history textbooks, and that endeavor, not the museum, was what supported them.

"Give me plumbing and electric that work any day. And a roof that doesn't leak," Caroline told her.

"I hear you," Sarah admitted. "But the house is magnificent. And in a year's time, I'll have it all set up as a bed-and-breakfast, and I'll run a collectibles and antiques business out of it, as well. You'll see," Sarah assured her.

Caroline laughed. "We should both live so long."

"Hey!"

"Sorry. You'll get it done. I just don't envy you the process. I grew up in the middle of constant renovations, remember? Every bad storm that came through, we were in the dark for weeks. No closets—they all had wardrobes back then. No whirlpool tubs." Caroline frowned. "And I'm not sure you should be staying there alone. It's too big. With everything that's going on, I don't think it's safe."

"What are you talking about?"

"I meant to show you the paper right away. I get sidetracked too easily."

"What happened?"

"Another missing woman. This one a local."

"Oh, no," Sarah said, reaching for the paper.

"A student from the community college," Caroline said. "She lived at home, but she went out a couple of night ago with a group of kids for a bonfire on the beach out on Anastasia Island . . . and didn't come back. There's her picture," Caroline said, tapping the paper.

"That's horrible," Sarah said softly. The picture was of a young woman, pretty and blond. It was her high school graduation photo. She had bright eyes full of hope, and long shining hair beneath her cap.

"Scary, huh?" Caroline said. "She looks a lot like the girl who disappeared last year, the one who was on vacation from D.C."

"That girl disappeared from Jacksonville," Sarah said. But she stared at the picture. The girls really had been similar in appearance. The big bright eyes, the long blond hair. Serial killers often picked a certain physical type, and if there was a serial killer working somewhere in the area, he had

27

obviously chosen his. Pretty blondes with large eyes. She looked at Caroline, who was still studying the paper. "They don't know that the other girl ever even came this far. Jacksonville is a big city, and with traffic these days, an hour away."

"What? Serial killers don't have cars?" Caroline asked her.

"I know, I know. But look on the bright side. Maybe this girl will turn up," Sarah said. "Thing is, you can't obsess, or you'd never leave your house. You just have to be smart and careful."

Caroline shook her head. "I'm not worried about me. I'm the world's biggest coward. I wouldn't live in your spooky old house alone for all the tea in China. I'm worried about *you*. Nothing scares you, and I think some things should."

"Not true, trust me. I have a healthy respect for being careful. I lock my doors, and I got friendly with my neighbors right off the bat," Sarah protested.

Caroline sniffed. "Oh, right. To the left, the pregnant teenager whose husband is in the service. And to the right, the octogenarian. They'll be a big help in a pinch."

"Brenda Cole isn't a teenager, she's twenty-one. And Mr. Healey is not an octogenarian, he's only in his seventies—and he has a dog."

"A teacup Yorkie!" Caroline said.

"One vicious teacup Yorkie, I'll have you know. He barks like a son of a bitch," Sarah assured her,

28

then laughed. "Which he is, of course. But seriously, I'm okay, honestly. I have a baseball bat, I *will* have an alarm system, and I can dial 911 faster than a speeding bullet."

"Just be careful," Caroline warned her.

"Yes, ma'am, I promise."

"Okay. Hey, want to have dinner?"

"I can't. I have to get home. Gary is at the house."

"And he's going to work all night?" Caroline asked.

"Until dark. He's trying to finish tracing all the pipes today. I have a leak in one wall. So I'm going to head home and call up for pizza delivery."

"Stop for a six-pack on the way home, too," Caroline warned. "Make Gary happy. He's the best. He's nice, and he can do anything. Funny how all that works out, huh? Gary was such a shop geek in high school, and now he's doing great. Pete Albright was a star, and I hear he's working in a fast food restaurant up in Atlanta. Go figure." She yawned. "Anyway, I'm meeting Will with Renee and Barry. You should grab Gary and go with us." When Sarah started to reply, Caroline waved a hand dismissively. "Never mind. I know, the house comes first. Anyway, let's go get changed."

"Will, huh?" Renee Otten and Barry Travis were fellow docents who had struck up a romance, and Will Perkins was Sarah's second cousin. Their mothers had been close, so he was almost like a brother to her, practically a fraternal twin, since they were both the same age, born a day apart, and shared the same coloring. And lately he and Caroline had become quite the item.

"He'll be disappointed that you're not coming. You haven't been home that long," Caroline said, turning on the reproach.

Sarah laughed. "I've been here six months. And Will and I see plenty of each other. In fact, he has threatened to move in once the place is done." While she had attended Florida State—not all that far away in Tallahassee—for her bachelor's degree, she had gone to Virginia for grad school, and then taken a job with an Arlington historical research and tour agency. But when Caroline's parents had needed another docent, especially one with her knowledge of local history and lore, she had decided it was time to come back. Virginia was beautiful, and she would always love it, but nothing could compare to the city in which she had been born and raised.

"Fine, be that way. In the meantime, I'm changing into something cute and cool and sure to wow them over at Hunky Harry's."

"Honey, all you have to do is walk into Hunky Harry's to wow everyone," Sarah assured her. "Trust me, you're 'wow' material even in what you're wearing now."

The lectures they gave covered topics ranging

from the coming of the first Spaniards to British rule, American rule, the Confederacy, Henry Flagler and the railroad, Prohibition and beyond, and they had different outfits to wear for each. Today they were focused on the Seminole Wars and the Civil War. So today they weren't dressed in silk and satin as would befit a pair of Southern belles.

Today they wore homespun cotton skirts and prim shirts that buttoned chastely to the neck. They were middle-class women of the era, those who churned butter and milked cows. And still, Caroline looked adorable. Sarah had yet to see a style from any era that Caroline didn't wear well.

"Why, Miss McKinley, you do go on," Caroline said with a mock simper. "And my, my, but if you aren't just a plate of buttered grits yourself."

"Yeah, yeah, Missy-yourself, let's just change and get out of here," Sarah said as they left the lecture hall. Barry Travis, in breeches and a homespun cotton shirt, was also heading toward the door marked Cast Members Only. He was a tall, handsome man of thirty, with longish brown hair that worked well in historical context.

"I hope you two can get changed quickly, because I'm starving. Renee is ushering the last of the book buyers out the front door, and we are officially closed," he said cheerfully.

"Sarah's not coming," Caroline informed him.

"Can't," Sarah said. "My house needs me." She

smiled to acknowledge that even she knew how silly that sounded.

"You know," he said, studying her and shaking his head, "you could have bought a nice new condo."

"There will be other nights," she said.

"What if the world ends tomorrow?" Barry demanded.

"My house will be one day closer to done, and Gary won't hate me," Sarah said.

"I give up," Barry said. "We'll miss you as we dine on succulent burgers—oh, wait. You didn't suddenly become a vegetarian, did you?" he asked her.

"She's a fish-a-tarian, I believe," Caroline.

"Pescatarian," Barry said.

"Whatever," Caroline agreed.

"Doesn't matter. You can torture me with thoughts of food and I won't care. Besides, I'm not sure anything at Hunky Harry's is actually succulent. Anyway, have a great time, and drink a beer for me."

"It's a good thing Harry didn't hear you say that. And it's not true—the food there is good," Barry protested.

"Yes, you're right. The food is very good, especially the fish. But I can't go. Not tonight," Sarah said.

She hurried into the women's locker room and quickly changed. Caroline had been right about one thing: she should stop and pick up a six-pack. Maybe a twelve-pack. Gary had a few employees working overtime right along with him.

She managed to escape without getting into further conversation, because when Caroline came in, she headed straight for the showers. Was she primping so hard for Will? Maybe. The two of them had always liked one another, but Sarah had never seen any signs that their relationship was anything beyond friendship. Then again, who knew? They said that friends made the best spouses. She certainly didn't know.

She'd fallen in love once, and it had been a brief and poignant affair. Clay Jenner had been a soldier. They'd met in Newport News, and had quickly discovered they both loved Buddy Holly, Peggy Lee, lounge music and historic ships. They'd spent a few months laughing, talking, listening to music and exploring historic sites. Then he'd been deployed. He'd been wonderfully romantic, going down on one knee when the cherry blossoms had been exploding all over the park, and he'd offered her the diamond she now wore on a chain.

He hadn't come home. That had been three years ago now, and although she would probably never get over the pain of losing him, she had accepted that he wasn't coming back. He had gone into the military for the schooling and the benefits, but, as he had told her, he'd signed the paper swearing that he would obey his superior officers and defend his country. It would have been nice if he could have served out his time somewhere safe, like Germany, but it hadn't happened that way.

He had been killed in a sniper attack. A bullet straight through the brain. He had probably never known what had hit him.

For that she was grateful. As her dad had told her once, every man and woman would die. An easy death was something that meant even though God might take a man early, he loved him enough to keep him from suffering.

Now she was glad to be home, where there were no memories of Clay, and glad to have moved into her house.

She didn't drive to work anymore; her house and the museum were in the area that was referred to as Old Town. After stopping for a twelve-pack and walking another four blocks through enclaves of tourist-centric businesses, she was thinking that a six-pack would have been fine.

She was almost at the walk that led up to her house when she saw him. The man she had noticed during her lecture.

While many buildings in Old Town sat right up near the sidewalk, there was actually a stretch of lawn in front of her place, along with a front walk and driveway—they'd needed a place for the cars and hearses to go. The man was only on the sidewalk, but he was right at the start of the coquina shell walk that led to her front porch. And he was staring at the house.

He must have sensed that she was watching him, because he turned, looked at her gravely, then smiled as she walked toward him, eyeing him carefully.

"Well, hello. It's Ms. McKinley, right?" he said. "Excellent lecture—thank you."

She nodded, staring at him warily. "Can I . . . help you?"

"I was admiring the house," he said.

She wasn't sure if she should say that it was hers or not. People had a tendency to be friendly in St. Augustine. In fact, there were dozens of B&Bs in the city, most of them homes that were open to strangers. In fact, she couldn't wait for her own house to be one of them.

But at the moment, she apparently had a bigger-city attitude going. And the first rule was never let a stranger know where you live.

He didn't look like a stalker. In fact, he was extremely attractive.

She reminded herself that many a serial killer had been attractive. They weren't all wild-eyed Charles Mansons. Ted Bundy had traded on his boy-next-door good looks.

She decided she was being ridiculous. The odds were strongly in favor of his being a tourist, one with an interest in history, given that she'd first seen him at the museum. Plus, there were still plenty of people about on the streets, and though the day was dying, there was still lots of light.

He didn't seem to need a reply. "The architecture is striking. It's quite a compelling place. Haunting, even."

"Thanks," she said. When he looked at her curiously, she added, "I own it."

He studied her for a moment, then laughed. "Of course, I shouldn't be surprised that a historian owns a piece of history. I see you have a lot of work going on."

"When you buy an old building, you have to be prepared for a lot of work," she told him. The twelve-pack was getting heavy but she fought against shifting the weight. She didn't want him offering to carry it and walk her up to the house. It wasn't a B&B yet, just a big old place without an alarm, and she didn't own a dog—not even a teacup Yorkie.

Of course, he didn't seem the menacing type. He looked far more likely to go after what he wanted with wit and charm. My, how her thoughts had quickly wandered.

"Well, congratulations on owning such a beautiful old place. Oh, by the way, my name is Caleb Anderson. And I know you're Sarah McKinley. It's been a pleasure to meet you."

"Likewise," she said. Then she startled herself by what she said next, because he had already turned to walk away. "Are you in town long?" she asked him.

She thought he hesitated before answering— only a half second, but a hesitation all the same.

"I'm not sure. I'll be around a few more days, at least. Thanks again. I really enjoyed your lecture— especially the way you handled those kids."

"Thanks," she said.

He lifted a hand. "Hope to see you again," he said casually and walked on, heading in the direction of Old Town and the shops that stayed open into the night.

She watched him go, then felt the heaviness of the twelve-pack again. She turned and hurried inside, and was immediately glad of her efforts. Gary Morton, all muscles and friendly smiles, kissed her cheek and told her she was brilliant. The two men working with him were equally happy.

"Although I did wonder when you were actually going to make it into the house," Gary said. "Who's the hunk?"

"Hunk?" she asked, pretending not to know exactly who he was talking about.

"Tall, well-built guy you were just talking to out front?" he teased.

"Oh. Just some guy who was at one of the lectures today. He was admiring the house. This is the historic district—people are supposed to admire my house."

He grinned. "Are you sure it was just the house he was admiring?"

She laughed. "Since he was staring at the house before I got there, I'm assuming that, yeah, it was just the house he was admiring. Anyway, we—as in you and me—were invited to dinner," she told him. "Will, Caroline, and Renee and Brad from the museum."

"What? You didn't invite Mr. Gorgeous?" he queried, grinning.

"Gary . . ." she said warningly.

"Okay, okay. Don't hit me." He put up a hand as if to protect himself, smiling all the while. "But pizza is good enough for me. I want to get this place in shape for you, so I need to knock out that last wall. I know it means a lot of work and a lot of mess, but you can't have a leaking water pipe. It will destroy the whole place on you, given time. You can go ahead if you want to. You don't have to be here wielding a sledgehammer."

"No, no, thank you, but I'm just as happy to hang around while you knock down walls," Sarah assured him, pulling out her cell phone. "I'm dialing the pizza guy right now. What do you guys want . . . ?"

"One cheese, one pepperoni, that'll be great, thanks," Gary said, then turned and disappeared down the hallway.

Sarah ordered the pizza, then took a minute and looked around.

At the moment, everything seemed to be coated in a thin layer of white dust. But even as she noted the dust, she was happy. It was such a beautiful place. So what if it had been a mortuary for a while? It had originally been built as the home of an American politician's aide soon after Florida became a territory. She had a sweeping porch that led to the original etched glass entry door. There was a small mudroom, still with the original tile. The house boasted a huge foyer, with a hall that stretched back toward a multitude of rooms that, while certainly viewing rooms during the house's tenure as a mortuary, had been planned as an office, a formal dining room, dual parlors—one for ladies and another for gentlemen—a music room and a laundry room. Somewhere along the line, a kitchen had been added to the house proper. The original kitchen had been a separate building out back; it was now empty but would one day make a beautiful apartment. The old carriage house had already been turned into an apartment, and though it, too, needed work, it was livable. The plumbing worked, and she'd put new sheets on the old four-poster bed in the large downstairs room. She'd put in sink, refrigerator and a microwave, just in case some of Gary's crew should ever need to stay. The carriage house stood just to the left of the driveway, creating an *L* with the main house. She couldn't help but take a moment to bask in the fact that she actually owned such a beautiful house. Well, she and the bank.

So far, Gary hadn't had to rip apart either of the front parlors. The men's parlor, on the right, was done in wood and dark tones. The ladies' parlor was light, with soft beige-toned wallpaper and crown molding painted to match. It was peeling, but that was all right. She could handle the cosmetic details later. There was a grand piano in the parlor, out of tune, but it had come with the house, and she intended to have it tuned and lovingly repaired eventually. There was also a small secretary, where she worked when she was home. Now she took one of the beers for herself, sat down at her desk and started looking at the articles she had collected on old St. Augustine, looking for anything about the house.

She found herself musing rather than reading.

There was no reason to think there was anything suspect about the man from the museum staring at her house. There was plenty to admire about it, and this was a tourist town, after all. And that was what tourists did. They stared.

He wasn't the usual tourist, though. Of that she was sure. He had an air about him. Like a . . . cop. No, not a cop. A CEO. No, not a CEO, either. She wasn't quite sure what it was that made him so striking, even over and above his looks. Maybe it was that build, sleek and powerful, and a stance that seemed to speak quietly of confidence.

Strange. Caroline had thought he seemed familiar. There *was* something familiar about him, but Sarah couldn't begin to figure out what it was. She was certain she would have remembered if she had ever met the man before.

"Hey!"

She had been so lost in her thoughts that she was startled when she heard Gary's voice.

"What is it?"

"Sorry, I think you should see this."

She looked at him, surprised. She didn't know a thing about construction, and she had told him so when she hired him to supervise the restoration of the mansion. Whatever he came across, he was supposed to deal with it. He knew what would fly with both the contemporary codes and the demands of the historic board. He knew walls and leaky water pipes. She didn't.

"What?" she asked again, worried by the look he was giving her. Things had been going so well, so incredibly well, and she didn't want anything to change that.

This wasn't going to be about leaking pipes. Instinctively, she knew that.

Just the tone of his voice was disturbing as if she had suddenly rounded a corner to find herself in an alien world. A creeping feeling of terrible unease began to fill her, slowly at first, then cold and sweeping, like skeletal fingers of ice reaching from a grave on a winter's day.

41

"Bones," he said, as if he'd read her mind.

"Bones?" she repeatedly blankly. "What, you found a dead squirrel?" she asked weakly, though she knew full well that wasn't he had found.

"No, Sarah. Human bones."

"Well, the house *was* used as a mortuary," she reminded him, though she knew she was being stupid. She just didn't want it to be true. It was as if everything had suddenly shifted. The world had been good, and now, from this moment on, it was going to be something altogether worse.

"We found them in the wall, Sarah. The *wall*. Mortuaries didn't usually wall up the dead," Gary said, then looked at her questioningly, as if waiting for her to decide what to do.

She nodded. "I'll call the police. I'll tell them we have a skeleton in the wall."

"A skeleton?" Gary repeated, staring at her blankly.

"Right," she said slowly. "Bones. A skeleton."

"Sarah, please. Just come look."

She stood at last and followed him back to what she intended to one day be a beautiful library.

She knew then what he had wanted her to see. There was no skeleton in the wall.

There were dozens of them.

2

"I heard you found a body," Adam Harrison said over the phone. Adam never did waste time with pleasantries over the phone, Caleb thought. No "Hey, how are you settling in? Good trip?"

In person, Adam Harrison—Caleb's boss and CEO of Harrison Investigations—was charming. One of the most dignified and courteous men who had ever walked the earth, Caleb was convinced. But he just wasn't a phone man.

"Yes, but nothing that has anything to do with our case. I just heard from that lieutenant friend of yours. The body is—"

"Frederick J. Russell, banker, who must have been speeding around that curve. He's been missing for twelve months, and if there's anything more, no one will know until the coroner's finished his report. A fine day's work, even if there's no connection," Adam said.

"Unfortunately, it doesn't get you any closer to what you're looking for. Have you discovered anything from talking to the locals?"

Caleb smiled, glad that Adam couldn't see him. "Adam, I've only been here twenty-four hours. But I'm out there, meeting people. I'll do everything in my power to chase down the girl who just went missing and see if we can discover some connection between her case and Jennie's. Frankly,

I'm hoping this girl just ran off with some guy. I'd just as soon not find her corpse." He was afraid he was going to find her dead, though there was always hope. As for Jennie, her own mother sensed that she was gone.

"Have you gotten a feel for anything?" Adam asked.

Caleb hesitated. *A feel for anything.* That could mean just about anything when you worked for Adam. Harrison Investigations specialized in the bizarre. The unexplained. The things that went bump in the night. Caleb didn't think they were going to find anything bizarre connected to this case, though. At any given time, hundreds of serial killers were on the prowl around the world. Most murders resulted from a moment's fury and were relatively easily solved. The husband who suddenly stabbed his wife with the carving knife over a burned meal usually wasn't smart enough to hide the prints or other trace evidence that would lead police straight to him.

But serial killers . . . they were hard to catch. All the DNA in the world couldn't help if the killer wasn't in the system. Ditto fingerprints. And they went after strangers, so linking their victims was a challenge, because the pattern connecting them wasn't obvious. And that was just when the bodies were found. At Quantico he'd once attended a lecture on the number of serial victims who went undiscovered. Swamps were a great place to dispose of bodies. Soft tissue decayed quickly; animals and insects destroyed evidence.

Complicating things further, serial killers were frequently mobile. They attacked when and where the moment—and the victim—was right; they might kill in one location and dispose of the body in another. The killer might move from Florida to Georgia . . . or Oregon—wherever life took him, killing all the while and counting on geography and competing bureaucracies to keep his victims from being connected into one ongoing case.

Caleb was afraid that Jennie Lawson might have been the victim of just such a killer, and because of that, her mother might never have the peace of burying her precious daughter's body.

But did any of that add up to a feel for anything?

"No gut intuition, not yet," he told Adam. It was barely a white lie. He genuinely wasn't sure he'd had a feeling for anything. Admittedly, he'd been interested in that house, the beautiful old colonial that was undergoing a lot of renovation work, as soon as he'd seen it. But had he actually been drawn to it? Beckoned?

And was it coincidental that it was owned by the gorgeous brunette from the historical museum? He was forced to admit that it probably was. The woman obviously had a passion for history, so there was nothing odd about her owning a piece of it. But was it odd that he had felt drawn to both?

Who wouldn't be drawn to such a beautiful

woman, with her flashing green eyes, the sense of fun touched with a bit of wickedness that had come out as she handled those kids, her obvious intelligence, and the lithe, sleek body that had been obvious even hidden under the dowdy clothing of a long-ago day.

"Caleb—you there?"

"Yeah, yeah, I'm here. I'm sorry. Like I said, nothing yet. Trust me, I'll be doing everything in my power to find Jennie Lawson. If she's here anywhere, I *will* find her."

"Of course. Don't forget, follow up on everything. No matter how off-the-wall you may think your hunch is, check it out. Those are often the signs that will take you where you need to go."

"Right. I'll keep in contact. Though I assume you're getting information from the police faster than I am."

"I'll keep you up-to-date on things."

"Thanks. And likewise."

Caleb hung up.

He stood and stretched, then wandered to the door.

He had chosen a bed-and-breakfast on Avila Street not for its charm—though it certainly offered enough—but because he could get a room on the ground floor with a private entrance. His doorway was on the side of the building, and a bougainvillea-shaded walk led straight out to the street at the rear of the rambling old Victorian.

Old Town St. Augustine was pretty much an easily navigated rectangle. On the coast, the massive Fort Marion, the old Spanish Castillo de San Marcos, served as the city's massive landmark, and the town had grown around it in the remaining three directions. Now the bay was lined with restaurants, hotels, shops and B&Bs. Beyond that main stretch were all kinds of smaller but interesting tourist attractions: the oldest house, the oldest schoolhouse, the oldest pharmacy—this was a city that prided itself on being old, and it was a historical treasure trove. Interspersed with the tourist attractions were more B&Bs, one-of-a-kind shops and even a number of private residences. At night, the backstreets were quiet, except when the sightseeing carriages and ghost tours went by.

With St. Augustine's notoriety as the oldest continually inhabited European city in the United States—with sixty years on Jamestown—naturally it was rumored to harbor a lot of ghosts.

As he stood on the sidewalk, feeling the Atlantic breeze that cooled the city year-round, he was startled as one police car went by, and then another, quickly followed by a third.

They were turning down St. George Street.

Caleb followed.

"Oh, my God. This is ghastly," Caroline breathed.

"Caroline, please," Sarah said.

"Horrifying," Caroline went on.

"Caroline!" Will protested. "Please, they're bones."

"Human bones," Caroline reminded him. *"Human* bones."

Will looked at Caroline, then rolled his light green eyes at Sarah as he ran a hand through his dark chestnut-colored hair.

St. Augustine could be a very small town. One officer had talked to another after Sarah had called the police, and the story about the bones in her walls had traveled like lightning, with a cop friend of Will's reaching him while he and the others were waiting for a table. The police had barely arrived before her cousin and her friends showed up, as well.

"This is history in the making," Barry Travis said, looking far more contemporary in jeans and a short-sleeved shirt.

"History?" Renee Otten protested. "As if we need more ghost stories in St. Augustine."

"I'll bet the undertaker was selling coffins to the families of the dead, dumping the bodies in the walls, then selling the coffins again," Sarah said. She felt tired. And despite the logic of her words, she was still unnerved. She loved this house, and she was pretty certain that she was right. In a few cases, something like mummified tissue remained on the bodies—enough to hold them together. And there were stained scraps of fabric left, as well, which seemed to date the interment to the mid to late eighteen hundreds.

She felt terrible, of course, that human beings had been treated with no respect and no reverence whatsoever. But she found it criminal, not ghastly. And she was aware, above all, that this discovery meant bringing in a team of historians and anthropologists, on top of the forensic specialists. She would be like a visitor in her own house. She had learned enough about dig sites when she worked as a historian in Arlington, charting relics and remains, to know that for a fact.

"How can you be so sure? Maybe someone who lived here was a monster. A murderer. There was a guy in Chicago who did away with whole families in the late eighteen hundreds. He was worse than Jack the Ripper—but they caught him," Will offered.

She glared at her cousin. "Will!"

"Sorry," he told her.

They were standing just inside the doorway. Behind them stood Tim Jamison, the police lieutenant who'd been handed the case. He was convinced that these weren't modern-day homicides, but there were still plenty of questions to be answered. He was supervising the arrival of medical personnel and forensic anthropologists. Gary was sitting in the kitchen, drinking beer. He had already given Tim his statement but didn't want to leave yet.

There were already a few reporters hanging around, and Gary didn't want to deal with them.

He just wanted to eat his pizza, drink his beer and stop the leak.

"Look at it this way," Caroline said, brightening. "They're obviously very old bones. They'll get them all out quickly and start studying them in some lab somewhere. You'll be able to get back to work on the house, and when you do open for business, it will be fabulous. People love to stay at haunted houses. There's some castle in Ireland that's supposed to be haunted and you can't even get a reservation there for years."

She offered Sarah a bright smile, then turned pale. "Those poor people. I bet they really do haunt the house. Can you imagine how terrible it must be to just get dumped out of your coffin? Oh! And we were just talking about Pete Albright this morning—and how we'd made up stories about people being buried in the house. And now it turns out those stories were true. I know I'd be furious enough to be haunting the place if *my* body had been dumped out of my coffin, wouldn't you?"

Sarah laughed at that. "Caroline, if someone dumped my body out of my coffin, I wouldn't care because I'd already be dead. My friends and family would have to be furious for me. And I don't believe we hang around after we're dead."

"You an atheist or something?" Barry asked, surprised.

She shook her head. "No, I believe in God and the afterlife, and I even like going to church. That's my point. We go to heaven or . . . wherever when we die. We're no longer tied to our bodies. So if I was dumped out of a coffin, I doubt if I'd know it, and if I did, I wouldn't care. I mean, we're organic, we rot. So I don't think that I'd be hanging around to haunt anyone, that's all."

"It's that time she spent in Virginia," Caroline said, shivering. "She worked in a bunch of old graveyards. I guess she got used to hanging out with dead people." She gave an exaggerated shudder.

"If you go over to the old cemetery just down the street, they tell you that you're only seeing half of it, that the street is paved right on top of hundreds of graves," Sarah said. "And the tourists eat it up. So if I get a good haunted-house story out of this, is that so bad?"

Renee shivered and moved closer. "When they said human bones, it scared me to death, I have to admit. I mean, with that girl missing and all . . ."

"Renee! You thought someone murdered her, then hid her body in my house—behind a wall, no less—and I never even noticed?" Sarah asked sarcastically. Renee turned bright red, and Sarah instantly felt sorry. Renee was a good docent; she just seemed to be a bit of an airhead in real life. She was pretty and sweet, and kids loved her, but Sarah couldn't quite understand how she and Barry had ended up in a relationship. Barry was inquisitive and intuitive, and knew a lot more history than what was contained in the training material the docents received. And Renee was . . . Renee.

"Well, of course . . . not," Renee said. "I'm sorry. It's just that that poor girl is missing and it has me worried, you know?"

"No, *I'm* sorry. I didn't mean to jump on you," Sarah assured her quickly. "Of course that missing girl was the first thing you thought of. I'm just grateful that 'my' bones do seem to be very old ones. You know, I've heard stories about this house, but never anything about a crazy undertaker filling the walls with his . . . clients. I'm going to have to do some more research and see what I can find out."

"The only way you would have heard the story would have been if someone had already discovered the bones and dug them out," Will said, his tone ironic.

She cast him an exasperated stare, but he didn't notice. He was looking out the open door to where a crowd had gathered on the street, a uniformed officer keeping them back. "Hey, I know that guy."

"What guy?" Sarah asked.

"Don't go staring," Will said.

"Why? Whoever he is, he's in front of my house," Sarah said. She gripped Will's shoulder and looked past him, then gasped.

"What?" Caroline asked, jumping.

"It's him."

"Him, who?" Caroline demanded, then gave a little gasp of her own and said, "Oh, my God, it's the guy from the museum!"

"He was here when I got home, staring at the place," Sarah said.

"I told you, I thought I knew him from some-where . . . oh, my God!" Caroline said. "You don't think that—"

"He was a creepy old undertaker after the Civil War and stuffed a bunch of bodies in the walls?" Will asked, laughing.

Caroline flushed. "No. It's just that—"

"I know who—" Will began. But he didn't get a chance to finish. Lieutenant Tim Jamison was striding their way.

"Let him in, Fred," Tim Jamison said into his radio, obviously speaking to the uniformed officer who was holding the onlookers back.

Sarah watched as Fred let the man from the museum step past.

"Hey!" she said as she caught Tim's arm.

He turned back to her. "What?"

"Tim, who is that? Why are you letting him in?"

"I know who he is," Will said. "I've been trying to tell you. He's a diver, and he just did some work with us."

"A diver?" Sarah repeated, confused.

"He's actually a P.I. with some firm out of Virginia or D.C.—*and* he's a diver," Tim told

Sarah. "He's connected, too. The captain told me to help him out as much as I can. Will you excuse me?"

Sarah let him go, though she wanted to protest that it was *her* house everyone was traipsing through, and she should be the one to tell any nonessential personnel whether they could or couldn't enter.

"He's a damned good diver. He found a body this morning," Will said.

"What?" Sarah, Caroline and Renee demanded in unison.

"The plot thickens," Barry said, twisting a pretend moustache.

Sarah shot him a glance telling him that his joke was in poor taste, then turned to Will. "The missing girl?" she asked.

Will shook his head. "We were looking for her, but it was a crapshoot. We don't know exactly when she disappeared, much less where she went, we don't know if she was killed . . . the bosses decided to send divers down since she'd been at a beach party when she was last seen. They called me in as the dive master and coordinator. We didn't find her—but your guy did discover a submerged car with a man in it. He knows his stuff—he's a good diver."

So he'd found a body. And now there were bodies in her house. Did that mean anything?

"His name is Caleb Anderson," Will supplied.

"I could swear I know him from somewhere," Caroline said.

And then, walking beside Tim, he was coming up on the porch. "I don't think this discovery can possibly impact your search," Tim was telling him. "This is a case for the history books—and new fodder for the ghost tours around here. Intriguing, though."

Caleb Anderson reached the group standing just inside the door, then reached out and shook hands with Will, nodded at the others, then walked over to stand next to Sarah. "Quite a discovery," he said to her.

"Yes, not what I was expecting, certainly," she said.

Caroline moved forward, offering her hand. "Hi. I'm Caroline Roth. I saw you at the museum earlier. And these are our fellow docents, Barry Travis and Renee Otten."

"Nice to meet you," Caleb said, shaking hands all around before turning back to Sarah. "You haven't owned the house very long?" he asked her.

"A few months," she said.

"But she's been in love with it forever—since we were little kids," Caroline said. "She was working in the D.C. area and just came home a few months ago to help out at the museum. And then she got the opportunity to buy this place and jumped at it."

Sarah stared at Caroline, wondering if her friend was going to give him her full biography. Then she wondered why it mattered. It wasn't as if her life were a secret in any way. Still, for some reason, she thought that the stranger should have to work for his information regarding any of them—maybe because she didn't think info about him was going to be easy to come by.

"I see. Well, it is a beautiful place—and the bones will add a nice touch of the macabre to its history—" Caleb said.

"Anderson?" Tim Jamison said, breaking in. "This way."

"Excuse me," Caleb said, and left them, following Tim to the almost-library, where the walls had been torn out.

"Come on," Will said to Sarah. "Pack a bag and let's head out. You can stay at my place tonight."

"Or you can stay with me," Caroline offered.

Sarah shook her head. "Will, you live in a studio. And, Caroline, no offense, because you know I love her, but your mom will just mother me to death. I'll go to Bertie Larsen's Tropical Breeze."

Bertie owned a charming little B&B around the corner. At any given time there were twenty to thirty such establishments operating in town, and the owners tended to help each other out. Sometimes business in the city was the proverbial feast, and sometimes it was famine, but the owners tended to stay friends, or at least allies. As a group they could advertise or petition the city for benefits like tax breaks, benefitting them all when they worked together. And since some places accepted pets, some accepted kids and some neither, they often passed on a competitor's name when they didn't meet a potential guest's criteria.

Bertie wasn't just a fellow businesswoman, she had become a good friend who had already given Sarah lots of advice. Best of all, her inn had a number of rooms with private entrances, and Sarah was in the mood for privacy. She crossed her fingers that a room with a private entrance would be available.

"If you're sure . . ." Will said.

"I am," Sarah insisted. "I don't mind spending the night away from home, but I want to be able to get in and out of my own house easily if I need to. And since we all agree I can't stay here tonight, please excuse me. I'm going to gather a few things."

Sarah didn't wait for an answer as she hurried up to her bedroom. She'd meant to just grab her toiletries and an outfit for the next day, but she found herself sitting down on the foot of her bed instead.

"This . . . sucks," she muttered aloud.

She loved her bedroom. The mattress was new, but the bed was original to the period, a massive four-poster, intricately carved. The dresser, freestanding mirror, secretary and bedside occasional tables matched the bed. The floor was hardwood, and she had stripped, stained and waxed it herself, then purchased the elegant Oriental carpet on eBay. Her clothing was hung in the wardrobe she'd gotten from Annie's Antiques, just down Ponce. The private bath featured a claw-foot tub and porcelain taps. She felt real pride in everything she had accomplished here and in the rest of the house.

But tonight there would be people in and out. Gary had agreed to stay to help as they used echolocation to discern whether there were additional bodies entombed in the walls. And despite her own credentials, Sarah—who had worked on many burial sites but had never managed one—had agreed that the excavation of the bones should be supervised by Professor Manning, an expert from the college who had one doctorate in history and another in anthropology. She was far too close to the situation here, too involved.

She just wanted those skeletons out of her walls and respectfully interred—somewhere far away.

It was definitely going to be one hell of a story. So far the police had agreed to her request that no press be let into the house until the researchers and police had carried out the necessary investigations. The bones wouldn't be going to a mortuary any time soon. While the circumstances leading to their presence in her walls were being determined, the bones themselves would be going to various institutes for study.

Study that would take time.

She let out a groan of frustration, stood up, grabbed her things and stuffed them into a small rolling suitcase, and then paused, looking around the room and catching sight of herself in the standing mirror. She looked too thin and too pale, she decided. *Why?* She wasn't afraid of the bones, wasn't afraid of being haunted by ghosts crying out for help. She firmly believed that the soul did not remain in the body after death.

Still, this discovery had somehow changed everything.

Her house had now become a small part of history, a part of local lore and legend, in a way she had never anticipated or wished for.

There was nothing genuinely tragic about the discovery—an undertaker of long ago had done all the right things in public, then made money by selling the same coffins over and over again. The souls of the people in the walls were long gone, and anyone who had loved them was long gone, too.

But for some reason it felt as if her life was going to be different from now on, and that made her uneasy.

At least I'm not a blonde, she found herself thinking, then winced. Where had that thought come from? A young woman, a blonde, was missing, and that was sad, but it had nothing to do with her house. It *was* odd, though, that there had been two disappearances in two years—two young women, both with blond hair. Maybe it wasn't the most admirable way to be thinking, but it was reassuring to know that at least she didn't seem to fit the profile of those recent victims.

She sighed and turned to leave. For tonight, she wanted out of here. Rolling her bag behind her, she hurried downstairs.

There was no one in the entry or hallway, but she could hear voices coming from the library.

The room where the grisly discovery had been made.

As she stood there, wondering whether she should let someone in charge know she was leaving, Caroline reappeared.

"Come on, at least come get a drink with us," Caroline suggested.

"All right, but let me run over to Bertie's and get a room first."

"I still say you could stay with me," Caroline told her, then gave in when she saw that Sarah's mind was made up. "Never mind. Go on and get your stuff over to Bertie's, then meet us at Hunky Harry's."

"It's a plan," Sarah agreed.

"You'll really show?"

"Yes, I'll really show," Sarah said. "I promise." She quickly gave Caroline a kiss on the cheek and headed out. From the corner of her eye she'd seen Will, Travis and Renee heading toward them from the hallway, and she wanted to get away from everyone. She desperately needed a little respite from the day's excitement.

She made it down to the sidewalk, where there was still a throng of tourists and a few locals. Friends. She found herself caught up in conversation, whether she wanted to be or not.

Luckily, the cops were there, too, clearing the area. As soon as she could manage it without being hated by every friend and acquaintance in the area, she escaped.

There was something about the house, definitely. It had drawn him from the first, and Caleb didn't think it was because he had somehow sensed that a long-ago funeral director had been playing fast and loose with the corpses of his "clients." Tim Jamison hadn't seemed surprised to see him standing on the sidewalk, but then again, a couple dozen people had been standing there. Still, he was glad when the police lieutenant asked him in. Maybe the fact that he had found a corpse in the water earlier that day somehow made him worthy.

Jamison had just finished clearing everyone unofficial out of the room where the skeletons had been found.

"Is this something, or what?" the cop was saying now. "I remember the newspapers being filled with something similar just a few years ago—the mortician comforting the grieving relatives, then dumping the bodies of the deceased and selling the coffins again. Coffins aren't cheap. Even cheap coffins aren't cheap, and the satin-lined, down-stuffed ones will *really* cost you. There's lot of money to be made selling those suckers over and over again. I guess there have always been people willing to make an extra buck or two off the dead, no matter how they do it."

Caleb looked around the library. Most of the plaster had been torn out, revealing piles of bones between the studs. Some of the bones were still attached to each other by bits of mummified sinew and tendon, preserved inside their plaster prison.

It was a gruesome sight, even for him. In some cases shreds of clothing remained. One of the corpses was wearing the remnants of a Civil War-era hat. It looked as if they had stumbled on a particularly bizarre scenario for a haunted house. Someone might easily think the remains were the result of an exhibit designer's mad imagination.

"Have you ever seen anything like it?" Jamison asked. "Hell, I'm a homicide cop. I've worked in Jacksonville, Miami and Houston—tough towns, all of them—and I've never seen anything like this."

The lieutenant shook his head, staring at the remnants of what had once been living, breathing human beings.

A small man was standing close to the wall, the epitome of the absent-minded professor with his glasses and tufts of wild gray hair, peering closely at the remains, a penlight in his hand. "You know, embalming started becoming popular after the war—the Civil War. They had to try to get those dead boys back home to their mamas and sweethearts. But it really came into vogue for most Americans because of Abraham Lincoln. When he died, his widow wanted him buried back in Illinois, so they held a public viewing as the body traveled cross-country by train, so they had to keep Abe looking good for the mourners. He was embalmed by injecting fluids through the veins, but I think these poor souls were embalmed in the much less efficient fashion of the day, such as disemboweling a corpse and stuffing it with charcoal, or perhaps just immersing the body in alcohol. I imagine they were given proper viewings to satisfy the families, and then they were walled up. You can see here—" he pointed out different shades of plaster that had been chipped from the walls "—that they were put in at different times. Just guessing from the look of the corpses, I'd say this was all done within a ten-year period. See how the bones have darkened just a bit more? That ten-year span was a very long time ago. Fascinating, the way some of the corpses have mummified. My office will retrieve the remains in the morning. Legally, we could arrange removal right now, but I want to bring in specialists to make sure everything is handled correctly. This is quite the find."

The man finally turned from his macabre monologue, saw Caleb and sized him up. He pocketed his penlight and offered him a hand. "How do you do? You're that out-of-towner who found that fellow who's been missing a year, aren't you? I did his autopsy this afternoon. I'm the M.E. here in town, Florence Benson—my parents were fans of the Ziegfeld follies, I'm afraid—so they call me Doc Benson or Floby around here. Nice to meet you. You solved a sad mystery today."

"Pleasure to meet you, Doc Benson, and I'm glad to have been of service," Caleb assured him. "Did you find out anything interesting regarding the body I found?"

"I sent what tissue samples I could gather out to the lab, but after a year in the water . . . it's hard going. I'm reserving my comments until I've completed my work."

"Very smart," Caleb said.

"Yes, especially given the circumstances. I'm working with little more than bone on that corpse, too, which is proving to be more tedious than you'd imagine. At least I know where all his body parts are. Here . . . well, as you can see, some of these skeletons are still more or less together, and some have fallen completely apart. This is going to be interesting, to say the least."

"So it appears," Caleb agreed.

The man studied him again, up and down, making an assessment.

"You work for some secret agency, huh?" the medical examiner asked him.

"Hardly secret," Caleb said. "We're just licensed

investigators, like lots of other firms. But my boss doesn't advertise. He's the quiet kind and only takes on cases that call for what we can offer that other agencies can't."

He knew that Tim Jamison was watching him as he spoke, intrigued. Tim had been asked by the mayor, who been asked by the governor, to bring Caleb in on the case of the newly missing girls. He was both wary, and curious. But he seemed open-minded enough, and that was all Caleb really cared about.

"So where has Miss McKinley gotten herself off to, Tim?" Floby asked.

"She left for the night. She grew up here—she's got plenty of friends around who would offer her a place to stay for the night. I'm not sure where she's headed. She loves this old place, though. This has to be a big setback for her."

"Not so bad—unless the whole house turns out to be riddled with corpses," Floby said cheerfully. "And I don't think it will. This seems to have been the . . . dump, shall we say? And as I said, I'll have the pros in tomorrow to clear out these unwanted tenants, you cops and that professor will do some investigating—though I'm sure you'll find out these people were already dead before they got stuck in the wall, just in case anyone was worried about that—and then everyone will get the burial they should have gotten years ago. And she's a historian with on-site experience, so she'll understand the significance of this find. And since she's not a shrinking-violet kind of girl, I'm betting she'll want in on the investigation herself."

"I'd really appreciate permission to help, too," Caleb said.

Floby looked at Tim Jamison, who nodded, giving Floby the okay to allow a stranger in on the find.

"We'll be starting bright and early, so we can catch all the light we can. Someone will be posted out on the porch twenty-four seven to keep the lookie-loos away, so you just check in with him whenever you get here," Floby told him.

"Thanks. I'll leave you two, then. I appreciate being let in on this, Lieutenant," Caleb told Jamison.

Jamison shrugged. "I don't know who you know, but they sure as hell know all the right people." He grinned. "You proved your abilities this morning. I'm happy to keep you in the loop—all the loops. And I'm sure you'll do me the same courtesy in return."

"Of course."

Two handshakes and Caleb was out the door. He took a minute to turn and stare up at the house— just as a small crowd was still doing from the side-walk, gruesomely speculating on the state of the bodies.

Caleb moved quickly past the crowd to avoid being questioned by those who had seen him leave the house and moved farther down the street, then stopped and studied the house again.

Brick, mortar and wood. The place embodied everything that old-town Southern charm should be. It was a decaying but grand old edifice. It wasn't evil, it was just a house. Still, he felt that there were things waiting to be discovered there, things that he needed to know.

But no ghosts danced on the wraparound porch. No specters wavered in the windows.

The house was just a house.

He turned and headed back toward his B&B, planning to check his e-mail and then head out for something to eat. He'd barely made it around the corner when he saw Sarah McKinley ahead of him, towing a small wheeled overnight bag along behind her. She was alone. That surprised him; she'd been with a group of friends last time he'd seen her.

Suddenly she stopped, as if sensing someone behind her. For a moment she went dead still. Then she swung around and stared at him before asking, "What the hell are you doing here?" Her eyes narrowed suspiciously. "Are you following me?"

3

"Man, that was really creepy," Caroline said, walking along Avila Street. She shuddered and moved closer to Will. It was strange. She had known Will most of her life. They had fought and teased one another as kids. They had become friends as adults. They had shared their trials and tribulations with other members of the opposite sex with one another.

Then . . .

They'd been together one night—at Hunky Harry's, as a matter of fact—and in the middle of laughing at something together, they had looked at each other and their laughter had stopped. And now . . . well, it wasn't as if they'd gone insane or anything, but they were both carefully negotiating the transition from friends to the realization that they wanted to be much more.

Will set an arm around her shoulders. "Leave it to Sarah. And what happened earlier today, that was pretty damn creepy, too."

"Yeah, tell us about it. Who *is* this Caleb guy, anyway?" Barry asked, strolling up alongside Will.

"Hey, wait! What about me?" Renee demanded, pushing forward.

"What are you trying to do? Block the whole sidewalk?" Caroline complained.

But they all wanted to hear what Will had to say,

so they crowded together and walked along in an awkward group, trying to hear him clearly.

"I think the guy is some kind of corpse magnet," Will said. "We were looking for that missing girl, Winona Hart, and Lieutenant Jamison said Anderson had to be on the dive team. He didn't explain why, just said the mayor had told him to extend every courtesy to the guy and let him work with us. He has connections in Washington. Some hotshot sent him down here. I have to tell you, we were ticked at first. But the thing is, in the last year, we've dived that area a dozen times, and no one ever found that car. But—he found it as easy as if he had a map. Now *that's* creepy."

"So who was the guy he found?" Renee asked.

"Frederick J. Russell, a banker from Jacksonville," Will said. "He was reported missing about twelve months ago."

"So what happened to him? How'd he end up in the water?" Renee asked.

Will sighed, shaking his head as he looked at her. "He was still in his car, so they figure he just drove too fast and wound up in the water. Not too hard to figure out."

"Hey," Renee protested. "Was he drunk? Had he been suicidal? Maybe someone was after him or something."

"She's right," Caroline pointed out. "What does the coroner say? Maybe someone shot him and *that's* why he drove off the road."

"There's no coroner's report yet," Will admitted, sounding slightly embarrassed, Caroline thought. "Who knows? He might have been drunk, though I don't know if they'll be able to figure that out this late in the game. The body . . . well, if you ask me, it was a lot creepier than anything in Sarah's house. Let's just say that on land, we eat the fish. But if you die in the water, the fish eat you."

"Oh, Lord!" Caroline exclaimed. "I was going to order fish. . . ."

"It's not going to be the same fish that ate the corpse," Barry said.

"And how do you know?" Caroline demanded.

"Good question," Barry admitted. "Cheeseburger for me."

"Getting back to Anderson, the guy is a little scary. I mean, he's okay. I like him," Will said. "But . . . he's been here a day and he already found a body we missed for a year. And then all those bones are found at Sarah's place and he just happens to show up? It's pretty weird, don't you think?"

Caroline moved even closer, and he hugged her more tightly to him.

"I don't think it's his fault that the bones showed up in Sarah's walls," Renee reminded him. "I mean, those skeletons have been there forever. Anyway, you said you liked the guy."

"I do," Will said.

"I sure liked him," Caroline offered.

"Oh, yeah?" Will said teasingly. "You just think he's hot."

Caroline laughed. "He *is* hot. But you're the only sizzling hunk of man flesh I'm interested in, mister. I'm thinking about Sarah."

"Sarah?" Will echoed.

"Of course Sarah," Caroline said.

"I'm not too sure about that. I mean, we really don't know anything about him," Will said.

"I don't think it's a good idea at all," Barry agreed. "We're going to have to check him out if we're thinking about hooking him up with Sarah."

Renee giggled. "What's the matter with you guys? Sarah is an adult, and she's not going to ask us who she can and can't date!"

"Besides, she knows him at least as well as we do, even if they just met today," Will said.

"Well, I think he's a corpse magnet, and I don't like it," Barry said flatly.

They all stopped and stared at him. "Hey, we have to look out for our girl, right?" he asked defensively.

"Okay, I'll ask around and see what I can find out about him," Will promised. "And we'll all try to get to know him—if he hangs around."

"He seems like a decent guy. I hope he does hang around," Caroline said.

"There you go again—you think he's hot," Will said, grinning.

"He's an inferno," she agreed. "And I'd really love a drink. Let's hope we can get a table." She shivered suddenly and looked at Will. "You know, with all this, we're forgetting that a girl from here and now is still missing."

"Well, your stud is on the case," Will said. "Maybe he'll find her."

"Yeah, and hopefully alive," Barry noted glumly.

"He's actually here looking for a girl who disappeared a year ago," Will said. "Her case was in the papers again today. The cops are wondering if there's a connection between the two cases."

"I saw the papers. I even showed the article to Sarah," Caroline told him.

A horse-drawn carriage full of tourists clip-clopped by on the street. "A young woman committed suicide in that hotel, on the top floor," the guide was telling his passengers. "They say her ghost still visits the room every new moon."

They all went still as the carriage passed, their gazes turning involuntarily toward the top floor of the hotel.

"I need a drink *now*," Renee announced, and hurried on ahead of them to Hunky Harry's, just a couple of doors away.

Caroline found herself standing alone on the sidewalk for a moment as the others passed her and went inside. She suddenly felt a chill, and she realized that a *frisson* of fear was sweeping through her.

She'd lived here her entire life. She knew practically every restaurant owner, bartender and shopkeeper in the city. She knew the people who worked in the hotels and museums, and owned the local B&Bs.

And she was suddenly afraid.

Something new had come to the city.

Or maybe something old, very old—and very evil—had been awakened.

Caleb caught up to Sarah McKinley, who was staring at him with suspicion. Even so, she was a beautiful woman.

At that moment, she reminded him of a small but ferocious terrier.

He stopped walking and stood dead still on the sidewalk, staring at her in return.

"Were you speaking to me? If so, no, I'm not following you. I'm headed to my B and B," he told her.

She blinked. A flush rose to her cheeks, and she winced. "Sorry. But . . ." She continued to stare at him suspiciously. "Where are you staying?"

"Roberta's Tropic Breeze, over on Avila," he said.

She closed her eyes, bit her lip lightly and let out a sigh.

"You're kidding? Are you saying that's where you're staying, too?" he asked.

"Bertie is an old friend," she told him. "There are

dozens of B and Bs in this city," she said. "I can't believe you're staying at the same one I am."

"Hey, I made my reservation before I left home," he told her. "I was definitely there first. And why are you staying there, anyway? You must have tons of friends in town."

"Precisely," she said.

He laughed. "Sorry, but I'm not checking out. I'd be delighted to help you with that bag, though."

"I'm perfectly capable of dealing with my own suitcase."

"I don't doubt that for a second."

She stared at him for a long moment.

"Okay, I won't help you with your bag. Nice seeing you."

She seemed to realize that she was being rude for no real reason and let out another sigh. "Sorry. Yes, thanks, I'd love the help."

He lowered his head, whispering, though there was no need. "It's okay—all the people who want to talk to you are still over on your street, staring at your house."

"Yeah?" she said, her voice skeptical. "I took one step outside and everyone thought that I had all the answers since it's my house. I have no clue as to how those bodies ended up in my walls."

"It was a mortuary. The answer should be easy enough to find," he told her, then looked at her quizzically, taking the bag as they walked. "You're a historian, right?"

"Yes. I have my master's degree in American history."

"You must find this fascinating."

"I would—if it wasn't my house we're talking about. I dreamed about buying that place when I was a kid. I love everything about it. Now I own it, but they have to hack into all the walls, and God knows when I'll get back in," she said.

"Oh, it won't be that long," he offered.

She glared at him. "Have you *seen* how the cops, not to mention all the experts, work?"

He laughed. "Okay, then think of it this way. Most people have a ghoulish streak. The value of your property is going to soar. People will be clamoring to take it off your hands."

"But I don't want to sell!" she protested. And then they were approaching Bertie's place.

Caleb saw Roberta Larsen standing anxiously on the porch, and she hurried down the steps as soon as she saw them, too.

"Sarah, you poor dear. Come on inside. I've got a nice cup of tea ready for you. And of course you're welcome to a cup, too, Mr. Anderson." She kept talking as she ushered them up the steps and through the door. "Sarah, you're right in here, first room behind the parlor. Mr. Anderson, if you'll just drop that bag in the room for Sarah . . . ? Sarah, come right into the parlor and catch your breath."

Roberta Larsen was closing in on seventy, but

she was still slim and beautiful, wrinkles and all. And she apparently knew Sarah well.

"Yes, ma'am," Caleb said.

"He's a Southern boy," Roberta told Sarah.

"Northern Virginia," he said.

"You can always tell the true Southern boys. They say 'sir' and 'ma'am,'" Roberta assured Sarah. "Not that there's anything wrong with Yankees. I just love it when those wonderful northerners come down to visit. But you can always tell a Southern boy."

Caleb saw that Sarah was trying to hide a grin, and he was glad. She needed to smile. Then he smiled, too. It had been quite a while since anyone had called him a boy.

Roberta's place was impeccably kept. The furniture was antique and polished to a high shine, and the parlor—where she served cookies, soda, wine and beer in the afternoon—was comfortable as well as beautiful, with coffee tables, plush sofas and wingback chairs, a fireplace, and rows and rows of books. Roberta had a full silver tea service set out on the central coffee table, though they seemed to be the only guests around at the moment, Caleb thought as he went to deposit Sarah's bag in the first bedroom, as instructed. It was next to his, but her room didn't have its own access to the outside the way his did, he noticed.

After setting the bag at the foot of the bed, he noted the large window on one wall. He had a feeling she might come and go via that window, if she got the urge to avoid conversation.

He returned to the parlor, where the two women were already seated. Roberta was pouring tea. "I just don't believe this," she said to him as he entered. "Or maybe I do. What a crazy day. Don't get me wrong, Mr. Anderson, it's not that St. Augustine is crime free. But we're a tourist town—have been for years. There used to be executions down in the square. The Spanish garroted their condemned in public. These days, though, we pride ourselves on being nice, on doing our best to share our remarkable past without any bloodshed."

"Bertie," Sarah said, sipping her tea, "it's all right. Whatever happened in my house happened a very long time ago, and no one thinks people were murdered and then stuffed in the walls. The general consensus seems to be that the mortuary owner was hiding bodies so he could resell coffins."

"Yes, but for Gary to have found them today, the same day . . . Mr. Anderson found that poor drowned man, and with one of our local girls missing . . ." Roberta's words trailed off, and she shook her head sadly. "I don't know whether to be glad or not that they didn't find the poor woman. And did you know that Mr. Anderson is here because *another* woman disappeared a year ago? Silly me. You must know that, because obviously you two know one another."

Sarah stared at him as if curious to see his reaction to that. He shrugged.

The phone rang just then, and Bertie hurried off to answer it.

"Just exactly who do you work for?" Sarah asked him suspiciously.

"An investigations firm," he said. "Harrison Investigations."

Her eyes widened with surprise and then she frowned. "You work for . . . Adam Harrison?"

"Do you know Adam?" he asked. It was his turn to be surprised.

"I've met him several times. I worked in Virginia for a while after I got my master's at William and Mary. I was working on a dig when Adam was called in. It turned out that some local college students were messing around at one of the local historic cemeteries, using light and sound effects to make the place seem haunted. Then I saw him again when one of my co-workers was convinced that a ghost was moving his equipment around. I don't know what the real situation was, but your boss arranged for a proper funeral and the reinterment of some bones we'd found, and, imagined or not, the problems stopped," Sarah told him. "So I know the kind of case your firm handles." She was looking at him differently now.

He had yet to meet anyone who didn't like, or at least respect, Adam, Caleb thought. And now he had a new in. Miss Sarah McKinley was not going to be so hostile and suspicious now, because he was connected to Adam.

Sarah was frowning again. "But I thought . . . Adam only investigates when there's a question of a ghost being involved? Not that I believe in ghosts," she said firmly.

"Ghosts?" Roberta said, returning from the other room in time to catch the tail end of the conversation. "Well, this *is* St. Augustine. We're supposed to be overrun with ghosts. Dozens of locals make their livings off the ghost trade. We would certainly never want to get rid of our ghosts." She hesitated, eyes narrowing. "Have you ever seen a ghost, Mr. Anderson?"

"Call me Caleb, please," he told her. What was he supposed to say to that? "I know several people who believe with all their hearts that they've seen a ghost or had some kind of paranormal experience," he said. That was vague enough. But she was still looking at him curiously, and he found himself going on. "Sometimes, when a person has lost a loved one, they're convinced that they've smelled that person's cologne or heard their footsteps. I had a friend in college who was certain his home was haunted by his grandmother. He swore he could smell her Italian cooking. What *has* been proven is that some people do have what we call extrasensory perception—you know, when a mother knows that her child has been injured halfway across the world, that kind of thing." Both

Roberta and Sarah were staring at him now. He was beginning to feel as if he'd suddenly grown horns. "Hey, what do I know? We're all in the dark, guessing about the great beyond. No need to fear, though, Roberta—I certainly wouldn't want to drive away any of your local ghosts. I say, if they're bringing in the tourist dollars, more power to them."

He saw a small smile start to brighten Sarah's features. Then she said, "Oh!" suddenly, and stood up as if she'd just remembered something. "You'll have to excuse me, but I have plans I almost forgot all about." She stared at Caleb again, as if carefully debating something, then apparently made a rather grudging decision to include him. "I'm meeting a few friends, and my cousin Will for drinks and dinner. You're welcome to join us."

"I'll be happy to, if you're sure you don't mind," Caleb told her.

"I just asked you," Sarah said.

Which didn't mean she didn't mind, he thought. Too bad. She *had* asked, and he was going to take advantage of that to spend some time with a beautiful woman.

"Sure. I haven't eaten yet. Sounds great," Caleb said, and stood, too. "I can even protect you from the curiosity seekers on the way," he said.

"I'm not really the type who needs protection," she said.

Everyone needs protection, he told her silently. *If you had seen half of what I've seen in this life . . .*

"You two have a good time," Roberta said. "I'll see you both at breakfast."

They thanked her for the tea and headed for the door. Outside, Caleb asked Sarah if she wanted him to drive.

"We're only going about four blocks," she told him. "Unless you can't walk that far," she added just a shade too sweetly.

"I should be fine," he told her. "Where are we going?"

"Hunky Harry's."

"There's really place called *Hunky Harry's?*" Caleb asked incredulously. "Is there really a Harry? And is he hunky?" he teased.

"There *is* a Harry, and he's been old as long as I can remember, so he's got to be . . . really old. And he likes to think he's hunky. It's a popular place with locals and tourists alike. So popular that he changes the name periodically, when he gets sick of the crowds."

"So Harry is a real character."

She shrugged, walking toward Avenida Menendez. "Maybe you'll get to see for yourself. He may or may not be around tonight. He comes in when he feels like it. When he does, he cleans tables, washes glasses, even cooks up a few appetizers. Yes, he's a real character."

She was keeping a definite distance between

them, he noticed. She still didn't trust him; he wouldn't be here at all, walking with her, planning to spend time with her friends, if it weren't for Adam.

"So exactly why are you here in town?" she asked.

"Jennie Lawson," he said.

She looked at him. "The woman who disappeared last year?"

"Yes. You heard about it, I take it?"

"I wasn't living back down here then, but Caroline showed me the newspaper this afternoon. Jennie Lawson was mentioned because of Winona Hart, the local girl who just disappeared. The article said they don't know that she ever got to St. Augustine."

"I know, but according to her mother, she was heading here."

"And you think you can find her—*here*—after all this time?"

"Her mother doesn't think she's still alive, but she *does* think I'll find out what happened to her, whether she got this far or not."

"You know, there's a possibility that . . . that she wanted to disappear."

"There's always that possibility. But . . ." He left off speaking and shrugged. "What I was saying to Roberta before? I've found that to be true. Whether it's instinct, extrasensory perception or what, I don't know. But when a mother feels her child is dead, she's almost always right."

She stared at him, obviously bothered by his words. "That's horrible."

"Of course it is," he agreed. "Any death is sad."

"No, I mean your attitude. How are you going to find her if you don't believe it's possible that she's alive? You need to . . . believe," she told him.

"I need to do everything in my power—whether she's alive or dead—that's what matters," he said.

She shook her head in disgust.

"All right," he said, "you tell me. What about the local girl? What's your feeling about her? Did she just run away? Is she trying to punish her parents? What do you *believe?*"

She kept shaking her head, pulling ahead of him a little. "No. But things . . . happen. Maybe she's hurt somewhere. And that's why it matters that people move quickly."

"Jennie disappeared a year ago," he reminded her.

"Maybe she has amnesia. Stranger things have happened," she assured him.

"I *will* find her. Alive or dead, I *will* find out what happened to her," he said flatly.

She fell silent for a few seconds, then, changing the subject, said, "You met Will Perkins this morning."

"Yes. Why?"

"He's my cousin."

"Cool."

She was walking very quickly now, as if she

were uncomfortable with him. "There's the restaurant," she said.

Avenida Menendez fronted the water. From where they stood, he could see the massive fortification of Ft. Marion, gleaming in the moonlight in all its historic glory. Horse-drawn carriages lined the opposite side of the street. Groups of tourists were walking around, some couples holding hands or arm in arm. There were several hotels nearby, and numerous restaurants. The downtown historic area was small, the streets busy with car traffic along with all the pedestrians. He saw tables in front of a café and bar. The neon sign, adorned with palm fronds and plastic alligators, advertised Hunky Harry's.

She preceded him, winding her way through the outside tables and walking straight to a table at the rear. He eyed the single empty chair as he recognized Will, Caroline and the other two docents from the museum, Renee Otten and Barry Travis.

"Hey!" Will saw him and stood, grinning. "Nice that you came along." He set an arm around Sarah's shoulders, drawing her against him to give her a rub on the head. They were obviously close. They resembled one another, too, with the same shade of hair and eyes, so much alike, yet Will was as completely masculine as Sarah was feminine.

"Sarah invited me along. I hope that's all right," Caleb said, after greeting everyone.

"It's great!" Renee said enthusiastically.

"I'm impressed you got Sarah here. I thought for sure she'd blow us off tonight," Caroline said.

"Here we go, another chair," Barry offered, pulling one over from another table.

"Thanks," Caleb said, taking the seat.

Everyone started talking at once, stepping on each other's words, and he tried to keep up the chatter until a waitress came and took their orders. He opted for the fish of the day and wondered why the others all gave him funny looks.

As soon as the waitress left, the conversation turned to the skeletons in Sarah's house.

"How long do you think it will take them to remove them all?" Renee asked.

"It can take months—years, even—at some sites," Barry said glumly.

Sarah glared at him.

"Sorry," Barry said.

"You don't have to let it take months," Caleb said to Sarah.

They all stared at him. "You have training in the field, too, so you can call the shots. So far, you've done all the right things, brought in the authorities and the experts. Now you can take control. You know the right people, so keep the process moving. Whatever crime took place, it was over a hundred years ago. You can see to it that everything is done right, that people are respectful of both the bodies and the historical record. And then

85

you can let the forensic anthropologists have their day once the bodies are out of your house."

Sarah stared at him and nodded slowly. "I . . . guess so."

Caroline tossed her hair back. "Don't just guess. Caleb is right. Take control."

"It's true. This is the kind of work I was doing in Virginia, but I certainly wasn't in charge. In a lot of ways, historians are really just record keepers, secretaries for the past. Once the bodies are removed and the remains dated . . . come to think of it, it will be intriguing to research the situation. And it *is* my house, damn it!" She slammed a fist on the table and grinned. "If there's investigating to be done, there's no reason why I can't do it."

"And Caleb there can help you, I bet," Barry said.

His words were followed by a moment of silence as everyone stared at Caleb.

"Well, you're an investigator, right?" Barry asked.

"Yes, I'm an investigator," Caleb agreed.

"Yes, but *I'm* a historian," Sarah said. "And the bodies in my house are over a hundred years old. It's not a police matter, because there's no one left alive to arrest. It's all a matter for the historians now," Sarah said, then stood, as if agitated. "Excuse me, I'm just going to say hello to a friend at the bar."

Caleb noted that no one standing at the bar

seemed the least bit interested in their little group.

He stayed at the table with the others. It never hurt to know as many locals as he could. It wasn't likely that this foursome could help him find Jennie Lawson, but they might know someone or something about the area that could be pertinent at some point.

And Sarah's house . . . well, he had to admit it fascinated him. Historian or not, he was drawn to it, and when he got a feeling like that, it almost always meant something.

"She's touchy tonight," Will said, apologizing for Sarah.

"I would be, too," Caroline said defensively.

"It will better once those bodies are out of her house," Renee said.

"Seriously," Barry said. "She just found out she's been sleeping with a bunch of bodies. You talk about a haunted house . . . Their spirits are probably all running around screaming, 'Let me out, let me out!'"

"Oh, Barry," Renee protested, giggling.

"So tell us about yourself," Caroline said, inching her chair closer to Caleb's. "You met Will today, right? Diving? And you found a body in a submerged car. Did he drive off the road?"

"I found the body, and it's in very bad condition. The medical examiner is on it now. As to how he ended up in the water, I'll leave it to the police to figure that out," Caleb said.

"There were no bullet holes in the car or anything like that?" Renee asked, intrigued.

"Not that I saw, but then again, I wasn't looking for any. The police have custody of the car now, as well, and they'll find out what happened," Caleb said.

"So Will says you're here to find a girl—but not our missing girl?" Barry asked, perplexed.

"Right," Caleb agreed. "You probably read about the case at the time. Her name wa— Her name is Jennie Lawson, and she disappeared a year ago on her way here. But of course I'll share whatever information I discover with the local police, because it could help with the search for Winona Hart. They might have been abducted by the same person."

"Maybe they both ran off to join a cult," Renee said. "That kind of thing happens, you know."

"It does, but usually someone who knows the person is aware that they're dissatisfied with their lives, or that they've fallen under the influence of some sect," Caleb explained.

"But the cases might not be related at all," Barry speculated.

"That's true, too."

"So where do you start?" Caroline asked him.

"Well, theoretically, you start with the person's last known whereabouts," Caleb said.

"But this girl you're looking for . . . the paper said no one even knows what she did after her plane landed in Jacksonville. She just disappeared," Barry said.

"She picked up a rental car," Caleb said.

"But after all this time . . . that car couldn't possibly yield any clues," Will said.

"You'd be surprised," Caleb said. "Trace evidence can survive an awful lot. But it's a moot point—unless we find the car. It disappeared, too."

Just then the waitress arrived with their meals, and Caleb thought his fish—which no one else had ordered, he noticed—was delicious. Despite the arrival of their food, Sarah remained at the bar, chatting with the bartender.

The others asked him more questions as they ate; he answered some and deftly sidestepped others.

Finally he managed to turn the conversation away from himself and learned that Will had grown up in St. Augustine, as had Caroline. Renee had been there about seven years, having fallen in love with the city while attending college over in Gainesville. Barry was the latecomer. He'd done historical tours in Chicago, his hometown, and Charleston, before seeing an ad for docents for the museum.

"I love it here," he told Caleb. "It gets chilly enough in winter for me to feel like there's been a change of season, but we pretty much never get snow, and even then, it's just a few flakes that melt on contact. It's a big deal when it happens, though, it's so rare. And because we're on the water, even summer is usually cool enough, better than a lot of other places. So I'm staying here for sure."

"Seems like a pretty laid-back town," Caleb said.

"Hey," Caroline protested. "We have plenty of nightlife. And if it's not exciting enough for you here, pop back onto the highway. In twenty minutes you're on the outskirts of Jacksonville. A few hours in the other direction and you're in Orlando, surrounded by theme parks."

"So where is home to you, Caleb?" Renee asked, breaking in before Caroline's lecture really got going.

"Virginia," Caleb said.

"So is this your first trip to St. Augustine?" Caroline asked, and he thought she seemed a little bit suspicious, even slightly troubled.

"Yes," he assured her.

"Hmm."

"Why?" he asked her.

"I don't know. I could just swear I'd met you, or at least seen you, somewhere before, that's all."

"Who knows? Maybe in another life," Will said, and yawned. "I've got work tomorrow, gang. I've got to get going."

They all rose in unison just as Sarah returned to the table. "Sorry, guys. Al and I just started talking and I lost track. Looks like I missed dinner," she added, staring at the lasagne congealing on her plate.

"Looks like," Caroline said. "Well, I'll see you tomorrow." She started for the door.

"Hey, wait, I'm walking you home," Will called after her. He gave the others an apologetic look. "She's a blonde. . . . I don't want her out there alone at night."

"Good call, stick with her," Sarah told him.

"Don't go thinking that just because you're a brunette, that makes you safe," Will said quietly to Sarah, then gave Caleb a speaking look before racing after Caroline.

"I'll see Renee home safe and sound," Barry said cheerfully, and something in the way he looked at her told Caleb that the two had been an item for a long time.

"We might as well head out, too," Sarah told Caleb when the others were gone.

"What about the check?"

"It's covered," she assured him.

"That's nice, but I pay my own way," he told her. "Besides, I can expense it."

"I'm so happy to hear we're a business expense," Sarah said.

He let out a sigh of aggravation, staring at her. "What the hell is it with you? You're the one who invited *me* here."

She was quiet for a moment, then shook her head. "I don't know. I honestly don't know. Anyway, don't worry about paying. Al—the bartender—told me that Harry was here earlier, saw us and told our waitress not to give us a check. So we were all Harry's guests tonight. And I have to show up to work tomorrow morning, too, so I need to get going."

"Let's go, then."

She waved to several people as they left, and a few called out to her in return, but at least no one was asking her about the grisly find in her house.

Even so, he was certain that the whispering would start as soon as they were gone.

They walked in silence for a few minutes. "So what will you be doing tomorrow?" she eventually asked him.

"Heading to Jacksonville," he said.

She looked over at him. "You think your missing girl is in Jacksonville?"

"No. I think she's here. And I think Winona Hart is going to be found here, too—eventually. But I want to go to the agency where Jennie rented her car. I would have done that today, but I had the opportunity to go on the dive, and I didn't want to miss it."

"There *is* the possibility that she just drove off into the sunset," Sarah said.

"No. She didn't get insurance on the car because her parents had insurance that already covered her. If she'd been planning on just taking off with the car, she'd have bought insurance so that her parents wouldn't be liable," he said.

"You overestimate people," Sarah said. "If she

was depressed or upset about something, she wouldn't have been thinking about insurance."

"But she wasn't depressed, and she wasn't upset."

"How can you be so certain?"

"I talked to her parents."

"The parents are often the last to know," she reminded him.

"Not these parents."

She was still skeptical, he could see, but he didn't argue with her.

"Do you really think you can read people that well?" she asked at last.

"Not always, but sometimes? Yes."

"Some people wear very convincing masks," Sarah pointed out.

"Very true."

"So how do you deal with that?" she asked.

"All masks crack with time, or under the right heat," he said. "So what about you? What will you be doing tomorrow?"

"Oh, I'll be going to work. I need the money more than ever now," she said, her tone slightly resentful.

"You're not going to hang at home, hovering over your property?"

"I'll let them tramp around a while on their own. Then I'll get involved," she said.

They had reached the B&B. Caleb used his key to open the front door instead of going around the side to his private entrance. "Thanks for inviting me tonight," he said.

"I'm glad you could come," she answered, but there wasn't a lot of warmth in her words. They were courteous, spoken by rote.

"Well, have a good day at work tomorrow. And . . . hey."

"Hey what?"

"Be careful. Something does seem to be going on around here," he said.

She smiled. "I'm not a blonde. And I'm sure not about to run out and buy a big bottle of bleach right now."

"Two blondes have gone missing, true. But that fact might be coincidence. If the two disappearances *are* connected, the real link might be something else entirely," Caleb said. "Everyone needs to be careful right now. No one knows yet what links the missing girls."

She smiled. "I'll be careful. And I'll see you at breakfast, anyway."

"Right."

She hadn't headed toward her room yet. The light coming from the parlor was dim, but he could see that she was staring at him closely. "Caroline is convinced that she's seen you before."

"Yeah, I know. But I don't see how. But anything is possible, I guess. Maybe we crossed paths in an airport somewhere."

She was still staring at him.

"Yes?" he said at last.

"I was just curious," she said.

"About?"

"When does *your* mask crack? When do we get to know the real you?"

Without even waiting for an answer, she turned then and headed into her room. He heard the click as she locked her door.

4

It was perfectly natural that Sarah had a bizarre dream that night.

She was at Hunky Harry's, but no one was what they seemed.

She was with her friends, but then she blinked and turned away, and saw that though a band was playing, the musicians were skeletons. They were dressed casually, in T-shirts and jeans, but a few wore top hats, as if they were planning to join an orchestra. They held their instruments with bony fingers, grinned wicked, lipless grins, and stared at her with empty eye sockets.

When she turned back to her table, everything about her friends had changed.

They were skeletons, as well. Will was drinking a beer, and she watched the amber liquid pass through his rib cage and disappear below the table.

Renee had a bandana tied around her head, just as if she were holding her hair in place, but there was no hair there. She was dressed in the home-spun cotton outfit she often wore when giving lectures at the museum.

Barry was wearing a stovepipe hat.

A bone forefinger touched her shoulder. She looked up and saw that it belonged to Al, the bartender.

"You having a beer, or would you rather a glass of wine?" he asked her.

She opened her mouth to answer him, but nothing came out. She wanted to scream, to ask them all whether they realized something was wrong—that they had all turned to bones.

Then she looked across the room and saw someone who wasn't a skeleton.

Caleb Anderson.

He was standing in the doorway, solid, living flesh.

His eyes met hers, and he shook his head, as if trying to make her understand . . . something.

"We all have masks on, all the time," he said. She couldn't really hear him because the music—an old Stones tune—was so loud, but she still knew exactly what he'd said.

"Look carefully at everyone," he added.

Then he started walking across the room to her, but the air was suddenly filled with flying bones. They were everywhere, like a gauntlet of flying ribs and femurs.

She leapt up and tried to reach him, but all she could see were the bones . . .

It was a dream, of course—nothing but a dream—and she wanted out.

She woke up, her eyes flying open while the rest of her felt almost paralyzed for a moment, and realized it was daytime. Despite the drapes in her windows, sunlight was filtering through.

She groaned, then rose and looked at her watch. Eight o'clock. Breakfast would be on the table in thirty minutes, and it would be large and elegant. Bertie served fruit, juice, a selection of main dishes, and a wide selection rolls and breads, along with butter and homemade jams. Most of the B&Bs in town prided themselves on their breakfasts, and the Tropic Breeze was no different. She used good china, silverware, and eclectic but elegant serving pieces. Somehow she managed to pull it all together seven days a week, though it helped that she paid her employees so well that every college student in the area was happy to help her. They began work at six, getting coffee out for six-thirty, and they had breakfast all cleaned up by ten, so they could head to class.

Sarah knew all that because, years ago, she had been one of those college students, having gotten the jobs thanks to her parents' friendship with Bertie.

But now she was a guest, so after a quick shower to wash away the uneasiness the dream had left in its wake, she neatly repacked, having decided that, as much as she loved Bertie, she was moving back home.

Bertie had refused to let her pay for her room, which made her feel guilty, and she had the carriage house, after all. She could live there while the academics and the authorities tramped through the mansion. She could keep an eye on everything going on, but she wouldn't have to deal with the mess—or the creepiness. She should have thought of it the night before. No, she'd been too upset last night; it was good that she'd spent the night else-where.

She thought about the dream from which she'd forced herself to waken. Strange. Though no stranger than yesterday's real-world events. She had been able to escape from the dream, but she wasn't going to be so lucky when it came to reality. Her house was going to be filled with strangers for the foreseeable future. Her carefully thought-out plan to get her own B&B started was going straight to hell.

It was, she reflected as she left the room, strange that all her friends had turned into skeletons in the dream, while Caleb Anderson had remained flesh and blood—and ready to come to her rescue.

"Morning!" Bertie called to her cheerfully as she walked into the dining room. The older woman was in the process of refilling the old Russian samovar she used for regular coffee. "How did you sleep, dear?" Bertie asked.

"Like a baby," Sarah lied. "Can I help?"

"No, but thank you for offering. Help yourself to breakfast, and let me know if there's something special you want to see on tomorrow's menu. You are staying tonight, too, right?"

"You know what? Thank you so much, Bertie, but no, I'm going to go home tonight."

99

"What?" Bertie demanded, aghast. "But, Sarah—"

"It's okay, honestly. It's not like I'll be sleeping with the skeletons, so don't worry. Anyway, I have the carriage house. It's all set up and ready to roll. I'm so grateful to you for making room for me last night, but I'd rather stick close to home in my carriage house until all those people clear out of my house."

"The dead as well as the living, huh?" Bertie said, shaking her head. "I still wish you'd stay here with me, Sarah."

"You're a sweetheart. And you know I'll run back here in a second flat if I decide I can't hack it staying in the carriage house anymore."

"You're always welcome here, Sarah, you know that," Bertie told her. "You still have that key I gave you in case of emergencies, right? If you get scared at any time, day or night, I want you to remember that you have a place here."

"I know, and I'm grateful."

Sarah gave Bertie a hug and sat down next to a family of four who introduced themselves as the Petersons. The twelve-year-old daughter seemed to be going on twenty. The son, who was ten, seemed to be going on four.

Still, when the son wasn't racing around, threatening one of Bertie's antiques, the family seemed pleasant. She talked about the museum, and they said they would come by, which would be good for

Caroline's parents, who needed all the business they could get.

She wasn't sure if she was relieved that Caleb Anderson wasn't there, or if she missed sparring with him. He seemed to have an amazing ability to control his emotions, answering her evenly no matter what she said to him. She still wasn't sure how she felt about the man. He worked for Adam Harrison, which was certainly in his favor. Granted, she didn't know Adam that well, but she certainly knew him by reputation, and knew that he was trusted by every government agency out there. Of course, there were those who might think that made him suspicious from the get-go, but she wasn't the type to see a government conspiracy around every corner. She had talked with Adam often enough to be convinced that he was an honorable man. But that only went so far. Caleb was his own person, and she had to judge him on his own merits.

As she and the Petersons talked, Sarah enjoyed her eggs Benedict, shaved potatoes with cheese and fruit with yogurt. When she had finished eating, she told the Petersons she would see them later and went back to her room. She still had a good fifteen minutes left to drop her bag in the carriage house and get to work.

When she reached her house, she saw a number of cars in the driveway, including the M.E.'s van that belonged to Floby, rumored to be the best of the local medical examiners. Sarah had met Floby shortly after her return to the city; he attended most community and city hall meetings, and loved St. Augustine with a passion.

She didn't recognize the other vehicles, except for the unmarked sedan that Tim Jamison drove. Poor Tim. He must have felt the way she did about so much happening at once. At least her only other stress involved getting the house ready to receive paying guests, while Tim was spearheading the investigation into the disappearance of Winona Hart. Sarah herself hadn't known the girl even existed until she saw the headlines trumpeting her disappearance and the fact that Tim was lead detective on the case, since she hadn't been part of the intimate world of the historic district.

Sarah was suddenly angry with herself for not taking the girl's disappearance more to heart. She argued inwardly that it was impossible for any one human being to take on the pain of the whole world, and the truth was that there was nothing she could do, nothing she could do that would help. If she *could* do something, she *would*. But she couldn't think of anything she could possibly do that the police weren't already doing.

She steered clear of the house and all the activity going on there and let herself quietly into the carriage house, deposited her bag, then left quickly, walking on toward the museum.

But as she walked, she found herself thinking

about the people whose remains had ended up in her walls.

She was sorry they'd ended up that way, of course. But they had probably lived and died in the normal way, and after that . . . well, the body was just a shell. It was nothing once death had taken the heart, mind and soul.

On the other hand, the grim discovery was bound to make for some great ghost stories, that was for sure. What better way to lure the tourists than with tales of misty figures who walked the halls demanding a proper burial?

She was suddenly anxious to get her hands on the historical records and learn more about the mortician who was undoubtedly behind the nasty scheme that had led to the deads' unorthodox entombment. Three hours of work, and then she would be off for lunch. That would be a great time to run over to the privately owned historical society library, which was open to the public several days a week.

In the grand scheme of things, coffin theft was morally reprehensible but not on a par with red-handed murder. She thought of some of the city's genuinely gruesome history. Under Spanish rule, executions had been carried out by the garrote. It wasn't a particularly bloody death—not like the spray of blood that accompanied the falling blade of the guillotine—but it was a painful one. The rope around the neck was tightened twist by twist.

Onlookers in the square often bet one another on how many twists it would take a man to die. Luckily that particular tradition disappeared at some point as the city burned to the ground, and went from Spanish rule to British, then back to Spanish, until Florida finally became part of the United States.

More recently, the city had had to cope with the notoriety of what they called "the murder house." In a nice part of town, in the nineteen seventies, two neighbors had gone at one another. Witnesses—who all mysteriously died or went mute before the trial—saw the owner of the house on the left emerge and slit the throat of the woman who lived on the right. He'd been furious with her for the insults she'd thrown at him after he'd called an animal control agency to take away the menagerie she'd kept in her yard. The murderer had lots of friends in high places, and once the witnesses disappeared, the charges against him were dismissed and he moved away. If anyone had a reason to haunt a house, it was that poor woman who had been so brutally murdered on her own front steps, but as far as Sarah knew, the people now living in the house had never experienced a single spectral incident.

In comparison, the skeletons of people who'd died naturally were nothing, even if they *had* ended up in the wall of her house. They made for a good story and some lively conversation, nothing else. But she did want to know the whole story of what had happened. It *was* her house, after all.

With that thought uppermost in her mind, she looked around and realized she'd reached the museum.

The morning traffic on I-95 heading north from St. Augustine to Jacksonville was light. Once Caleb neared the city, he took the 295 extension leading around the downtown area and toward the airport, which was north of the city center. The car rental agency he was seeking was just half a mile from the airport. When she had arrived in Jacksonville a year ago, Jennie Lawson had deplaned, waited for her luggage and boarded a courtesy shuttle for the rental agency.

Then she had driven away in her rental car and disappeared. There was no record on her credit cards of any later purchase, and the car she had rented, a silver Altima, had never been found.

He cautioned himself to be methodical, to start at the beginning and, no matter how tedious and repetitious, get the facts straight before he started trying to extrapolate his way to a conclusion.

Those were simple rules of any investigation, and Caleb always followed them.

As he drove, he tried to keep his mind on the case, but he couldn't help it: his mind kept wandering back to yesterday, and all those bones.

They'd been the unknowing victims of a mortician's greed, pure and simple. Another ghoulish story to add to the repertoires of the multitude of ghost tours that wound through the city by night.

Nothing to do with the real tragedies of two missing girls, at least one of them presumed dead.

Caleb wondered why the chronologically separate cases seemed linked together somehow—if only in his mind. And then there was the house where the long-dead bodies had been found. He had felt drawn to it from the moment he had seen it. A natural fondness for architecture? No, definitely something more. Something instinctive had made him stop in front of the house and study it.

Maybe instinct had something to do with his fascination with the house's owner, as well. Sarah McKinley was decidedly attractive. But he was equally drawn by her ability to speak, and her fascination with history and people.

But he was here because of Jennie Lawson, he reminded himself. He needed to forget about the bones in the wall and get his mind back on his assignment. Jennie hadn't disappeared into thin air. He had to find out what had happened to her.

Caleb parked outside the rental agency, strode inside and took his place at the end of the line, which at least moved quickly. When he got to the front, he asked the cheerful young woman at the counter—who wanted to offer him an upgrade before he even got out a word—if he could speak with the manager. She immediately looked crestfallen, as if she hadn't been cheerful enough. He explained that it was about a previous rental, and she directed him to a small glassed-in office to the left. The manager rose, looking concerned as Caleb entered, but he offered a hand and introduced himself as Harold Sparks. Sparks looked at Caleb suspiciously after studying his credentials and shook his head. "The cops were all over us about this a year ago. I wish I could help, but I can't tell you a thing."

"Would it be possible to speak with the rental agent she saw?" Caleb asked. He had taken out his notebook, and now he looked down at the page. "Mina Grigsby."

The other man's jaw tightened. "She's been through this before, too."

"I understand," Caleb said patiently.

Sparks shrugged, looking abashed. "Sorry. Sure. Either of us would do anything to help find the woman, it's just that . . . there's nothing else to say or do. She came in the courtesy shuttle, she rented a car—and she disappeared. The cops kept coming back because once she left here, everything's a dead end. We're all they've got. Her picture ran in all the papers, and no one came forward to say they'd seen her anywhere, not a gas station, a restaurant, or a hotel, bowling alley, movie theater or bar. It's almost as if aliens came down and swept her up. But I'll call Mina into the office, and you two can chat."

"Thank you," Caleb said. He knew that the police had been here; he knew that the manager and the poor clerk had been through it all before. And he didn't think he was going to learn anything new, but that was half the job, doggedly repeating what had been done, always searching for whatever little bit of information might have seemed insignificant at the time but now just might become a clue.

Mina Grigsby was one of those thin, nervous-by-nature people, but she didn't seem to have a problem talking to him. She nodded when her manager explained that Caleb was a private investigator, and she quickly perched on the edge of her boss's desk, looking expectantly at Caleb as Harold Sparks excused himself.

Caleb smiled reassuringly. "I'm sorry," he began. "I know you've been asked about Jennie Lawson before."

"Oh, it's okay. Really. I'm glad to hear that someone is still looking in to what happened to her. She was very pretty and very sweet. And polite. I think that's why I remember her so clearly. We didn't have the exact car she had requested, but she wasn't nasty about it, the way some people are. I mean, the rental forms say 'a certain vehicle or its equivalent.'"

Caleb agreed. "I've rented plenty of cars, and you're certainly right about that, Miss Grigsby. Mina. I know that she came in, got the keys and left, and that her agreement for was two weeks. And I know that you two just met to transact business, but I was hoping she might have said something, given you an idea whether she was meeting up with friends or what her plans might be. Something that might have come back to you in the time since she went missing. If I had anywhere to go from here, it would be very helpful."

"Well, let me think . . . I mean, she didn't say where she was staying. She did say that she wasn't leaving the state with the car."

"Did she say anything about her plans? Anything at all?"

Mina was thoughtful for a moment; then she smiled. "Well, to be perfectly honest, people don't always get too excited about Jacksonville. They're all heading somewhere else—down to the beaches, or St. Augustine, or Daytona, the space center . . . even the theme parks. But Jacksonville is a great city, with a really nice river walk and lots of history. It's old, too, you know."

"Of course. Was she planning on visiting Jacksonville?"

"Yes—but on her way back. She was anxious to see St. Augustine. She said that she'd be heading straight there. I told her where there were some very good restaurants . . . but she wasn't planning on eating for a while. She had a bottle of soda in her purse, and some PowerBars. She wanted to get started seeing things right away."

"Did she say what things?"

Mina shook her head slowly again. "No, not exactly."

"Not exactly? Think, please, Mina. What exactly *did* she say?"

"Well, she said that she was going to take a ghost tour—but that wouldn't have been until that night."

"Did she say anything about a hotel reservation? Or maybe a B and B?"

"No. She was going to head into Old Town and find a place that appealed to her—I do remember her saying that."

Caleb waited, because she appeared to be thinking with intensity. She let out a sigh after a moment, and he decided he had gotten all he could from her, and that it wasn't terribly helpful. He could—and of course *would*—speak to the ghost tour operators, guides and ticket vendors, but since Jennie Lawson's picture had been up all over the city and no one had come forward, he didn't think that avenue would take him far, either. Still, he had to follow where the trail led.

"There *was* one more thing," Mina said, surprising him.

"Oh?"

"I'd forgotten all about this. She told me she was going to get a reading. You know, a palm reading or the cards or something. She wore a pentagram around her neck, and I asked her if she was a witch. She said no, she just liked it. There was a ruby set in one of the points of the star. She said she wasn't a believer, but she liked the stories. I guess that's why she was going to take that ghost tour." She fell silent, then sighed again, shaking her head as she looked at him. "I'm sorry, but I really can't think of anything else."

"Do you remember what she was wearing?" Caleb asked.

"Yes. Jeans and a red T-shirt, and she was pulling a black, white and purple suitcase. She said it was wonderful—she could always find her luggage at baggage claim."

"You've been very helpful," Caleb assured her.

"Really?" She seemed genuinely pleased. "It's terrible. And sad. And now another girl's missing, and she looks . . . so much like Jennie Lawson."

"Yes, she does," Caleb acknowledged.

"I hope you find her. Jennie Lawson, I mean. And the other girl, too, of course," Mina told him, then stood and offered her hand. He thanked her again as they shook, and then she left and went back to work. He would have thanked Harold Sparks again, but the man was behind the counter, pretending to be busy. He nodded Caleb's way, so Caleb nodded in return and left.

He had learned something new, something no one had mentioned, something that wasn't in any of the police files. Jennie Lawson hadn't been on her way to explore Ft. Marion. She hadn't been planning to explore the bar scene or seek out a dance club.

Jennie Lawson had been in search of something scary.

Sadly, it seemed that she had found it.

The United States took control of Florida in 1821, and it became a territory in 1822.

Sarah already knew that her house had been built that year as a home for Thomas Grant, a statistical consultant advising the politicians and military men intent on making Florida a state. Apparently he'd been talented enough with numbers to parlay his own earnings into a small fortune. The home had originally been built to accommodate his wife and seven children, and he'd owned it for thirty years, after which it had been sold to the MacTavish family. It had remained in their possession through the Civil War, after which it had been abandoned when Cato MacTavish had suddenly left the state.

Sarah had always known the basic facts and figures that went with the house, and she'd heard the rumors that it was haunted in the way *all* old places were supposedly haunted. There was a rumor that Cato's father had a woman working for him who was the child of a Haitian—descendent of refugees from the Haitian revolution—and an Indian, though no one knew exactly what tribe. There was a white man somewhere in her genetic background, as well—a plantation owner or an overseer. She had been the "spell queen" of the area, selling love potions and other such supposed magic.

There were stories, too, that women had died and disappeared during those years, and that Cato MacTavish had killed his wife, or possibly his fiancée, and that he had abandoned the property rather than face justice and the hangman.

What she knew for a fact was that the MacTavish family had used the house as a mortuary at the beginning of the Civil War, and that it had been abandoned after the war, then bought for back taxes by the Brennan family—who had used the house as an address both before and after the sale, which was very strange, unless it was an error in the record keeping. They had used it as a mortuary again, and it had remained in the family until it had been more or less abandoned once more, before finally being then purchased by Mrs. Emily Douglas, who had eventually sold it to Sarah.

What she wanted to do was hunt down the truth behind the rumors, to see what was smoke and what was fire. She knew how to dig through old records—she had a master's degree, after all—and the historical library was very good, so she didn't expect to have too much trouble.

The first thing she came across were a number of

blueprints showing the changes that had taken place in the house over the years. She was immediately grateful to the person who had put the kitchen in at the turn of century—one of the Brennan clan—and even more grateful that the house had been built from the start with full plumbing and bathrooms. Electricity had gone in during 1904.

None of that seemed to have anything to do with the bones in the walls, other than the fact that she discovered that nothing had been done to the walls in the library where the corpses had been found—not on record, at least—since 1857, when some cosmetic work had been done after a fire had damaged the plaster. Of course, then as now, people had often done whatever they wanted to *inside* a house, despite codes and regulations. These days St. Augustine had a very strict historical preservation policy, but even so, and even by those who honored it when it came to the exterior of their houses, inside work was generally at the discretion of the owner.

The guilty mortician must have been one of the MacTavishes or the Brennans, since it was highly unlikely that an outsider could have sauntered in with a string of bodies and walled them up. Now all she had to do was find the criminal in question.

Sarah glanced at her watch and realized that an hour wasn't nearly enough to finish her digging. It was time to return to work.

She left the library—a historic building itself—and headed back to the museum. On her way, she saw that flyers had been posted everywhere.

Have you seen this woman?

The picture was of the missing local girl, Winona Hart. She was smiling and bright-eyed in her photo, a beautiful young blonde whose innocence and zest for life had been captured by the photographer's lens.

Sarah felt a tightening in her heart, and she wished there was something she could do to help find the girl, but she doubted that a master's in history qualified her to be of much help in a missing persons case.

But . . .

Caleb Anderson was here to search for another woman. Could the two disappearances be related? She wished she knew more about the psychology of crime. Would a serial killer hang around a city like St. Augustine so he could kidnap and most likely kill two women a year apart?

She realized that she was still staring at the picture. It was one thing to read about the girl in the paper, see a grainy photo and impersonally hope for the best. Now, looking at such a lifelike image, she felt as if she had somehow become involved. Those big bright eyes seemed to stare at her. Winona was so young, so pretty, and so full of life and laughter.

She was surprised when she reached out to touch

the picture, as if she were actually reaching out to touch Winona Hart's face.

And she was even more surprised by the electric sizzle that streaked along her arm when she made contact with the paper.

"I'm so sorry," she caught herself saying aloud. "I'm so sorry, but I don't know how I can possibly help you."

Then, feeling like a fool, she looked around and hurried down the street, walking quickly now, since her lunch hour was definitely over.

A year ago, the usual had all been done. Jennie Lawson had made a cell phone call to her mother when she had landed. That was the last call she had made, though her cell records and voice mail showed a long list of calls coming in, from her mother—growing more frantic with each message—and various friends who had hoped to make it to St. Augustine to meet up with her. The friends all had alibis; none of them had ever even come to St. Augustine, because they had never been able to contact her.

She had last used her credit card at the car rental agency, and no one had accessed her bank account since her disappearance, so presumably she hadn't been killed in the course of a robbery for financial gain.

She had left with her rental car and, as Harold Sparks had suggested, disappeared as thoroughly as if she had been beamed up by an alien spaceship.

But that hadn't happened. Which meant that someone, somewhere, had to know something.

Caleb stopped at a few gas stations on his way back down to St. Augustine, but she had left the rental agency with a full tank of gas, so it was unlikely she would have stopped at any of them. Still, despite what she'd told Mina Grigsby, she might have stopped for a soda or a cup of coffee, even something to munch on or a more detailed map of the area than the rental agency had provided.

A tedious and time-consuming canvas of local businesses was likely to get him nowhere. Still, it had to be done.

If he were visiting St. Augustine for the first time and was anxious to find out the best things to do, the local tourist agencies would be a logical place to start. There were several, not to mention the booking offices for all the hearse tours, carriage tours, tram tours, walking tours and train tours.

He pounded the pavement with Jennie's picture in hand, and at each stop he was told that no, they hadn't seen Winona. Each time he explained patiently that this was a girl who had disappeared a year ago.

Finally, toward the end of a long and frustrating day, he entered a booking office offering a variety of tours and went through the usual spiel.

"This isn't the girl who just disappeared. This

girl's name is Jennie Lawson. She came down a year ago on vacation and disappeared. We think she might have been looking to take a ghost tour," he explained for what felt like the thousandth time.

The young guy manning the place frowned, taking the picture again. He looked at Caleb, then studied the photograph again.

"Wow. They really could be the same girl, except—" He broke off, his face wrinkled in concentration.

"I can't tell you how many tourists come through here," he said apologetically.

"It's okay, I know that. I appreciate you trying," Caleb said.

"I'm thinking about what she might have looked like with her hair up, and I'm thinking I just might remember her. Because she was asking about the scariest, spookiest thing it was possible to do. Naturally I told her all our tours are great, it just depended on what she was looking for."

Caleb waited, tension filling him at the possibility of a break in the case, as the kid remained silent, studying the photo.

At last he said, "I think I do remember her, but her hair wasn't down like this. She'd put it up, because of the heat and all."

"Do you remember what tour she decided on?"

"She didn't. She took all the brochures and said she'd be back, that she'd probably take several of them. It really is uncanny. Those two girls, they really could be the same person." He looked up at Caleb again. "I'm sorry. I wish I could be more help."

"You *have* helped. More than you can imagine," Caleb told him. "Thanks." He gave the guy his card, asking him to call if he thought of anything else, and left.

The sun was setting, and his feet hurt; it felt as if he had been walking around forever. But thanks to the kid at the tour office, at least he had some new information and an avenue to explore. Because the kid was right. The missing women didn't just fit a general type. They looked so much alike that it was uncanny.

Whoever had taken Jennie Lawson was the same person who had just snatched Winona Hart. He was sure of it. And the trail leading away from Winona's last known whereabouts would be much warmer than that of the one leading away from Jennie's.

He was going to find the person behind Winona's disappearance, and when he did, he would also find out what had happened to Jennie.

He started back toward his B&B then changed direction.

Five o'clock had come—and gone. Businesses— and museums—would be closed.

And the locals would be headed for Hunky Harry's.

Caleb stood still for a long moment, remembering, as he watched people moving past him on the sidewalk, how Adam Harrison had asked him if he'd gotten a feel for anything. The tram was running a block away, and he could hear the conductor talking about Henry Flagler and the beautiful hotels he had built.

A cannon boomed from nearby Ft. Marion.

A horse-drawn carriage clip-clopped by, and a cloud slipped over the sun, casting the area into shades of silver and gray. The facades of the old Spanish buildings seemed to catch hold of the resulting shadows and recede back in history.

Had he gotten a feel for anything . . . ?

Yes.

Yes, Adam, I have.

I have a feeling a very old house whose walls have been hiding hundreds of bones is somehow connected to what's been going on here.

Not only that, but I have a feeling that its very beautiful owner is somehow—innocently, I'm sure—connected to the mystery, too.

Hunky Harry's it was.

Sarah was tired and aggravated, and longing to get home.

While the morning had gone well, everything seemed to have gone to hell while she'd been gone for her lunch break.

The news about her house had gotten out, turning her world upside down.

The bones had been pretty much the only topic of discussion that afternoon. The receptionist had done nothing but field questions and interview requests from dozens of radio and television stations, not all of them local, which really amazed her. Even the visitors to the museum had heard about the discovery and wanted to talk about it; local history had flown right out the window.

When the first reporter had called, Sarah had taken the call. The man's questions had all been about ghosts and haunted houses, and how did she feel about living with ghosts and wasn't she afraid? After that she'd refused to come to the phone and ended up with a stack of messages that were all variations on that original theme.

She opted to work in the bookstore, leaving the lectures to Caroline, Renee and Barry, because that way, at least, when she faced the same ghoulish questions over and over again, she wasn't interrupting history to answer.

"We're heading to Hunky Harry's, just for drinks," Caroline told her as they closed the doors at last. "And you need a drink more than any of us. My parents said you should take a few days off, by the way."

Sarah stared at her friend, dismayed. "They don't want me here?"

"No, no, it's nothing like that," Caroline assured her. "They don't want you pestered to death."

"Well, tell them thanks, but I don't want to take

any time off," Sarah said, then almost immediately thought better of it. She *did* want time off. She wanted to uncover the truth. She didn't want other people telling her about her house. She wanted to do the research herself.

"Come have a drink and then see how you feel," Caroline suggested.

"Okay, but I'll have to meet you there. I just want to run by the house, see what's happening," Sarah said.

"I can go with you," Caroline offered.

"No, I'll be all right. You go with Barry and Renee. You should be with people—preferably including a big strong guy—right now."

"Why?" Caroline asked, startled. Before Sarah could answer, she said, "Oh. Right. You're worried because I'm a blonde with big blue eyes, and the hair and eye color of both girls were the same—as noted in the news reports."

"It never hurts to be careful," Sarah said.

"And," Caroline added, a smile teasing her lips, "you want to be alone with your precious . . . mortuary."

"It's not a mortuary anymore, and it's not likely I'll be alone," Sarah told her. "I just want to see what's up. You go on, and I'll be right there."

"You'll bail on us," Caroline said.

"I won't. I swear," Sarah promised.

Oddly enough, Sarah found herself hoping that the people prowling her house would be done for the day and really, they should be. After all, what needed to be done had mostly been done the night before. They had brought in Floby, they had taken a thousand pictures of the bones in situ, and they had used special equipment to check the rest of the walls to see if they, too, were hiding something, so they wouldn't have to tear her entire house apart.

"Okay, okay. I'll walk over with Renee and Barry, swear," Caroline said.

"Is Will going to be there?" Sarah asked.

Caroline blushed, nodding in answer to the question.

"I feel like kind of a fifth wheel," Sarah said.

"Never. So don't you dare bail," Caroline told her.

"I won't, I won't, Scout's honor," Sarah said.

"As if you were ever a Scout," Caroline countered.

"If I *had* been a Scout, I'd have had tons of honor badges. I'll be there, promise."

Sarah managed to get out before Renee or Barry could give her an argument and hurried toward her house, half-afraid that strangers were going to stop her on the street to ask about the bones.

But no one did.

She reached the house and was pleased to see that no one was there. Not a car remained. She hurried up the steps to the porch, fitted her key in the lock, turned it and entered.

The house greeted her with an eerie silence.

"Hello? Anyone here?" she called, even though she already knew everyone was gone. Her voice sounded far too soft and tentative, she thought, so she cleared her voice and called out again. "Hello? Is anyone here?"

Unsurprisingly, there was no answer. She walked through to the back and saw that the library was indeed empty.

Tentatively, she moved forward and looked inside the walls, then breathed a sigh of relief. No bones. They had been removed.

She walked on into the kitchen. On the counter there was a note from Floby, who said he'd been there all day, working with the different experts and agencies. He also said they would probably be in and out over the next few days, just to make completely certain that she wouldn't be living with more remains.

She smiled. Floby was a sweetie, a charming old guy, despite holding a job many people considered to be morbid. But he simply saw himself as an investigator, discovering clues in the bodies of the deceased, just as detectives sought them on the streets.

She walked back down the hallway toward the front door and froze. The door was open, and an old man was standing there.

He was so thin he was practically skeletal.

Just like the bones in the walls.

Was he real?

He walked closer to her. She could see that his cheeks were hollow. There were only a few silver tufts of hair on his head, and his nose looked like a narrow perch.

To her astonishment, she opened her mouth but no sound emerged.

What on earth was going on? Could he actually be a ghost? But she didn't believe in ghosts.

Did she?

5

The man had to be real.

He also had to be ninety if he was a day.

"Young lady," he said, taking another step forward, supporting himself with a cane and moving slowly, yet with purpose. "Young lady, I am Terrence Griffin the Third. How do you do?"

He *was* real, she thought in silent gratitude, and he couldn't possibly offer her any harm. A breeze would blow him over.

"Hello," she managed to respond, her voice sounding like a croak. She was angry with herself. She'd left the door open. The discovery of the bones in her walls was bound to bring out the sightseers, and it was likely that a serial killer was at work in the city, and like an idiot, she had left the door open.

"I've come to talk to you," he said. His voice was dry and low, like the rustle of leaves.

"Okay," she said.

"Because you have to know the truth about your house. It's evil."

"A house can't be evil," she said, staring firmly at him.

"Think whatever you want, but people do evil here because evil was done here before," he told her gravely.

She didn't know what to do. He was so old and

looked so frail that she didn't want to upset him, but his intensity and the craziness of his words were disturbing. She fought the urge to scream, push him aside and rush out of the house, and considered calling the police.

In the end she just kept standing there, still staring at him.

He took another step closer to her. "You must listen. It's important. You can do something, you can . . . communicate with them. You need to find out the truth and stop it from happening again."

She wanted to tell him that whatever had happened here a hundred or more years ago couldn't happen again now, because whoever had perpetrated the crime was long dead.

"It started during the Civil War," he told her. "When the house was owned by the MacTavish family."

He knew his local history, she thought, drawn in despite her best intentions to ignore anything he said.

"Old man MacTavish was ill, and he was against the war, so his heart had been broken when his son Cato went off to fight. Cato was planning to marry Eleanora Stewart after the war and take over the mortuary his father had set up. He and Eleanora were madly in love, but when he was wounded and sent home, he discovered that Eleanora had disappeared right after he'd been back on leave. He had been the last person to see her. His father had died while he was gone, so he was left to run the business alone, with just a housekeeper to take care of him, and a boarder and his daughter to help. Pretty soon young women started disappearing. Only a few bodies were found, but the others were presumed dead. Everything was in an uproar, with the war still being on and all. And pretty soon Cato was being accused of kidnapping and murder. People started putting two and two together, and they figured he must have killed Eleanora, so he had to be responsible for what had happened to those other girls, too. So he left, he just left. Or hid out in the woods, as some speculated. The housekeeper went away, too, or so some said, though others thought she had been lynched. The only ones left in the house were the boarder, a man named Leo Brennan, who bought the place when it came up for taxes, and his daughter. He must have learned the trade from Cato, because he kept it as a mortuary, and eventually his son took over. And then . . . well, it happened again."

"I don't understand, Mr. Griffin. What happened again?" Sarah asked.

"The disappearances. Young women just . . . disappearing. I know because my own daughter left the house in the summer of 1928, and she never came back. She came here to get together with Louise Brennan and another friend, Susannah, and she and Susannah both disappeared. They were never seen again," Mr. Griffin said with the sadness of years in his voice.

He had been the father of a teenager, at least, in 1928. How old *was* he? she wondered.

Once again, the question invaded her mind.

Was he even real?

Yes, he was flesh and blood. She was sure of it.

"The housekeeper . . . she knew voodoo, the black arts, magic," he said.

"Mr. Griffin, you said she left right after Cato did," she reminded him gently.

"The evil remains, it resides inside these walls," he said.

He was in his dotage, she told herself. He had never gotten over the loss of his daughter. And now, with all the publicity about Winona Hart, he was simply seeing the past reflected in the present.

"I'm very sorry about your daughter," she offered, not knowing what else to say.

"She's here, in these walls," he said. "Like Eleanora, like the others."

"Mr. Griffin, there's no one in these walls . . . anymore. The medical examiner came, and the bones have all been taken away. My house isn't evil."

"You'll feel them. You'll know. You'll find out the truth," he told her.

He was just a sad old man having a hard time, she told herself. Other people, people who weren't personally involved in any way, were morbidly fascinated by what had happened, but for Mr. Griffin, it was a terrible trip back in time.

"Mr. Griffin, honestly, no one knows for sure what took place in this house, but no one believes it was anything horrible. They think an undertaker was making money by selling coffins, then hiding the bodies in the walls so he could make extra money by reselling their coffins. With the war and then Reconstruction, people were pretty desperate for money," she said gently.

He pointed a finger at her, and in the lengthening shadows of evening, the effect was eerie enough to make her shiver.

"You'll find out the truth. You have to. They'll haunt these rooms until you do. They have no choice, don't you see? The evil in this house will keep coming back unless *you* stop it."

Sarah wanted to do something, to run away screaming or shake the old man and make him see that he was wrong, that her house didn't have a personality, especially not an evil one. It was just a house.

But she didn't want to hurt him, not even his feelings. He'd been through enough, losing his daughter, and he was so earnest.

Before she could speak again, or make up her mind what to do, they were interrupted by a voice coming from the porch.

"Mr. Griffin? Oh, dear God. Mr. Griffin, where *are* you?"

The voice was feminine, and clearly concerned.

"We're in here!" Sarah called.

She heard footsteps, and then, coming up the hall behind Mr. Griffin, she saw one of the most strikingly beautiful women she had ever encountered. Blue jeans and a T-shirt hugged the woman's perfect form. She had long, curling blond hair, a classically beautiful face and slightly tilted cat's eyes so brilliantly blue that Sarah could discern their color even in the dim hallway.

She set an arm gently around Mr. Griffin's shoulders and looked at Sarah apologetically. "I'm so sorry. We were out walking when his hat blew away, and when I ran to get it, Mr. Griffin walked off on me." She flashed Sarah a hopeful smile. "I am so, so sorry. I hope he didn't scare you. He's the kindest man you'll ever meet."

"It's all right. We were just talking," Sarah said.

The woman looked relieved as she offered Sarah a hand. "I'm Cary Hagan. I work for Mr. Griffin. Nurse, companion, secretary, all-around best girl. Right?" She turned to him as she spoke, and he nodded. "He's one hundred and two years old, and absolutely remarkable," Cary said.

"And standing right here," Mr. Griffin said flatly. "You needn't speak about me as if I can't hear you. I came to see this young lady because I saw her go into the house, and she needed to hear the things I know."

Cary lowered her head for a moment, then looked back up at Sarah. "It's the hoopla about the missing girl, and then the bones. His daughter disappeared years and years ago—one of a dozen or so girls who disappeared at the same time—and this has brought it all back," she explained.

"It's perfectly all right," Sarah said. She stepped forward and took one of Mr. Griffin's hands. "It's been a pleasure to meet you, sir. Thank you for coming to see me."

A look of gratitude lit Cary's eyes. "You're very kind and understanding."

"It's fine, seriously," Sarah said. "And Mr. Griffin is more than welcome to come back and see me anytime."

"You're beyond kind," Cary said. "Right now, though, he—*we*—need to get back. He's due for his medication, and timing is important."

Mr. Griffin was staring intently at Sarah.

"I didn't mean to frighten you," he said.

"I'm not frightened, so don't worry," she said. And it was true. She *wasn't* frightened. He was solidly real, and there was a perfectly reasonable explanation for his presence.

And even for most of his words.

"But you believe me, don't you?" he implored suddenly. " 'It' happening again. The evil—it's back again."

"Mr. Griffin, we really have to go," Cary said.

Mr. Griffin nodded, but he was still staring at Sarah. "It's all right. I'll go. Sarah knows. And she'll find out the truth."

He turned and started down the hallway, leaning heavily on his cane. Cary Hagan flashed Sarah one last smile, then turned as well, slipping her arm through his.

They left the door open behind them, and Sarah watched them all the way down the steps and out to the sidewalk. The man *was* pretty remarkable. He was over a hundred years old and still getting around on his own, and he appeared to still have all his marbles. Well, most of them.

But the loss of a child had to affect a person's reason; she didn't have children, but she knew that after losing a child, life would be irrevocably changed.

Evil.

Twilight had come, and the shadows were deepening, and his characterization of her house suddenly reverberated in her mind.

She reminded herself that she didn't believe a building could be evil. Even so, she found herself unnerved.

Suddenly she didn't want to be there any longer. She felt inexplicably afraid to turn around, afraid to look in the corners and see what might be lurking there.

She grabbed her purse and fled.

Caroline had hit the nail on the head harder than

she could have imagined with what she had said earlier.

Sarah was certain she had never wanted—*needed*—a drink so badly in her life.

He'd been right on the money.

As Caleb sat at the bar and sipped a beer, Caroline Roth entered along with her coworkers, Barry Travis and Renee Otten.

Unfortunately, Sarah wasn't with them.

The threesome took a table. As they got settled, Renee noted him. The look she gave him was slightly wary, which didn't bother him. He was a stranger, and there were unpleasant things happening in town. But she nudged Caroline, who looked up, smiled and walked over.

"How are you doing? Enjoying the city?" she asked.

"Of course. It's beautiful," he said.

She smiled, but her smile quickly faded. "Isn't it bizarre? The bones they found in Sarah's place, I mean."

"Bizarre and sad. How's Sarah doing?"

"She's a trouper, but this was a rough day for her. Even the tourists have heard about it now, so on top of the media driving her nuts, visitors were asking her about it all day. And since she just bought the place, really, what could she say to anyone?"

"Sounds like a pretty uncomfortable position."

"She's wanted to live in that house since we were kids. Its history always fascinated her. I think she was born to be a historian—she knew every bit of local history, ever, by the time she was about ten." Caroline was studying him with the look of a matchmaker. He was careful to listen without smiling or showing his awareness of her purpose. "She was always the best student in school. We all thought she should be a model, but she's a bookworm at heart. Not in a bad way, of course."

"Of course not." He allowed himself a smile then. "Where is she now, anyway?" he asked.

"She wanted to run by the house. But she'll be here soon."

Caleb felt an almost overwhelming desire to leap up and run to the house to check on her, suddenly worried that she was there . . . alone.

Of course, maybe she wasn't alone.

"Why don't you come over and join us?" Caroline asked.

Bingo.

"I don't want to intrude."

"I wouldn't have asked you if I thought you'd be an intrusion. Come on. Will's going to show up, too. He's totally dependable, and Sarah swore to me that she wouldn't bail on us."

"If you're sure you don't mind . . ."

"I'm sure. Really."

He placed money on the bar for the beer and followed her over to the table. Renee greeted him with a smile, and Barry Travis smiled as if he were welcoming a long lost friend.

"Any luck on finding that girl?" Barry asked as Caleb sat down.

"It's a pretty old trail," Caleb said.

"Yeah. Tough to find anything out, I imagine," Barry sympathized. "Do you have a deadline or anything?"

"No. I'm here until I find out something," Caleb said.

"Until you find . . . a body?" Renee asked tremulously.

"Until I have something to tell her parents."

"So," Barry said, "how do you handle money in your line of work? Do you get expenses and all that?"

"Barry!" Caroline said, horrified. "That's like . . . asking him his age or something."

Caleb laughed. "No, it's all right. I do what the boss man tells me to do, and the finances are his concern."

"Do you make a good living?" someone asked over his shoulder.

He turned. Will had shown up. Caroline jumped out of her seat to greet him with a hug.

Will was smiling. "Sorry," he said, grinning at he sat. "Since it seems like we're giving you the third degree, I figured that was the next logical question."

"I make out all right," Caleb assured him. "How's the dive business going?"

Will made a face. "I spent my day in the muddiest piece of the St. Johns known to man."

"Still looking for Winona Hart?" Caleb asked.

"Yep, and why anyone thinks she wound up in the St. Johns, I don't know. Anyway, we didn't find squat."

"No one told you why you were looking there?" Caleb asked.

"I'm just the hired help," Will said. He drummed his fingers on the table for a moment, then shrugged. "*You* could probably find out."

They all stared at him, wondering why he had such pull with the police.

"Trust me, it's the guy I work for, not me," Caleb said.

"Adam Harrison, Harrison Investigations," Barry said. "Boo. Aren't you guys ghost busters or something?"

Caleb was careful not to hesitate too long before answering. He drew his finger through the frost on his beer glass as he spoke. "We're an investigation agency like any other. Licensed, all that. I spent today tracking down information the police already had, just double-checking. Tedious and time-consuming. Most of our work is slow and not at all exciting, much less eerie, in any way."

"But I read somewhere that you were called in by the government because some weird shit was going on in a couple of government buildings and people were saying it was ghosts," Barry argued.

"We were. We get a lot of calls like that. Most of the time, the supposed whispers are coming from old pipes or the wind coming in through leaky window frames."

"Here she is," Caroline interrupted suddenly. With a huge smile, she stood up, waving.

Caleb looked over to the door and saw that Sarah had just arrived, looking stunning in a simple black dress and low heels.

Her hair was flowing around her shoulders like shining velvet, and she was as model-perfect as Caroline and all her friends thought, but she appeared tense. Her face was ashen, and even as she hurried between tables toward them, the look in her eyes seemed distant.

She didn't notice him at first. She took a seat next to Caroline and swiped her beer, taking a long swallow.

"Hey, I said you needed a drink," Caroline told her, "not an entire keg!"

"What's wrong, cuz?" Will asked, looking concerned and leaning forward to meet her eyes.

"Terrence Griffin the Third is what's wrong," she said, then saw Caleb and nearly spilled the beer as she set it down. She stared at him.

"I saw Caleb sitting all by himself at the bar and asked him to join us," Caroline said.

As if jolted into remembering her manners,

Sarah quickly said, "How nice. Nice to see you again, Caleb."

He could tell from her body language that she didn't think it was nice at all, but that was okay. He was making points with Caroline, and maybe even the wary Renee. Will had accepted him when they'd first met, but maybe that was only professional courtesy.

"Who is Terrence Griffin the Third?" Caleb asked when no one else said anything.

She shrugged.

"Sarah, seriously, what happened? Who is this guy?" Caroline asked.

"A very, *very* old man," Will answered for Sarah.

She turned to stare at him, frowning.

"You know him?" she asked.

"Yes, and you do, too—in a way," Will answered. "Twenty years ago, we ran through his yard and got in trouble for it. That wall in front of his place isn't historic—he built it to keep kids out. The guy was ancient, must've been eighty, at least. A cranky old hermit. What brought him up now? Were his bones in your walls?" he asked.

She shook her head. "I don't even remember whatever incident you're talking about."

"So you guys were the evil hellions torturing your poor old neighbors?" Renee said.

"Oh, yeah, whoopee. We trespassed," Sarah said, shaking her head. "It couldn't have been that bad. I don't remember it—or him."

"So what about Mr. Griffin?" Caleb prompted.

"He can't still be living," Will said.

"He is. He wandered into my house," Sarah said.

"What? Impossible—he has to be dead. He was older than time twenty years ago," Will told her.

"He's one hundred and two," Sarah said.

"And off his rocker, I'll bet," Will said. "You might not remember what happened, but I do. I was grounded for a week when he called my mother. Just for running through his yard!" He snorted indignantly.

"Why are you so bothered by seeing him tonight?" Caroline asked.

"I'd like to know how the hell he got into your house," Caleb added.

Sarah looked at him, the silver in her eyes shimmering like mercury. "I just stopped by the house to see if anyone was still working, and they weren't. I was on my way back out when he walked in."

"You didn't lock the door?" Will demanded.

"Sarah!" Caroline said.

"Please, you should know better," Barry told her.

"Oh, come on. Don't start on me!" Sarah protested, turning to stare at Caleb. It was obvious in the way she looked at him that she thought this was all his fault for asking how the man had gotten into the house.

Well, she might be pissed, but too bad. He was glad that he had spoken. With this much pressure from her friends, she wasn't likely to make the mistake again.

But it sure as hell wasn't going to help him any in his quest to get to know her better.

"What did the man say?" he asked quickly. Maybe if he shifted the conversation's focus, it would improve his position with her.

She hesitated briefly, then shrugged. "He said that my house is evil, that it's haunted. He's convinced that it . . . did something to his daughter back in the nineteen twenties."

"He thinks the *house* did something to her?" Will asked, confused.

"What? Does he think your house *eats* people or something?" Renee asked, bewildered.

"No, no. I feel sorry for the man, actually. His daughter was on her way to my house to meet a friend—a mutual friend of one of the Brennan girls, the people who were living there then—and she disappeared," Sarah explained.

She had finished off Caroline's beer. Caroline picked up her empty glass and studied it sadly.

Caleb turned around and motioned to the waitress, making a circle in the air to indicate a round of drinks for the table. She nodded.

"Poor man," Caroline said. "Imagine, living all those years—and never knowing what happened to your kid."

"What if her bones were in the walls?" Sarah said.

"What?" Will demanded, grimacing.

"We don't know anything yet, really," Sarah told him. "Maybe his daughter was killed and put into the walls eighty years ago."

Caleb leaned forward. "Floby thought the bodies were all from around the same time period, back around the Civil War," he told her.

"I hope he's right," Sarah murmured.

The drinks came. When the waitress set a beer in front of Sarah, she frowned, as if wondering how it had gotten there. Then she shrugged and drank.

"Here's the thing," Renee said. "You really shouldn't go back to that place."

"That place has my life savings invested in it," Sarah said.

"Stop being a cliché," Caroline said, exasperated. "Every stupid horror movie aggravates the audience for the same reason—if a place is that bad, get the hell out! Come on. Your life is worth more than some building, even one you've coveted since we were kids. Come and move in with me."

Sarah laughed and hugged her friend. "Caroline, my life hasn't been threatened. Nothing bad has happened to anyone in that house for . . . well, maybe ever. I mean, dumping bodies out of coffins and stashing them in the walls is gross, but if Floby is right, it all happened a long time ago, and that means there's nothing for me to worry about."

"But you're not going to stay there tonight, are you?" Barry asked her.

"The *house* hasn't done anything," Sarah said again, reaching for her drink.

Caroline was holding onto her own glass tightly now.

"That old guy startled me, that's all," Sarah said, looking around from one to the other of them. "It's terrible of me to be so upset."

"Not so terrible. He was a mean old bastard," Will said.

"That's a horrible thing to say!" Sarah protested.

"Well, he was."

Sarah looked at Caleb. "So how was your day?"

"Not very eventful," he said, keeping his new information to himself for the moment. "A lot of running around. But it was a start, and at least I'm not going to have to do it again."

"Nothing in Jacksonville?" she asked.

"Just a lot of legwork," he said.

He had a feeling she was trying to get him to talk because she didn't want to be pressured anymore; he had a feeling, though, that she hadn't told the group what she was really thinking, or maybe she hadn't told them everything Mr. Griffin had said. But he wasn't about to say that he might have taken a few steps forward and was certain now that Jennie Lawson was dead, and that she had been killed here in St. Augustine.

He lifted his glass to Sarah and turned the topic right back to *her*. "So how did your encounter with Mr. Griffin end?"

"His nurse showed up looking for him. Her name is Cary Hagan, and she's the most beautiful woman I've ever seen," Sarah told them.

"Oh, yeah?" Caroline said. "Well, *you're* the most beautiful woman *I've* ever seen." She looked at Caleb as if for confirmation.

Sarah turned to stare at her friend, completely baffled. She had confidence in herself, Caleb realized, but she had a complete lack of vanity and was genuinely dumbfounded by what Caroline had said.

"No, I mean she was perfect. Like walk-off-a-magazine-cover perfect. If you ever see her, you'll know what I mean," Sarah said. "I bet she'll show up in here one night."

"Come on, the city isn't *that* small," Will argued.

"Shh, don't look now," Renee said suddenly. "I think she just came in."

Of course they all turned to see.

"I said *don't* look," Renee said. "And she's not just here—she's here with Tim Jamison."

"You don't know that," Caroline argued. "She walked in and he walked in, but that doesn't mean they came together. Besides, we don't even know if we're talking about the same person."

"That is one of the most gorgeous women I've ever seen," Barry said, and Renee whacked him playfully on the arm. "Hey! I'm not blind, you know. And as a totally objective observation, she's stunning. So, Sarah, is that the woman you were talking about?"

Sarah, who was staring wide-eyed at the door, simply nodded.

"Look," Caroline said. "She's talking to Tim. Maybe they *did* come in together."

"Tim is married," Renee pointed out.

"I'll go say hello and introduce you all," Sarah said.

"You don't need to do that," Caroline protested.

"Why not?" Sarah asked, clearly puzzled.

Caleb hid a smile. She obviously didn't realize that Caroline was trying to steer the two of them together.

"Well, because—"

"Don't be ridiculous," Sarah said, and left them, winding her way through the tables. All of them were silent, staring at Cary, who seemed startled when Sarah reached her. She quickly smiled, though, and then, as Sarah spoke, she looked toward their table—and caught all of them staring at her. She smiled and waved, and they had no choice but to wave back.

Sarah led Cary over to their table. As they approached, Caleb stood, followed by Barry and Will.

Sarah was smiling like a cat with a canary as she introduced everyone. "Cary Hagan, I'd like you to meet my cousin Will, and my friends and coworkers Renee Otten, Barry Travis and Caroline Roth. And this is Caleb Anderson, who's just in town for a visit. Everyone, Cary Hagan."

"Hello, everyone. It's a pleasure to meet you. I haven't lived in the area very long, and on the rare occasions when I get out, I usually head up the coast. Now that I've met you guys, maybe I won't feel like such an outsider coming in here."

The woman really was stunning, Caleb thought, right down to the dimples that flashed when she smiled. They added a touch of mischief to her features and countered her regal stature.

"Consider yourself an insider now," Will said gallantly. "Come and hang with us anytime. In fact, join us now."

"Really? Thank you."

Caleb had the sense that Sarah was feeling proud of herself, certain she had proven that the other woman wasn't there with Tim Jamison.

"So you're a nurse?" Caroline asked.

"Yes. The thing is, Mr. Griffin is in excellent physical health. He moves slowly, but he's never broken a bone, he exercises every day, and he takes his medicine without complaining. He's the perfect patient. Most of the time, anyway. Today . . . well, I guess Sarah told you what happened? The news keeps going on about that missing girl and the bones in the walls of the old Grant house, and his daughter disappeared years and years ago on her way there. I think all this talk has caused a mental . . . tremor, I guess. He's a real sweetie, really. I swear."

"Well, if it isn't a class reunion," Tim Jamison

said, suddenly looming up beside their table. He didn't seem pleased as he pulled up a chair, nudging in between Caroline and Sarah.

"You look grouchy," Sarah told him.

"What can I say? I get cranky when a local girl disappears without a trace," he said, shaking his head. "I see you've all met Cary."

"So how do you two know each other?" Sarah asked, looking from Tim to Cary.

"Mr. Griffin had a bit of a weak spell one day when we were out walking. . . . I was trying to flag someone down for help when Tim came by. Nothing better than being helped by an officer of the law," Cary said with a smile.

"Tell us about yourself, Cary," Sarah suggested.

Cary explained that she was from North Dakota and had gone to school in Chicago, but she loathed the winters. She'd started looking for nursing positions in warmer places, and when she'd gotten the offer to come to Florida, she'd jumped on it. She'd only been living there for a little over a year.

Drinks kept coming, then eventually food, and the talk was casual. Then Renee yawned and said she needed some sleep. Barry didn't move until she stood and tapped him on the shoulder. Then he started and rose to join her, setting down money for his part of the bill. The two of them said goodbye and left, but Caleb caught Barry glancing back for one last look at Cary as he was heading for the door.

"I've got to go, too. I need a good night's sleep," Sarah said, rising.

Caleb rose, as well. "I'll walk you," he said.

She tensed slightly, and for a moment he thought she was going to argue with him, but she seemed to think better of it and simply said, "Thanks."

Tim leaned back in his chair, staring up at Caleb. "Before you go . . . how was your day? Find out anything?" he asked.

"I'll call you first," Caleb assured him, thinking that Tim looked like the perfect image of the over-worked and weary cop at that moment.

"Yeah. Come see me. I'd just like a rundown of everything you're doing."

"Sure," Caleb agreed.

"Well, good night, all," Sarah said. She added money for the bill, and Caleb did the same.

"Good night," Caroline said, grinning—no doubt pleased with her matchmaking efforts and relieved that he wasn't staying to hang out with the perfect blond newcomer.

She moved closer to Will.

They waved and left, and Caleb noticed that Tim Jamison didn't return the gesture or even look up. He was too busy staring morosely into his beer.

"Where am I walking you?" Caleb asked Sarah as they reached the street.

She smiled. "You're not going to tell me that I shouldn't go and stay in my own carriage house, are you?" she asked.

"I could, but it wouldn't do any good, would it?"

Walking at his side, she grinned wryly. "No," she admitted. "I'd just get more adamant about it being my house."

"You have good locks on your doors, and you won't make the mistake of leaving a door unlocked again, will you?" he asked.

"No," she said seriously, and added a quiet, "I was lucky today."

They walked in silence for a few minutes, and then she suddenly said, "You *did* learn something today, didn't you?"

He laughed. "Very insightful. Okay, yes, I'm pretty sure my missing girl was here. And that the same person or persons snatched her and Winona Hart. Now it's your turn to answer me. What freaked you out so much about Mr. Griffin's visit?"

She thought hard for a minute.

"His whole bit about the house being evil . . . I really don't believe that a house can be evil, but bad things did happen there, and there was just something so . . . so creepy about the way he talked about it."

She still wasn't telling him everything, he thought. But he wasn't going to press her for the moment. They were actually beginning to make a connection, and he didn't want her closing any doors in his face.

They reached her walkway. The house looked

old and, yes, spooky in the moonlit darkness. There seemed to be a lot of trash around the yard now, too, which was unusual for the area. Then again, a lot of people had come by to ogle the place today, and they were probably responsible for all the trash.

They bypassed the main house and headed for the carriage house, where Sarah took out her keys. "You can check the place out for me, if you want," she said lightly, but he could read the need for reassurance in her tone.

"Certainly," he assured her.

The carriage-house-turned-apartment was definitely impressive, Caleb thought. There was still a slight feel of decaying grandeur about it, but there was fresh paint on the walls and a huge four-poster in the center of the single large room. She'd put in a wide screen TV, a sofa sat between it and the foot of the bed, and a small kitchenette had been built into one corner.

"Very nice," he told her.

"Thanks. There are two smaller rooms upstairs. Once I get the place going as a B and B, I can rent it out to couples and families."

He opened the bathroom door, revealing both a claw-foot tub and a new glass-enclosed shower stall.

There was obviously no one lurking in the bathroom.

He checked the closet and looked under the bed,

then went upstairs to make sure everything there was secure. When he came back down, he checked the lock on the single window, which had been added when the carriage doors had been removed. "Everything looks good to me. Bolt your door and keep your cell phone close, and you'll be fine," he advised.

"I will. I don't see Mr. Griffin trying to break down my door, though," she said with a hint of a smile echoed in the dazzling silver of her eyes.

He walked past her to the door, careful to keep his distance from her. "Good night. You can call me any time, you know."

"Thanks."

"I'm not a mass murderer in investigator's clothing, you know. I work for Adam Harrison. Trust me, his background checks would do any intelligence agency proud."

"I'm sure that's true," she said, ready to close the door behind him.

The thing was, he could tell that she *did* trust Adam. She just didn't trust *him*. Not yet.

The carriage house was like her own little castle. She had kept the historical tone of the house, but with just one nicely updated room, no one could sneak up on her, not with only one window and one door, both of them well-secured.

Sarah wanted to sleep, but she felt wound up. She didn't want to admit that Mr. Griffin had managed to send a few chills down her spine. She wanted to blame his bizarre behavior on dementia, then realized what a cruel thought that was. She found herself hoping instead that it was the pain that never went away that made him so certain there were ghosts in the house—and that they would talk to her.

Also, she reminded herself, this was the carriage house. She was certain that no equine ghosts were going to come back to life and haunt her.

She scrubbed her face, showered, washed her hair and, as it dried, gave herself a pedicure and manicure. To make sure she didn't catch the news, she turned to a cable channel that showed nothing but old movies. *The African Queen* came on and seemed like a good choice.

Finally she turned off everything but the bathroom light, determined to get some sleep. It didn't help. Her mind continued to race. She kept recalling the arrival of Terrence Griffin III and everything he had said to her, and when she wasn't thinking about him, she found herself thinking about Caleb. She hadn't even considered a relationship since Clay's death, and she certainly wasn't envisioning a deathless romance with the man, but she was only human, and she *was* imagining sex. She groaned, determined not to imagine the man naked or think about his hands touching her, and she would absolutely not hear the deep, rich tone of his voice in her dreams.

She slept, and woke, and slept again, tossing and turning until she woke herself up again. She sat up at last, ready to punch her pillow into a more comfortable lump.

Instead she went dead still, a scream frozen in her throat. This had to be a nightmare, she told herself. The kind where danger came, and there was nothing you could do about it, because panic had seized you and deprived you of the ability to move.

There was a man standing at the foot of her bed. Or was there?

Was she dreaming? She had to be, because he was dressed in the kind of outfit Barry wore at work. Except . . .

He didn't look like someone wearing a costume, the way Barry always did. There was something authentic about him. Maybe he wore the vest and frock coat with more comfort. Maybe it was the tilt of his sweeping hat. Maybe it was his face, his eyes, haunted, distant and oddly familiar.

She let out a croak, desperately trying to scream. Because dream or reality, he was standing at the foot of her bed and she was scared.

But she never had a chance to scream, because he spoke then, his tone full of pain.

"I didn't do it. I loved her," he said.

She continued to stare, still caught in a twilight world between life and dreams. He looked different and yet . . . so familiar. He had long sideburns, a goatee and moustache, and long tawny hair, but she couldn't escape the sense that she should recognize him.

"I *loved* her. Do you understand?" He sounded so agitated. "But I had to leave."

She closed her eyes, clenched them shut, and furiously commanded herself to awaken.

When she opened her eyes, he was gone.

She glanced at her bedside clock. It was 5:00 a.m. It must have been a dream, brought on by a combination of all that had been happening and Mr. Griffin's insistence that her house was haunted.

She lay back down and closed her eyes, then opened them again and looked toward the foot of her bed. There was nothing there. Of course not. She had imagined the man there, imagined his claim that he hadn't done it.

Hadn't done *what?*

Put the bones in her walls?

She groaned and closed her eyes.

Worthless. She looked at the clock again. It was 5:03 a.m.

It didn't matter. She wasn't going to get back to sleep. She threw off her covers and, swearing at herself, Caleb and Mr. Griffin, she headed into the shower. It bothered her that her memory of the man at the foot of her bed was so perfectly clear. She could remember exactly what he had looked like.

So familiar, and yet . . .

She didn't know. She showered unhappily, thinking that she was going to call in and take the day off—after all, it had been offered.

When she emerged from the shower, the sun was beginning to rise. Wrapped in her towel, she walked over to turn on the television, opting for a children's show rather than the news. As she walked back toward the bed, she looked down and was startled to see bits of mud and grass on the carpet.

As if they had been carried in from outside.

Like footprints.

Her heart skipped a beat.

Then it occurred to her just why the man at the foot of her bed had reminded her of someone.

He had looked just like Caleb Anderson.

Give him some facial hair, long curls and period clothing . . .

"That bastard," she breathed aloud and hurried to the door. It was still bolted. It would have been impossible for him to have gotten in.

On the other hand, the man worked for Adam Harrison, who seemed to have the ability to get just about anything done.

So what the hell had Caleb been doing? Trying to scare her to death? Trying to make her give up the house so he could . . . what?

It didn't matter. She dressed as quickly as she could and headed out on the warpath. She was going to confront that wretched son of a bitch right away, while her temper was flaming at a thousand degrees, and if he didn't watch his step, she was going to sock him in his ridiculously rugged jaw.

6

Caleb woke suddenly from a sound sleep, his sharp senses aware of footsteps on the walkway outside his room.

He looked at the clock. It was barely 6:00 a.m. but the footfalls were light, a woman's. Probably just someone heading home after a late night.

And then, even though he heard the steps marching straight toward his room, he was stunned when he heard a pounding on the outside door of his room, and even more stunned when he got up and opened the door to reveal Sarah standing there with a murderous look on her face.

For a moment she simply stood in the doorway, shaking with rage. Then she stepped inside and closed the door behind her.

"You . . . bastard," she began. "I should call the police. I should have you arrested. And I still may. What in God's name did you think you were doing?"

Without waiting for his answer, she walked to the bed, still trembling with fury, grabbed a pillow and threw it at his head with a vengeance.

"What the hell . . . ?" he demanded as he caught the pillow.

She went for another. "What kind of an idiot are you? You could have scared me to death. Or what if I kept a gun? I could have shot you!"

The second pillow came hurtling his way.

He tried to figure out what the hell she was talking about as he dodged the pillow. She had one hell of an arm on her. She would have been great at a company softball game. "What are you talking about? And I *do* carry a gun, so it was dangerous as hell for you to burst in here!"

Before she could send the last of his pillows flying his way, he rushed her, wrenching the pillow from her hands and tightening his arms around her to stop her from starting on the rest of the bedding, his momentum bearing them both down on the bed. Glad that he'd slept in boxers, he tried to keep a distance as he held her down, but it was difficult. She was on fire. Her eyes were wild with a passion for revenge over something he couldn't fathom, and her skin was soft as silk. She was vital and vibrant, and he found himself fighting the rise of desire while he attempted to subdue her and get to the root of the problem.

She stared at him, silver eyes as sharp as knives, her breasts heaving with the exertion of her breathing.

"Do you think this is all a game? What did you think you were doing, playing dress-up and sneaking into my house at night?"

"Calm down," he insisted. He wasn't the only guest, and Bertie was undoubtedly somewhere nearby, too, and there was Sarah, pinned beneath him, screaming accusations that made no sense.

No one would ever believe that he'd been the one being attacked.

"Don't you ever set foot on my property again," she warned him. "I was an idiot to come here. I should have called the cops immediately."

"Sarah, listen to me. I swear to God I don't have the faintest idea what you're talking about," he vowed.

She blinked, and for a moment she seemed on the verge of believing him. Then she apparently discarded the thought as totally impossible.

"You were in my carriage house," she accused him.

He answered carefully. "Of course I was. I was there with you. But that was the only time I have ever been there, I swear."

She was still a ball of tension beneath him, but he could feel her trying to control herself. She was seething, but she'd stopped trying to escape his hold.

"Let me up," she demanded.

Carefully, he did so. To his astonishment, she began ransacking his room, looking through the closet, the drawers and his open luggage. He was glad that his computer was sitting open on the small antique desk; she might have sent it flying, otherwise, as she hurled his clothing over her shoulder.

He didn't even think to try to stop her. It would only have made her madder.

At last, exhausted, she stood still for a moment. From her expression, he could tell that she hadn't found what she was looking for.

"What did you do with it?" she demanded.

"With what?" he asked.

"The clothes!"

"You've just seen every piece of clothing I have with me," he said, sitting on the foot of the bed and staring at her. "Maybe *I* should be calling the police."

"Be my guest."

"Sarah, can you tell me what's going on and what you think I've done?" he asked, hoping he sounded patient, since he certainly didn't feel that way.

"You came to my house and stood at the foot of my bed, pretending to be a nineteenth-century ghost. And I don't care what you say, I know it was you. The facial hair was great, and the wig was even better, but it was you."

He frowned. "Someone broke into your carriage house?"

"Not someone—you!" she accused.

"In nineteenth-century clothes?" he said skeptically. "Did it ever occur to you that you were dreaming?"

"Oh, no. It was no dream. It was real, and I have your footprints to prove it," she announced.

He stood. She backed away from him.

"Sarah, I walked you home, then came back

here, and I never left this room after that. I did not bring a period costume with me to St. Augustine. I don't know what to say to convince you, but I would never break in to someone's house and play a joke like that. Aside from the fact that it's cruel, it's also illegal. You must have had some kind of a nightmare."

"It wasn't a nightmare, it was a . . . a play. And you were the flesh-and-blood star," she said. She stared hard at him, then said, "Shoes!"

She went back to the closet and pulled out his shoes, turning them over and looking at the soles.

At last she stood, hair a wild tangle about her face—but now with just a trace of doubt on her features.

"I told you, after I said good-night to you I came back here and went to sleep," he said evenly.

At that moment there was a tap on his door, and Bertie called, "Excuse me, but is everything all right in here?"

Sarah winced, closing her eyes tightly for a moment.

"Everything's fine, Bertie," he called. "Just give me a minute." As he spoke, he was pulling on a pair of pants.

As soon as he was decent, he went to the door and opened it for Bertie, who walked in hesitantly, a wary look on her face.

He couldn't blame her. This was her home as well as her business. She could hardly be expected

161

to ignore the sounds of a heated argument and flying objects coming from a guestroom.

"Caleb? What's going on here?" she asked, taking in the state of the room. Then she saw Sarah and just stared.

Caleb crossed his arms over his chest. "Sarah will explain," he said.

Sarah shook her head. "Someone . . . someone dressed up and played a trick on me, tried to scare me. He looked just like Caleb," she said.

"When did this happen?"

"About an hour ago," Sarah said.

Sarah might have known Bertie longer, but at this moment, Bertie seemed to be taking his side, Caleb thought.

"So you came here—and trashed his room?" Bertie asked quietly.

Caleb stood, took Sarah by the shoulders and steered her toward the door. "Bertie, I think Sarah needs a cup of coffee. Why don't you give me a few minutes to take a shower, and then I'll go back with her and try to get to the bottom of the situation. Will that be all right, Sarah?" he asked, as if he were talking to a particularly slow-witted child.

She was still angry, but now she also looked uncertain, even mortified. Maybe she was finally accepting the idea that a nightmare had sent her marching over here to accost a half-naked and innocent—at least of dressing up and scaring her, he thought, hiding a grin—man in his bed.

"Be quick," she said scathingly, gathering her anger around herself like a shield.

"Sarah . . ." Bertie said, leading Sarah out and closing the door in her wake.

He locked the door, and then with the women gone, took a quick shower and dressed with the speed of lightning. When he emerged, the kitchen help were just arriving and Sarah was nursing a cup of coffee.

"Come on," he said. "Let's go see what's up at your carriage house."

"Would you two like some breakfast first?" Bertie suggested.

"Thank you, but I think this needs to be resolved. Now," he said. "And don't worry about the room. Nothing's broken, and I'll deal with the mess when I get back later today."

He didn't let either woman protest as he maneuvered Sarah out the front door. She was as stiff as a two-by-four, and waves of heat and hostility seemed to be sweeping off her into the morning air. She hurried to get ahead of him, but his strides were long, and he soon caught up to her.

When they reached her property, she turned on him again. "Just admit that you did it. I promise I won't call the police."

"I didn't do anything," he told her. "Now, tell me why you're so convinced this was something more than a dream. Was the door open after your . . . visitor left?"

She looked away. "No. But you're a private investigator, and you have . . . skills, maybe some kind of a key."

"A key that opens the lock *and* the dead bolt?" he demanded.

"It's possible," she said defensively.

He stepped past her with disgust. "I don't have a magic key, okay? So would you be so kind as to open the door?"

She did so. "Be careful where you walk. I don't want you to mess up the evidence."

"What evidence?"

"The mud and grass you—*someone* tracked in. See? At the foot of the bed."

He hunkered down and studied the rug. There were indeed bits of mud and grass on the floor, as if they'd been tracked in by someone who had come through the door, circled the sofa to stand at the foot of the bed, and then . . . vanished.

He stood, puzzled. "You do need to call the cops, I think."

She sank down on the arm of the sofa, staring at him. He was sure she was feeling desperate, still wanting it to have been him, wanting the mystery to have a solid answer.

"They'll think we tracked it in when you walked me home last night. They'll think I'm crazy. Especially when I tell them that he was dressed in period clothing."

"Is anything missing?" Caleb asked her.

She shook her head. "No . . . it was . . . I'm telling you, it was *you*. In costume."

"And *I'm* telling *you*, it wasn't," he said firmly.

She looked lost—still prickly and defensive, but lost.

"Sarah, it really might have been a dream."

"Explain the dirt and the grass."

"Maybe we did track it in last night."

"We walked on the sidewalks. The driveway is paved and the walk is stone. Neither of us stepped off the walk onto the lawn," she said.

"All right, what did this person say or do? Did he just stand there looking at you?" Caleb asked.

"No. He kept saying he 'didn't do it,' that he had loved her," Sarah told him, getting up and pacing agitatedly.

"I see," he said consideringly.

She socked him on the shoulder. Not hard, but enough to make her point.

"Don't you dare patronize me. I'm not crazy."

"I didn't say you were," he protested. "Sarah, it had to be a dream. There's no other explanation. Unless you think I have a doppelganger with a bad sense of humor hanging around the area? Because I swear to you, I wasn't here. I wouldn't play that kind of a joke on anyone. Ever. So . . . it wasn't me. We can call the police, if it will set your mind at rest. In fact, I was heading to the station this morning anyway. You can come with me and make a report, and they can search my room again, my

165

car, anything that you want. You can have them dust for prints, too. Of course, you will find mine, along with yours, but . . . maybe they'll find someone else's, too."

She shook her hear. "It wasn't anyone else," she said stubbornly. "It was you."

He hesitated. "Look, when you came into the bar last night, you were already upset, because of Mr. Griffin showing up at your house. I think he said more to you than you shared with the others. Want to tell me now?"

She sat down again, deflated, staring at the floor. "I have to admit, he looks kind of scary, very old and very skinny. He talked about the history of the house, and he kept saying it was evil. That part's crazy, but I have to admit, he had the history right. Before the Civil War, the house was owned by a family called MacTavish, and the father was a mortician. The son, Cato, went off to fight when the war started. He came back wounded, only to find that his father was dead and his fiancée had disappeared right after he left. Then other young women started disappearing. He ended up being accused of murder, so he just took off, abandoning the house. His housekeeper—who supposedly practiced voodoo and magic—left right after he did. A man named Brennan had been living here with Cato, learning the mortician's trade, and he ended up buying the house for back taxes after the war. The Brennans hung on to it for generations, and then—like I was saying last night—Mr. Griffin's daughter disappeared on her way to meet a friend here back in the nineteen twenties. Cary said a bunch of girls disappeared at the same time. Anyway, Mr. Griffin is convinced the house itself is evil. I think he heard about the bones being discovered, and now he believes that people's souls have been caught here." She hesitated. "He thinks I can communicate with them, and that I have to talk to them and find out . . . something, or else women will keep disappearing and . . . dying."

"Wow. He laid a lot on you," Caleb said.

"I don't believe in ghosts, or that a house can be evil," she told him.

"I don't believe it, either. But I believe that human beings are capable of some pretty hideous things, and that madmen can walk around looking like saints. And if there's a legend that goes with the house, some bastard may find it useful in carrying out his own crimes." He lifted her chin, looking into her eyes. "Look, Sarah, you don't have to believe in ghosts to have been subconsciously influenced by what Mr. Griffin said. You had a dream, and I was the last person you saw before you went to sleep, so . . ."

"So . . ." she repeated softly, staring at him. "So where did the mud come from?"

"We tracked it in somehow."

She stood. "I've got to call the museum and leave a message. Caroline's parents suggested that

167

I take a few days off, and I'm going to. I want to look at the historical records and whatever newspaper files I can find. I want to see what went on in the house over the years. So you can go on to the police station without me."

"Are you sure you'll be all right?" Caleb asked her.

"I'll be fine. So go do whatever you have to do," Sarah said.

"I'm going to help hunt for Winona Hart," he said.

"What about Jennie Lawson?" she asked.

"Jennie was here. I found someone who saw her. She wanted to go on the spookiest ghost tours she could find." He hesitated. "When I showed her picture around yesterday, a lot of people thought I was showing them a picture of Winona Hart, so logic says that the same person snatched both girls. If we can find Winona, I'll find out the truth about Jennie."

"Do you think Winona might still be alive?" Sarah asked. "She hasn't been missing that long."

"We can hope. But I want to get moving quickly. That means a trip to the station to tell Tim Jamison what I learned yesterday and find out everything the police have on Winona, and then I need to follow up on every last person who was near her and every possible clue."

"I hope you can find them both. Alive."

He nodded. "I hope so, too."

"You don't think it's possible, though, do you?"

He shrugged. "I saw Jennie's mother. She said she knows that her daughter is gone. And Jennie was a good kid. She wouldn't have just disappeared. She wouldn't have run away with a man. So . . . quite frankly, it doesn't look good. But people need closure. They need to bury their dead, and they need to grieve." He stepped toward the door. "Maybe I should walk you wherever you're going."

She smiled. "Thanks. But it's broad daylight now. Someone will be by to get into the house soon—Floby left me a note that they still had some things to do. And I can walk to the library on my own when it opens. It's a whole three blocks away—maybe."

He paused at the door, looking back at her. "You believe me, don't you?" he asked her.

She nodded. "Yes, it's just that . . . it was so real." It took her a minute but she finally gave up. "I'm sorry," she said slowly. "I'm sorry about your room and your stuff. I can go clean up if you want, since you'll be busy."

He shook his head. "No, that's all right. I can manage. But, by the way . . ."

"By the way . . . what?"

He grinned. "If you ever show up at my room again, it had better be for sex."

She flushed, and her lips parted, but she didn't speak.

He let himself out.

• • •

Sarah knew that legal documents would only back up what she already knew.

What she needed were newspaper articles, diaries and letters from the period. Such things existed, she was sure. St. Augustine had been occupied by Union forces long before the war's end, and it had never been burned to the ground. Many of the old houses had attics, and those attics often yielded treasures offering insights into the past. Even now, despite the intervening years, people often found old trunks in crawl spaces, or stashes of Confederate bills stuffed into cubbyholes or under old floorboards. Even Spanish coins still surfaced now and then.

It wasn't a hopeless case.

Vicky Hind, one of the librarians, was happy to assist Sarah.

"Those old bones got you thinking, huh?" she asked sympathetically. "Well, legend and history are often one and the same, you know. Here's a memoir written in 1908 by a woman whose father came down after the Union established command of the city. She was born in 1860 and came here with her mother when she was just two years old. She self-published her journal in 1908, when she was nearly fifty. She died a few years later, so we're lucky she got it out there. Anyway, take this and have a seat in the General's Room, and I'll see what else I can find for you."

Sarah thanked her and took a seat in the room that had gotten its name because a Confederate general had been born there. He hadn't surrendered when Lee had. Instead, he'd gone to Texas, hoping to lead his unit into Mexico to establish a new order. His mother had remained in the house until her death, a feisty old woman who reveled in causing trouble for the "damn Yankee invaders," as she called them.

Sarah started reading and found a charming personality developing as she turned the pages. She found herself fascinated by the writing alone. The author, Sadie Hanrahan, didn't remember much about the war, but she did recall the days after. There had been a great deal of bitterness in the city, despite the fact that it had been in Federal hands for years, and that many of the citizens had never wanted Florida to secede—they had always needed their Yankee tourist dollars. It had been a difficult time. President Lincoln had been assassinated. John Wilkes Booth had been hunted down and shot, and his co-conspirators hanged, but many blamed all Southerners for the death of the president. And so many in the South had been stripped of their homes, their heritage and more.

Sadie's first pages were filled with tales of growing up and vivid descriptions of buildings that hadn't changed to this day. There were also some very funny anecdotes about learning to deal with the cumbersome clothing women had to wear, even in the summer heat. And then Sarah hit the jackpot.

It was on a Saturday late in 1865 that I walked by the old Grant place with Scotty Kehoe. It was near dusk, and in front of the building, in the drive, we saw the mortuary's glass-encased hearse with a coffin inside. At first I was enthralled by the two horses that were to draw the funerary wagon; they were glorious big black beasts, wearing black-feathered headdresses. But Scotty was drawn by the coffin within the hearse. "Come on!" he said to me. "What are you doing?" I protested. Then he called me a chicken. Well, I couldn't have that. He'd cluck at me every single day at school. So I crept with him through the brush that was kept neatly trimmed around the entrances to the main mansion and the carriage house and then we crawled up on the conveyance to look in. I'd never been to a funeral. I was shocked by the coffin. It was beautifully carved, but there was a glass window above the face. I saw the girl in the coffin. She was young, with beautiful wheat-colored hair, and she had pale skin, like all her blood was gone, but her lips were a bright red. She looked as if she was sleeping. "Look, she's opening her eyes!" Scotty teased, and I nearly screamed. I did slide from my perch. That was when the elder Mr. Brennan came out on the porch. I had always hated him. We weren't bad people, not most of us—even if they did call us carpetbaggers. But Mr. Brennan had rather taken over the place before he had bought it. We'd heard tales that the previous owner's father, Mr. MacTavish, had been a kind man, forced to turn his home into a funeral parlor to survive once his plantations had failed and his son was gone to war. MacTavish had died, and his son had returned from the war only to have his heart broken when he found his father dead and his fiancée gone, so I'd been told. Some people remembered the son kindly, too. He had been dashing, and a valiant soldier. Always charming and kind and caring, especially to children and the elderly. But other people whispered about him, saying that he was really the devil incarnate and a murderer. But at least some people had liked him, and no one liked old man Brennan. I especially didn't like Mr. Brennan after that day. He was furious; he yelled at us and promised that kids or no kids, next time, he'd have his shotgun out, that we were defiling the dead. We ran. I thought he would tell our parents about the incident, but he never did.

I found out who the girl in the coffin was that night, when my father's housekeeper was talking to him about it.

"A carriage accident, my foot. That young'un disappeared more'n three weeks ago. It's something afoot, just like that Madison girl who disappeared in 'sixty-two. She died in a carriage accident, too—so they said. I didn't believe it then, and I don't believe it now. Not Miss Della Bentley. It's them carpetbaggers that run this place that say what isn't is, and ignore what's going on. They say one girl rode off with her Rebel lover, and another girl ran off to meet her Yankee lover, and it just ain't so. They're just saying it was a carriage accident 'cause poor Mr. Cato MacTavish isn't around for them to be blaming this on! Why, they've even tried to start the rumor that Cato is out hiding in the woods—that he comes back to stalk and hunt women—just in case someone realizes there weren't any carriage accidents."

My father was a good man. He tried to soothe her. He said it was a tragedy about the poor girl, but we couldn't go believing in wild fantasies made up by folks who were bitter about the war and had little else to do.

Our housekeeper walked away, muttering.

My father kept a sharp eye on me after that, though. I wasn't allowed to walk around town anymore with the other children. But by then, we weren't really allowed to be children at all anyway. Maybe it had to do with it being the aftermath of the war. I was a child at the time. My father trusted the authorities. I trusted my father.

After that day, whenever I saw Mr. Brennan on the streets, I ran. One day, when I was much older, I asked my father about Brennan and the house on

St. George. He was silent for a long time. "There was a lot of tragedy there," he told me at last. I asked him why the young Mr. MacTavish had left. I understood a broken heart—half the women not too many years older than I was had broken hearts, on account of their fellows had died in the war. But he had abandoned such a beautiful house.

"The disappearances," my father said. "Or the murders," he added after a moment of reflection. "I didn't believe it at the time." He rattled off a list of names. Women's names. "They all disappeared, starting right when Cato MacTavish came home. We assumed then that they had run off—it was a war, conditions were miserable. Only two of the girls were ever found—and the doctor on call said that both had died in the streets. Carriage accidents. But . . . they didn't look right." He stopped. He wasn't going to tell me any details of the corpses that had been found. "Cato's fiancée had disappeared right after he left to fight, and since he wasn't here, he was a good scapegoat. When he returned from the war, people said he'd killed her because she was pregnant or he was just tired of her. He tried to fight the accusations—they weren't official, there was no evidence—but bear this in mind, child. Words can be as cruel as any weapon; they give rise to battles and wars, and in the end, he was a soldier who could not win the battle of words, I'm sad to say. Thing is, soon after he left, the housekeeper disappeared, too. She wasn't actually his housekeeper, she had come with Brennan. But the whole city was terrified of her." "Why?" I asked. "Black magic." "You don't believe in black magic," I told him. He shook his head. "I didn't want to believe. They said that she mixed voodoo with Indian lore, black magic and more. Some thought it was her spells that made the girls disappear. Or made them run away. Or perhaps she was the one who killed them. The truth, Brennan was allied with the powers that controlled the city at the time. Cato MacTavish was not. And MacTavish was a man who could bear no more. Perhaps he changed his name when he went north—or south. All anyone knows for sure is that he rode out of town one day on his father's big bay, crying out his innocence and cursing the city, never to be seen again. Brennan, now, Brennan is a dangerous man. He conned Cato into teaching him the business, and he managed to make MacTavish leave and get hold of the place for himself. It's always dark, that house, always covered in a pall of black and mourning. I told you once, years ago, to stay away. And I want you to do so now and forever, even if you're growing into a woman."

And so I did. But as the years went by, I found myself walking past the house, time and time again. It was on St. George, just a block from my home, so it was easy to take that route. The house remained sheathed in black, black veils, black drapes, black wreaths. And the death carriages came and went, and I still wondered why old man Brennan had never told my father about my crawling up on his hearse and looking into the coffin of the beautiful young woman.

Sarah just finished the entry when her cell phone rang, nearly sending her flying from the chair as it broke into her intense concentration.

"Hello?" she said a bit breathlessly.

"Sarah?" It was Caroline.

"Yes, hi."

"Are you all right?"

Sarah laughed. "Yes. The sound of my phone just startled me, that's all."

"I know you're taking the day off, but can you stop by the museum for a minute? Come in the back. No one will even know you're here."

"Okay. But are *you* all right? You sound . . . disturbed."

"There's something I need to show you," Caroline said.

"What?"

"Just get over here. You really need to see it for yourself."

Sarah frowned and glanced at her watch. "Okay. Should I head over now?"

"Please. I'll meet you at the back door."

Sarah returned the book to Vicky Hind, aware that it was valuable and should be put away carefully, so she was surprised when Vicky told her that she was welcome to take it home to read.

"I know you, Sarah. You'll treat it like gold. Here—let me put one of these dust jackets over it, and then you won't have to worry about a thing."

Once the book was duly encased, Sarah put it in her shoulder bag and left, thanking Vicky for her help. Vicky assured her that she would dig around for more references to the house.

Sarah hurriedly walked the few blocks to the museum and headed around to the back.

Caroline was already standing there with the rear door open, dressed in homespun antebellum attire. Her face was knitted in a frown, and she was anxious.

"Get in, get in!" she urged, as if they were on a secret spy mission.

Sarah stepped through the back door into the employees' break room, nicely set up with a slightly worn but comfortable sofa, a refrigerator, microwave, television and coffeemaker. A door on a side wall led to the hall, and the restrooms and lockers.

They were alone in the room, but even so, Caroline looked around worriedly, as if the walls themselves might be watching surreptitiously.

"Caroline, what the hell is going on?" Sarah demanded.

"He's so striking—Caleb Anderson, I mean. And I admit I've been trying to throw you at him. It's time for you to start dating. I mean, your fiancé's been gone for longer than you knew him. . . ."

"Caroline! What are you trying to tell me?"

"All right. Remember how I told you I was sure I'd seen Caleb Anderson before, and you thought he looked familiar, too?"

"Yes," Sarah said warily.

Caroline looked around again, then reached into the pocket of her homespun cotton skirt and produced an old photograph.

It had been framed and placed under glass to preserve it—the museum was careful with all its artifacts. It was dusty, probably from being in the storeroom, since they rotated exhibits.

"Okay, it's a photograph. An old photograph," Sarah said, taking a quick glance, then looking back at Caroline. "I think it's a Brady, and since it's in good condition, probably very valuable."

"Look at it," Caroline insisted.

Sarah did—and nearly dropped it.

It was the same man she'd seen standing at the foot of her bed.

It was Caleb.

In nineteenth-century garb, complete with one of the sweeping plumed hats that had been in vogue at the time.

"The name is on the back," Caroline said. "It's Cato MacTavish. *MacTavish*. This guy owned your house, Sarah, and Caleb Anderson is his spitting image!"

7

"I've had my men cruising every street, we've searched in the water, and we've questioned every kid that was at the beach party before Winona Hart disappeared," Tim Jamison told Caleb. "We've checked out the parents—because when a kid disappears, right or wrong, we look at the parents first. We've interviewed every ex-boyfriend and all her girlfriends—we never kid ourselves. Girls can be jealous and vicious." He was sitting behind his desk at the station, and now he leaned back, looking weary. "We were on this faster than a brushfire. If she was there to be found, we would have found her. Here's what's really sad," he admitted, leaning forward and folding his hands on his desk. "Last year, when we started the search for Jennie Lawson, it was impersonal—we just didn't believe that it had anything to do with us. Unlike you, we couldn't find anyone who saw her after she picked up her car in Jacksonville, so we assumed she never got here, that she went somewhere else or was taken before she got this far. As time went by, we assumed it was a random crime, tragic, but a one-off. You and I both know that the percentage of violent crimes that go unsolved is staggering. Old cases get shoved to the back burner when new crimes are committed. But now . . . now we've got two women who've as good as vanished—into thin air."

There was a tap on the door. A young officer came in at Jamison's bidding, handing him a file, which he in turn handed to Caleb. "Take it with my blessing. Anything you can find, we'll be grateful to hear about."

Caleb nodded. "Thanks. I'm really hoping I can find something here, because I think we're looking for someone who's going after a certain physical type, and that the two cases are related."

Jamison shook his head. "I don't know. I've only taken a few classes in behavioral crime, but you'd think this guy would escalate, not snatch one girl a year."

"Maybe he was somewhere else in between, or maybe there's a method to his madness," Caleb suggested.

"No one sees anything, and we've got nothing at all to go on," Jamison said glumly. "They say there's no perfect crime, but this guy seems to be getting away with what he's doing pretty fucking well. No bodies, no blood, no signs of a fight or fingerprints, footprints, no witnesses—*nada*."

"Criminals are often strangely brilliant," Caleb reminded him. "This guy may study people. Follow them, watch them, looking for the perfect victim, making the perfect plan to get her. But sooner or later—and I hope like hell it's sooner—he'll make a mistake. I'm going to start by talking to the kids from the beach. You never know what will jar a memory, or what little overlooked piece of information might come out."

"Like I said, you have my blessing," Jamison told him. It looked to Caleb as if Jamison hadn't been sleeping. As if there were more on his mind than just the missing girl.

Caleb stood and thanked him. For a moment he toyed with the idea of mentioning that someone might have broken in to Sarah's carriage house, but he refrained, seeing as she still seemed to half believe that that someone had been him.

He left the police station, leafing through the file he had been given. He was completely convinced that the parents had nothing to do with Winona Hart's disappearance. He was working on the theory that the same person or persons had abducted both girls.

He had a list of the kids who had been at the party. A well-organized list, with notes by each name, and the names weren't in alphabetical order, but in an order based on who among those who had seen her last had the closest relationships with Winona.

One of the boys she knew well worked at an open-fronted ice-cream shop along the pedestrian mall. Nigel Mason. According to the notes, he should be working now, and that meant *he* had a place to start.

Feeling newly invigorated, Caleb headed down the street.

"That's . . . amazing," Sarah said to Caroline.

"Amazing? It's uncanny," Caroline countered.

Sarah felt as if the air had been knocked out of her.

The picture depicted the man she had seen at the foot of her bed—exactly.

Chills raced through her. Her throat was dry. She didn't want to show Caroline just how much the photograph disturbed her, but her knees were buckling. She pretended to be studying the old photograph with keen interest as she headed for a chair and sat.

For some reason—maybe to preserve her own reputation for sanity—Sarah didn't want Caroline to know anything about the night's strange events, at least not yet.

Events—or nightmare?

"Now I understand why Caleb looked so familiar when we first saw him," Caroline said, following her and perching on the sofa by the chair. "We both saw this photograph before when it was part of that display on how the city was divided during the Civil War. You and I took down that exhibit when we replaced it with the one on Henry Flagler's wives."

Sarah let out a long breath and almost laughed aloud as she handed the photo back to Caroline. Of course. That was it. She had seen the photograph before, and that was why she had thought Caleb looked familiar. She just hadn't put the two together. And of course this was why she'd been so sure Caleb himself had been in her room. Now, with a fair amount of time having passed between the morning and this revelation, it all made sense. In a way, at least. She'd had the photograph catalogued neatly somewhere in memory. She'd met Caleb. Mr. Griffin had come into her house and given her quite a jolt with his crazy fantasies. And then she had dreamed, and in her dream, she had dredged up her memory of the photograph and put the Caleb she knew into the body of a man who had lived long ago.

"Caroline, I could kiss you!" she said.

Caroline stared at her as if she'd gone nuts. "What?"

She decided she still didn't feel ready to share what was proving to be only a nightmare, however terrifying, with anyone else. She'd already made a fool of herself in front of Caleb.

"This photograph. It explains everything," Sarah said. Caroline was still looking at her blankly, so Sarah smiled and went on. "Don't you see—I've been wary of him because somewhere in my subconscious I remembered this photo. Now I understand why he seemed so familiar, so . . ." She faltered, at a loss for a way to pull things together. "Now it all just makes so much sense," she finished lamely.

"*That's* all you can think of to say? You've got to be kidding," Caroline said.

"No, I'm not kidding. Why?"

"Didn't you hear me? This is *uncanny*."

"I admit, the resemblance is startling."

"It's more than a resemblance. There's got to be a genetic connection. I mean, how else could Caleb possibly look so much like Cato? His great, great, great . . . whatever grandfather must have been Cato MacTavish, who used to own *your* house. Maybe it's destiny that Caleb's here now. We have to show him the picture. We have to tell him about it," Caroline said excitedly, and then her smile faded. "Although I have to admit, when I came across the picture today, my . . . mind went a little crazy. For a minute there I actually thought maybe Cato was back from the dead to take vengeance on the people who drove him away."

"Oh, Caroline . . ."

"Well . . . you have to admit it's pretty weird. I mean, Cato's double shows up in the city when all this . . . stuff is happening."

"Caroline, *Caleb* is here searching for a girl who disappeared a *year* ago, and then he plunged right into the efforts to look for the girl who only just disappeared, but be reasonable. He wasn't here when either one of them disappeared," Sarah said, then looked away for a moment. She'd been scared for a minute herself when she first saw the photograph, yet here she was, completely prepared to defend Caleb Anderson with all the passion she had.

185

And it wasn't because he was good-looking and articulate, not to mention capable, charming and charismatic.

He worked for Adam Harrison, and that meant he was the one thing that really mattered: a good man.

"I know. I realized right away that I was being ridiculous. I can't wait to show the picture to him, though. There's obviously *some* connection here. He has to be related somehow to Cato MacTavish. I know—when Cato MacTavish left St. Augustine, he changed his name to Anderson."

Sarah shook her head, smiling. "Even if he is somehow related—and I admit it looks likely—the connection might have come down through the maternal line."

"Maybe. But I'll have to research it later. Right now I have to get back out there and talk about Henry Flagler," Caroline said, glancing at her watch. "What's up at your house today, by the way?"

"I don't know. I've been at the library, but I think I'll head back home now. And, Caroline, I don't think you should look into Caleb's connection to Cato here at the museum."

"Why not?"

"Because . . . Caleb is here on business. I don't think he'd want to become a sideshow oddity."

"You're right." Caroline studied the photograph

186

for a long moment, then offered it to Sarah. "You hold on to it."

"Thank you, Caroline."

Caroline looked at her and smirked. "You're really going to go back to the library to try to trace Caleb Anderson's background, aren't you?"

"Yes."

Caroline studied her. "You like him, don't you?"

"Yes," Sarah said, then hesitated for a moment. She felt silly for keeping secrets and decided to confide in her. "Caroline, here's what's so strange. I must have remembered this photograph in the back in my mind somewhere, because last night I had a nightmare about this man, dressed just this way, standing at the foot of my bed, telling me that he was innocent."

"Innocent?"

"I didn't know what it could have meant then, but now that I know this is Cato, I think he meant he was innocent of kidnapping and killing those girls."

"How bizarre." Caroline grinned suddenly. "Did you think you were dreaming about Caleb all dressed up or something?"

Sarah grimaced and said, "Actually, I thought it was really him and he'd broken into the carriage house. I went over to Bertie's and burst in on him, and accused him of trying to scare me half to death."

Caroline gasped, then laughed. "You didn't! What on earth did he say? No, wait. More importantly, does he sleep in the buff?"

"No." Sarah said. She hesitated. "He was wearing boxers."

"Still . . . oh, Sarah!" Caroline started to laugh.

"Stop it."

"Sorry. So—does he think you're crazy? Too crazy to maybe go out with? Wait—how did he look?"

Sarah paused, then admitted, "He looked damned good. Now let me out the back," Sarah said. "I don't want to run in to anyone right now. Be sure to lock the door behind me."

"Okay, okay, come on."

Sarah had just stepped outside when Caroline stopped her. "Sarah?"

"What?" Sarah asked, turning back.

Caroline was grinning. "Go for it. If he looks good *in* boxers, chances are he looks equally good out of them."

Sarah groaned and made her escape.

Nigel Mason looked like a typical high school kid, hovering between adolescence and adulthood. He was tall, and extremely lean and lanky, with long hair that he had tied back and covered with a bandana as he served ice cream. Caleb recognized him instantly from his picture in the file Tim Jamison had given him.

He observed the boy before approaching the window. He saw Nigel perk up when a trio of young women came to the stand, and after they had paid and departed, he leaned an elbow on the counter and looked glum.

Caleb approached him. "Nigel?"

Nigel looked up and straightened, a wary look coming into his eyes.

"Yes?"

Caleb offered him a handshake. "Hi. My name is Caleb Anderson."

"You another cop?" Nigel asked.

"Private investigator."

A flash of pain crossed Nigel's features, making him young and vulnerable all of a sudden. He looked around for a moment, as if praying for someone to come over to buy ice cream. "You're here about Winona, aren't you?" he asked Caleb.

"Yes."

"I wish I knew something," Nigel said.

"Can you just tell me about the night she was last seen? I'm coming in fresh, and something might hit me that the cops missed, or maybe you'll remember something new."

Nigel looked around again, still hopeful that a customer would appear from nowhere. "I wish I knew something," he repeated.

"Anything that you know will help me. Where were you? Who was there? What was the night like? Like I said, I'm not a cop. I'm not going to turn anyone in, or tell anyone's folks they were drinking or smoking pot or anything else," Caleb assured him.

Nigel inhaled deeply, then exhaled loudly, as if he'd made a decision. "Okay, so we had this party at the beach—out on Anastasia Island, not far over the bridge. There's a place that's kind of off the beaten track. We had a bonfire going, and . . . and yeah, there was booze and grass." He went quiet, remembering.

"You dated Winona for a while, right?" Caleb asked, prodding him.

"Yeah, kind of. Last year. But it felt too weird. We'd gone to grade school together, you know?"

"There were no hard feelings when you split up?"

"Hell, no." He stared at Caleb suddenly. "You think I could have done something to her?" he asked incredulously.

"No," Caleb assured him. His gut told him that this kid couldn't have carried off a white lie, much less an abduction. "I'm just wondering if she would have confided in you. If she would have told you that she was going to run away, for instance. Or if she was meeting someone."

"She wasn't running away. And she wasn't meeting anyone." He was quiet for a minute, then looked at Caleb as if sizing him up. "She was pretty wasted, though. Just on beer—she didn't smoke weed. But she had a lot of beer. She was dancing around the fire and pretending it was some kind of an old Maypole or something."

"Really? Why do you think that was?"

"She liked to read creepy stuff, books about black magic and crap like that. She was kind of Goth for a while even."

"So did she believe in ghosts and that kind of thing?" Caleb asked.

"Oh, yeah. She wanted to experience all that spooky stuff, you know? See the real thing. She was the kind who would turn out the lights and make noises to scare you, and then laugh. She wasn't afraid of anything. She used to climb into cemeteries at night and dare us to come after her."

"Did she know anyone who she felt might help her experience the real thing?" Caleb asked.

"I don't think so," Nigel said, his brow furrowed in concentration. Suddenly he brightened. "She did talk to a weird woman on the beach."

"A weird woman on the beach?" Caleb asked, trying to sound casual. This was something new, and maybe it meant nothing. On the other hand . . .

"She came over while we started setting up." He stared at Caleb. "She looked like a hippie. She scared us at first," he admitted, flushing. "She just walked out of this grove of scrub right when we started building the fire. We thought she lived nearby or something, and that maybe she was going to threaten to call the cops on us. But all she said was hello, and that we should be careful. Hey wait!" he said suddenly.

"What is it?" Caleb asked.

"She said that she was there communicating with the elements, that she was some kind of medium," Nigel said. "I figured she'd been hiding out back there, smoking weed. But now . . . I hadn't even thought of it. There were only three of us there. Mindy Marshall, Winona and me. She told us to be careful, said the moon was at its most powerful peak or some weird shit like that, and it brought out all kinds of spirits. I thought she was a kook. Winona thought she was cool and talked to her for a little while, but I wasn't really paying attention. I can't believe I forgot all about her 'til now."

"What happened then?"

"She walked away."

"To where?"

"I don't know. Probably down the trail that led back to the road."

"Did you see her again?"

"No. She just told us to be careful and left."

"What did she look like?"

"I told you, a hippie."

"A tall hippie? Short, dark, light?"

Nigel frowned in concentration. "I don't know. She was wearing some kind of a kerchief thing on her head, and she had on really big sunglasses."

"Okay, was she tall or short?"

"Medium," Nigel decided after a moment.

"Five-five?"

"Yeah, maybe."

"Do you remember anything else about her? Anything at all? Was she wearing perfume? Did she walk with a limp? Did you see her hands? Anything."

Nigel looked away for a moment, then faced Caleb sheepishly. "I'd had two beers, maybe three by then. I was pretty looped by the time I saw her. You really won't say anything to my parents, right? You're really not a cop?"

"I'm really not a cop." Caleb drew a card from his wallet and handed it to the boy. "I want you to do me a favor. If you think of anything else—and I want you to really think about this woman and see if you can remember something more—give me a call. Please."

Nigel took the card and looked at Caleb again. "Okay. You might want to talk to Mindy. She might remember something." He looked down, wincing. "Thing is, the three of us . . . we had a twelve-pack to start and it was pretty much gone by the time the woman showed up. So . . . I kind of doubt she'll remember anything, either, know what I mean?"

"Point taken," Caleb said. "But I'm going to go talk to her anyway. So where exactly was this beach party?" he asked. He had directions; they were in the file Jamison had given him. But he wanted the kid's directions, as well.

"I'll draw you a map," Nigel said, taking a napkin from the counter and a pen from underneath the cash register.

"While you're at it, draw me a map of the area and show me where the woman came from, and where you think she walked off to," Caleb said.

Nigel did as asked, then looked Caleb straight in the eye and asked, "Do you think you'll find Winona?" he asked. "Alive?" He looked a little sick, as if he were afraid of the answer.

"We're all trying."

When he left Nigel, Caleb headed back for his car. Mindy Marshall was next on his list of people to question, but before he talked to her, he wanted to walk on the beach where Winona Hart had last been seen.

He had just found another connection between the two missing women.

Both of them had wanted to be frightened.

Frightened—to death?

Vicky Hind was pleased when Sarah returned. "This is so exciting," she said. "Well, sad, too, but not *that* sad. I mean, Mrs. Abrams was ninety-two, and she died in her sleep."

"Pardon?" Sarah said.

"Not ten minutes ago, we received a donation from Ethel Abrams. Well, from her estate. She lived in the old Pickens-Aubrey house down the street. You must remember her," Vicky said. "She was always trying to do something good for the city."

"Mrs. Abrams . . ." Sarah mused. "Oh, yes, I do remember her. She seemed old even when I was young, but she was always dressed up, wearing a hat and gloves."

"That's her. Was her," Vicky corrected herself. "She passed away about a week ago. Anyway, she left us some old boxes of papers from her attic, and I thought that you might enjoy looking through them. Her husband inherited the house from his grandmother, and she was here during the Civil War. I found a journal I thought might help you, and you can help us, too. You're a historian, so you can catalogue the contents."

"That's wonderful. I'd love to read it," Sarah said. "Would you mind, though, if I logged onto the computer for a few minutes first?"

"Help yourself," Vicky told her.

Sarah was familiar with all the genealogy Web sites and immediately signed onto her favorite— and entered Caleb's name.

Then she paused. Where was he originally from? Virginia? Worth a try.

She filled in the state, without a clue as to the city, then paused again. She didn't have his date of birth or a current address.

Giving up on that approach, she filled in Cato MacTavish's name instead. Birthplace, St. Augustine, Florida. Year of birth? She gave a range in the 1830s. He'd served in the Confederate Army, so she entered that information, too, along with the address of the house that was now hers, then clicked on Search.

Thirty seconds later, she had her results.

A death certificate had been filed for a Cato MacTavish in 1901, in Fairfax, Virginia. He'd left behind one son. There was no mention of a wife, just a son, Magnus, who in turn had died in 1919.

Magnus had been survived by his three daughters, Emily, Elisabeth and Edna.

Sarah kept filling in information and refining her search.

In 1901, Emily MacTavish had been granted a marriage license and wed a Mr. John Anderson of Colonial Beach, Virginia.

For a moment, Sarah stared at the screen, amazed that she'd found the proof she was looking for so easily.

Then she started searching again.

John Anderson and Emily MacTavish had one son in 1903, Ellsworth. Ellsworth married a woman named Dorothy Sweeney in 1926. They produced two daughters, Michaela and Genevieve, and one son, another John. In 1950, John's son, Andrew, was born, and then . . .

Andrew and his wife, Cynthia, had their first child, a son named Caleb.

Caleb Anderson.

The beach was exquisite. Off the beaten path, it was surrounded by pine trees and washed by gentle waves.

Caleb found the place where the kids had built their bonfire. Though they had conscientiously doused the flames and broken down the remains, the evidence was clear in the scraps of burned wood. They had picked up all their beer bottles, cans and leftovers, though. The place was amazingly clean. It was also the kind of place a person had to know about to arrive at, secluded from view and at least a third of a mile off the road.

Caleb had followed the single path from the road to the beach, found the darkened pit in the sand and done a cursory visual search. Pine and bracken to the left, pine and bracken to the right, and pines and oaks behind him, many draped with the Spanish moss so common in the area.

Winona Hart had been here with her friends. She had met a woman coming from the northern side of the beach area—a hippie who had told them she was a medium, and that they needed to be careful because of the moon. The woman had left via a path that led back to the road.

There was no other access to the beach, unless you came by boat. It was possible that Winona might have been taken by boat, but none of the kids had mentioned seeing one. The file had told him that the last kids on the beach had been Nigel and Mindy. They had made sure that the fire was dead—and the garbage had all been cleaned up.

Winona had disappeared at some previous point, but no one remembered when she had left the party. There had been too many kids, most of them drunk or stoned.

Caleb walked into the pine forest to the north. A trail of beaten-down vegetation led away from the sand, and he followed it.

It curved around and joined the main path between the beach and the road. The kids might have been followed by the kidnapper, who broke off into the woods and observed them from there until he—or she—found a chance to grab Winona. Could the mystery woman have been the kidnapper? It was certainly possible.

And Winona, fascinated as she was, might have gone looking for the woman again. And the woman might have led her to the road while the others were busy drinking and smoking and pairing off in the moonlight.

Winona would have gone willingly, fascinated by everything the woman had told her.

He took a seat on the sand about two feet beyond where the waves washed up and closed his eyes.

There was a reason why he had gone to work for Adam Harrison, and this was the time and place to put his mind to work. He still had a tendency to balk at the idea, but he'd learned that whatever it was—logic operating in the far recesses of his mind, an ability everyone possessed but didn't know how to tap into—it helped stopped murderers. And if he could prevent the death of another human being, then it would be cowardly, perhaps even criminal, not to do everything he could. His mental re-creations, as he thought of them, weren't available on call or at all times, but sometimes, when he concentrated, he could see the little thing that everyone else had missed and gain insight into the truth, find a clue to follow.

The sea breeze drifted by him, and he remembered the day when he had discovered that he could use intense concentration to somehow intuit what had happened at a crime scene. He still refused to believe that he was actually seeing the past, that something psychic was at work. The way he saw it, he just put the pieces together and, like a filmmaker, created a visual image.

But that first time . . .

He'd been on a beach then, as well.

His cousin Elisia, just seven years old, had somehow strayed from a family gathering at a busy beachside picnic area. People had been everywhere, eating and laughing. A man dressed as a clown had been making balloon animals for a donation of a dollar apiece to delight the children. It had been easy to lose track of one little girl.

She hadn't been gone more than a few minutes when Aunt Julia had begun to grow frantic.

Everyone had assumed she was still with the other children, who were all playing hide-and-seek, until his aunt had realized Elisia wasn't with them anymore.

Caleb had been twelve at the time, and the last time he had seen Elisia, she had smiled and winked at him before hurrying away to hide.

The police had been called immediately, and while everybody rushed around shouting and searching, Caleb had stood to one side, retreating somewhere deep into his mind. As he lost himself in thought, his cousin's pretty and precocious face had risen before his eyes. He'd seen her smile and wink again. He saw her looking for a good place to hide, and he saw the balloon man bring a finger to his lips and smile, showing her that she could hide inside the restroom.

Someone had already looked inside the restrooms, but he'd shouted and gone running toward them anyway. You couldn't see her at first. Her killer had folded her tiny body and left it on a toilet, then jammed the door shut.

If he lived to be a hundred, he would never forget the look on his aunt's face when her child was found. He would never forget the sound of her hysterical sobs. He would never forget anything about that day, the heat of the sun, the feel of the breeze, the smell of saltwater.

But they'd caught the clown. And a cop had told Caleb that the man might have gotten away in the time it would have taken them to put the pieces together, if it hadn't been for Caleb. It had been small comfort for the loss of Elisia.

He'd been enamored of Jacques Cousteau up until that point, convinced that he was going to become an expert diver and deep sea explorer. He'd planned to find lost colonies and sunken treasure.

After that day, he'd known without question that he wanted to be a cop. To do something, anything, to stop predators like the one who had killed his cousin.

He never forgot the past, but he didn't dwell on it. For years he hadn't known how to use his "talent," not through his days in the military, college or the academy. He hadn't understood his ability until he met Adam Harrison, who had sought him out, and then funded him through his master's degree, asking only that he consider coming to work for Harrison Investigations to use his talent in return.

But to this day, Caleb hated clowns.

And today . . .

This lonely beach was the perfect spot. If he opened his mind, he was sure he would see the past, the flames leaping, the kids celebrating, and Winona . . . He would see what had happened to Winona.

And he had to do it, because there was a killer on the loose. The threads were beginning to fit together, and he had to add to the pattern with whatever he could discover in the depths of his mind.

For a moment he just listened to the sounds around him. The surf, moving in gently. The wind, barely a whisper in the trees. In his mind, he saw shadows, the coming of twilight.

The first kids arrived, carrying a big cooler. Nigel had one side of the cooler, Winona the other. They were laughing as they kept dropping one side or the other. Winona accused Nigel of being a weakling; he said even if she was a girl, she had to manage her half of the weight.

Mindy Marshall was right behind them; he recognized her from her picture in the file. She was a tall girl with long dark hair, carrying bags of chips and a box of garbage bags. They knew they had to clean up. If a single beer can was found, they would be busted.

Nigel told the girls to start finding wood for the fire, while he dug in the sand to create a pit.

In his mind's eye, Caleb imagined the birth of the fire, the way it smoked at first, then took hold. He saw Winona dancing around the rising flames, chanting something she had learned from a book, teasing Nigel and Mindy and the others, perhaps telling them that she was ready to meet with the forces of darkness. . . .

Then the woman walked out of the woods. Large, dark glasses covered not just her eyes but most of her face, hiding her features. She wore a scarf around her neck, and she smiled at Winona, who had stopped and gone silent at the sight of her. She spoke in a pleasant tone, assuring the kids she wasn't going to report them and asking Winona about the words she'd been chanting.

The woman saw something in Winona, and Winona saw something in her, as well. The stranger stepped closer to Winona, who was separated from the others by the leaping bonfire. The woman said something to Winona in a hushed tone, and the other two were totally unaware of the conversation. Seconds later, the woman left them, laughing, waving, telling them to be careful.

Moments later, more partygoers began to arrive, bringing food, booze and pot. A boom box played in the background, and he could hear the laughter, the teasing, see kids pairing off and heading into the shadows. . . .

He concentrated, and he saw Winona Hart, looking around, then starting along the trail back toward the road. She was seen by dozens of witnesses, yet not seen at all.

He opened his eyes, rose and dusted off his jeans.

The sun was beginning to set. The view was spectacular as the sun crouched low on the horizon, painting the sky with bands of gold and orange, and creeping purple.

It was a beautiful place, giving the impression of being wild and even a little forlorn in its beauty, despite its relative proximity to the road.

Caleb walked down to the water.

And found the corpse.

8

Sarah had expected to hear from Caleb Anderson. After all, she had barged into his room that morning and trashed his belongings.

And he had told her not to do it again unless she was looking for sex.

Despite everything else she'd had to deal with that day, the idea of having sex with Caleb crept in unbidden time after time.

And why not?

She was an adult. The rest of the world had sex all the time. She had just put the very possibility on a mental back burner somewhere after Clay's death. She wasn't against the idea of having sex again someday. She didn't even think that it needed to be with the one and only love of her life, someone with whom she was hoping for a future. Which was a good thing, since she hadn't met anyone else . . . she thought she might be able to fall in love with. She hadn't even met anyone who intrigued her for more than a cup of coffee or dinner out.

But Caleb Anderson . . .

Frankly, he was just gorgeous, the kind of man any woman would want to have sex with. . . .

When Vicky came into the room—clearing her throat politely and saying that it was time for her to lock up—Sarah was forced to realize that it was long after five, and Caleb had made no effort to contact her.

Then again, why would any man—especially an exceptionally handsome and charismatic one—want to spend any more time with a woman who had not only been convinced that he dressed up in costume to play a practical joke on her, but had also come crashing into his room at the crack of dawn to accuse him? She was anxious to see him, though, because she was dying to explain about the picture—and what she had discovered about his ancestry. Once he had all the facts, her seemingly crazy behavior would make sense.

Meanwhile, her afternoon had been a productive one. She'd printed out the records she'd discovered online, and she'd begun reading the journal from Mrs. Abrams's trunk.

It had been kept by Nellie Brennan, daughter of the nasty undertaker Leo Brennan, and it had been every bit as intriguing as the memoir she'd been reading earlier. Nellie's mother had died young, and her father's housekeeper, who had come to live at the Grant mansion with them, was, in Nellie's words, "a witch." And not just figuratively, either. The woman scared her; she served her father faithfully, but she treated Nellie badly. Nellie thought that was because she herself wasn't a pretty girl. The housekeeper, Martha Tyler, though an octoroon of mixed blood, was extremely beautiful and seemed to be ageless.

Nellie believed she kept a book of spells hidden in her room, and *knew* she kept jars containing all sorts of loathsome things, dried and preserved animal parts, herbs and potions, and other similarly repulsive bits. But she ran the house—and the mortuary—faultlessly, so Leo wasn't about to fire her.

Sarah would have loved to take *that* journal home, but it was both fragile and a brand-new acquisition. She knew she was lucky to be reading it. When Vicky stretched out a hand, still smiling, to take it back, there was nothing to do but hand it over and thank Vicky for her help.

"Oh, I enjoy helping someone who's as fascinated as I am by the personal details of history. People love stories about real people." She waved a hand dismissively. "Do children remember dates and figures? No. But give them exciting events and real people, and they'll love learning history."

Sarah agreed, and said, "Vicky, that journal is a true find. I barely got started reading, but I can already tell it's full of insight into the era. I'll be back tomorrow. I want to know more about the housekeeper. Nellie said she was a witch."

"A witch?" Vicky said. "I'll see if I can find anything about her in the morning."

"Thanks, I'll see you bright and early."

"Oh? Are you off tomorrow, too?"

Sarah hesitated. "Yes, I'm taking tomorrow off, too."

Vicky looked at her sympathetically. "People still driving you crazy about those bones, huh?"

"Yes."

"Just go on one of the big talk shows—get it over with," Vicky suggested.

Of all the people who had called, Sarah thought wryly, unfortunately Oprah hadn't been one of them.

"I'll see you in the morning," Sarah told Vicky, then left the library and headed home. She stood on the sidewalk staring up at her house, so many things racing through her mind. The things she'd just been reading. The bones in her walls. Mr. Griffin's words.

She didn't care what he said. Houses weren't evil.

There were no cars parked in front of her house. Still, she didn't go inside, but headed for the carriage house instead.

It felt . . . lonely.

She turned on the television, opting for music videos over anything requiring her to pay attention.

She curled up on the bed, intending to read more of the memoir, but her mind was too full. She finally admitted to herself that she hadn't just expected Caleb to call her, she'd hoped he would. She couldn't wait to show him the proof of his heritage that she had printed out at the library, not to mention the picture. She was eager to prove her sanity to him.

She turned back to the memoir, and as she read, she wondered about the words the man in her dream had spoken. *I didn't do it.*

Clearly she didn't want to make Caleb look guilty, even in her dreams, though she had no idea what he could actually be guilty *of.* After all, she was attracted to him. He had been the one to mention sex, but it wasn't as if she hadn't already been thinking of it.

As for Cato MacTavish, nothing she had read proved that he had been guilty of the disappearance or the murders. In fact, the crimes had continued after he'd left town, which seemed to indicate the opposite: that despite the rumors swirling around him, he'd been entirely innocent. But there had been rumors—purposely circulated—that Cato remained in hiding. So, through the years he remained a suspect.

She was restless, and though she was enjoying the memoir, she found her mind wandering every few pages.

Finally she put the book down and tried calling Tim Jamison. He was theoretically a nine-to-fiver, but often a case made him run late, sometimes even keeping him on the job well into the night. But not tonight.

She tried Floby, but he wasn't available, either.

She looked out the window at her house. Twilight was just beginning to arrive. The heat of the day was waning, and everything seemed a bit softer without the glare of the sun.

She left the carriage house, marched up the steps of her home and let herself in.

Someone had been sweeping.

And, she discovered in the kitchen, someone had been using her coffeepot—and her coffee. There was even a half-full cup still sitting out on the counter. All of which was fine, of course. She just felt a bit like one of the three bears, trying to figure out who Goldilocks might be, and whether Goldilocks was still in the house somewhere.

No. She could feel the emptiness.

She walked into the back, where the library was—or would be. The walls were still knocked out, but someone had tried to sweep up in here, too, though despite their best efforts the plaster dust was still ubiquitous.

Floby hadn't left her a note that day. She wondered idly whether the medical examiner had been the one making coffee.

It suddenly occurred to her that she might have made the same mistake she'd made the other day: forgetting to lock the front door behind her. She raced back to the front door and was relieved to discover that she *had* locked it. But as she stood there, awash in relief, the emptiness suddenly seemed to be overwhelming.

She turned and found herself studying the beautiful entryway, the double doors leading to the two parlors, and the hallway that led deeper into the house. If she closed her eyes, she could picture herself in the house as it must have been before the Civil War. It would have been beautiful then. Cato MacTavish would have been handsome, dashing and young, with an affectionately teasing light in his eyes as he flirted with his beautiful Eleanora. He wouldn't have been scarred yet by the horror of the war, by seeing his fellow soldiers and friends fall. Eleanora wouldn't yet have disappeared. His father would have been alive, and Eleanora might have come over to play and sing for both the elder MacTavish and the younger, the man she loved. The swish of taffeta would have accompanied the sound of laughter. Sarah could almost see them. . . .

But that had been long ago.

I didn't do it. I loved her.

Sarah wasn't afraid of ghosts, didn't even believe in them. Still, she didn't want to be alone. The silence and emptiness were unnerving.

She went outside, conscientiously locked the door and headed for Hunky Harry's.

"Anderson's a corpse magnet, I'm telling you."

Will's back was to the front door, and Caleb knew the other man had no idea he'd just walked into Hunky Harry's.

Caroline, Renee, Barry and Sarah were all there, and they all saw Caleb and looked up at him in mortified silence.

211

Will spun around, realized he'd been overheard and blushed. "Sorry, buddy," he said, "but you have to admit it's true."

Caleb was glad to see that the chair next to Sarah was open, and he didn't hesitate to take it.

He wondered if he looked as drained as he felt. He'd spent the last few hours on the beach as Tim Jamison and his crew barricaded the area with yellow tape, then the crime scene unit had arrived, quickly followed by Floby.

"Was it . . . do they think it was Winona Hart?" Sarah asked him.

Apparently the news of his find had preceded him. Will knew a lot of cops, and even with Lieutenant Jamison putting a gag order on the information, Caleb wasn't surprised that it had traveled.

"No," he said.

"No?" Caroline said, surprised.

"It was a young woman, though, right?" Renee asked, hesitant and yet intrigued.

"Yes," Caleb told them. There was no reason to lie. No matter how much Tim might have wanted to keep it quiet, word was going to spread.

"So who was it?" Sarah asked.

"We don't know yet. The body was in pretty bad shape. The fingers were missing, so they won't get any prints. They'll have to use dental records for an ID." He turned away, motioning to the waitress for a beer, the same young woman who seemed to wait on them every night. She saw him and nodded, but the smile she gave him was no-nonsense. The waitresses at Hunky Harry's were there to work. They didn't wear short-shorts and skimpy tank tops. Jeans and T-shirts that advertised Hunky Harry's were the uniform here.

"This is going to be terrible for business. The whole city will start to empty out," Caroline said. "And of course those poor, poor women . . ."

"My God. We have a serial killer right here in St. Augustine," Renee said.

Barry put his arm around her. "Don't worry, I won't let you out of my sight," he told her.

"I think you should dye your hair," Will told Caroline.

The waitress set Caleb's beer down, and he waited for her to leave before speaking.

"Let's not jump to conclusions. For all we know it was a boating accident. Maybe it has nothing to do with anything else that's going on."

He didn't believe it, though. The corpse had been in such an advanced state of decomposition that it was impossible to tell how the woman had died, but no boaters had been reported missing, so violence seemed likely. Floby had refused to say much of anything until he could get the body to the morgue and do a full autopsy. All he'd been willing to commit to was the fact that she appeared to have been dead for some time, although he'd then contradicted himself by saying that if she had been dead that long, more of her should have been lost to the salt water—and the creatures whose home it was. Which made Caleb suspect that she'd been dead for a while before her body had been consigned to the ocean, but he would leave it to Floby to figure that out.

"Will said Jamison is trying to keep it quiet. Why?" Sarah asked.

"Because he doesn't want a panic like Caroline was talking about, that's why," Will said.

"I'm thinking that he wants to have something more to say before he makes a statement," Caleb said. "But with or without more information, he's going to have to call the papers quickly. It's better to have what facts there are out in the media than have a pack of half truths floating around."

"How did you discover the body?" Sarah asked him.

He looked down at his beer and winced. Hadn't she been listening to Will? Because he was a corpse magnet, of course.

"I had gone to the beach—I was trying to get a sense of the layout on the area where Winona Hart disappeared," he said. "The body had washed up on shore. It had been there several hours, by the look of things. I really don't think I attract dead bodies." He stared at Will.

"Yeah, he wasn't even in Sarah's house when those bones showed up," Renee said, trying to be helpful.

"She might have washed up from anywhere," Sarah said quickly, clearly eager to turn the conversation away from the goings-on at her house. "It could be a case of domestic violence. A husband up in Jacksonville or down in Daytona, out on a boat, getting into a fight with his wife. Maybe it was accidental. He didn't mean to kill her, and then he panicked and threw her overboard. Or something else we haven't even thought of might have happened. Or . . ."

Sarah looked down at the table. "Maybe it's another in a long line of disappearances. Just like before."

Caleb saw that the others were staring at her blankly.

"What are you talking about?" Renee asked.

"Oh, you mean the old stories . . . about your house and Cato MacTavish? It's not as if they ever had any evidence or anyone was ever arrested," Caroline said.

"What are you two talking about?" Barry asked.

"Oh, come on, all the ghost tours go by there and tell stories about the mortician who supposedly abducted and murdered women," Caroline told him.

"Yeah, and Osceola walks around at night looking for his head, too—right on Castillo Drive, so I hear," Barry said. "We deal in facts at the museum, and I've never heard any *facts* about Cato MacTavish killing anyone."

"Maybe, but I've read a number of references lately to women who disappeared back then—including Cato MacTavish's fiancée," Sarah said.

Caleb noticed that she looked at him strangely as she spoke. Then Caroline leaned over to whisper to her, but he could hear her words.

"Did you show him?"

Sarah shook her head. "Caroline—he just got here." Her voice was equally low.

"What are you two whispering about?" Will demanded.

He didn't get an answer, because at that moment Barry, who was directly facing the door, let out a soft whistle. "Don't look now, but—I mean—do not look now!" He let out a sound of disgust as they all ignored his words and turned as one.

"Hey, it's Ms. Perfect," Caroline said.

"And look who's right behind her," Barry added.

Lieutenant Tim Jamison was walking into the bar, perhaps five feet behind Cary.

Caleb found himself reflecting that if Jamison *was* having an affair with the woman, it wouldn't be the most startling thing in the world. He was a good-looking man, and he'd been married long enough to have developed a roving eye.

"His wife is such a sweetie," Caroline said sadly.

"They might not be together," Sarah said.

"Right. Twice in a row. They suck at being discreet," Renee said.

"There—he's not with her. He just went to meet

216

up with those officers at the bar," Will said. "And tall, blond and gorgeous is coming over here to say hello to us."

The men stood, all at once.

"Hello, all," Cary greeted them. "Sit down, please, though it's certainly nice to see there are still gentlemen in the world." She had on hip-hugging jeans and a tailored shirt that, admittedly, emphasized her narrow waist and high breasts.

She oozed sensuality, Caleb thought. And she didn't seem the least bit aware of it.

Or else she was very aware of it and had the whole act down pat.

"How are you?" Sarah asked. "Want to join us?"

"Thanks," Cary said. "But I'm just going to grab a quick beer at the bar and take off—I'm pretty tired tonight."

"How is Mr. Griffin?" Sarah asked her.

"He's been kind of upset lately, which is part of why I need to get back. But I will join you one of these nights, now that I see you're always here," Cary said.

"Not really," Caroline said, then flushed and admitted, "Though we *have* been here an awful lot this week, haven't we?"

"It's that place 'where everybody knows your name,' I guess," Will offered.

Caleb, quietly watching the exchange, also noted that Tim Jamison was watching their table closely from his seat at the bar, and he didn't look pleased.

He nodded in Caleb's direction when he noticed he was being observed in turn, then swallowed the last of his drink and exited the bar.

Cary was only pretending not to notice, Caleb thought. She quickly said her goodbyes to them, went to the bar and drank a beer in record time, and then she, too, left.

"Interesting," Caroline said as her eyes followed Cary out the door.

"It's really none of our business," Sarah commented.

"But his wife is a doll," Caroline argued.

"So what are you suggesting?" Sarah asked. "That we should call her? Ask, 'Do you know where your husband is at night?' For one thing, he's a cop, so he could be anywhere, and for another, we don't actually know that anything is going on between them."

Will stared across the table at Caleb and grinned. "She was always a little bit on the naive side."

"I'm not naive—I'm sensible. We don't want to start any rumors, and that's all we'd be doing," she said firmly.

"What's your take?" Will demanded, turning to Caleb.

Caleb was startled by the question. "I'm new here. I don't know any of the players well enough to guess."

"Sorry, I changed the subject on you. You came down here looking for a girl who disappeared a year ago. So far you've found a guy dead in a sunken car and some other girl dead on the beach. Unless . . . you don't think she's the girl you're looking for, do you?" he asked.

"No, definitely not," Caleb said. He'd thought at first that she might be. But the woman on the beach had naturally dark hair—Floby had pointed that out. She was also petite, maybe five feet even, and Jennie Lawson had been taller, around five foot seven.

"So do you think everything's connected?" Will asked. "Except for the guy in the car, I mean."

"Yes, that's what I think," Caleb said.

"Do you think you'll ever be able to prove it?" Renee asked him, shivering.

"Yes. Because all killers mess up eventually," Caleb said.

"Not Jack the Ripper," Caroline pointed out.

"With today's science, he'd have been picked up," Caleb said.

"But we all know that killers get away with it all the time," Barry said, shaking his head. "It's terrible, but it's true. There are tons of unsolved murders."

"Let's get off the subject of murder, okay?" Caroline asked.

"Okay, here's another subject," Will said. "I need another beer."

"We all need food," Sarah said.

"Yes, Mom," Will said.

"I'm going to smack you in two seconds," Sarah promised him. "Don't eat if you don't want to, but I'm going to." She stood, looking irritated, and headed for the bar. Caleb stood and joined her.

"Are you all right?" he asked, standing next to her while she waited for their waitress to finish at the draft taps.

She looked at him. "Actually, I've been anxious to see you all day," she admitted.

"It was the sex comment, right?" he said, hoping he wasn't coming off as a total jerk.

She flushed slightly, looking away. "In a way, yes."

"Oh?"

"You have to admit, it was pretty memorable. But the thing is, now I know exactly why I thought what I did."

"Really?"

"Really," she said firmly, looking at him again. "I don't want to show you now, and I don't think you want me to show you now, either. Since you're down here working, I'm assuming you don't want to become the lead story on the local news. Those guys," she said, indicating the table, "are a great bunch of people, but you saw the way they hopped right on Jamison. No secret is safe with them."

He stared at her, trying to follow her words. "Well, thanks for thinking about my reputation, but I have no idea what on earth you're talking about."

She laughed. "Walk me home. I'll show you then."

Their waitress turned to them then, apologizing, and Sarah told her that they just needed menus. She ordered another beer for Will, too.

He thanked her when she returned to the table, depositing the beer in front of him, and asked, "May I have a menu, too? Please? I won't be obnoxious anymore, I promise."

"You can't help it," Sarah said, but she handed him a menu.

They spent the next few minutes poring over the menu, but in the end, they ordered a round of fish and chips for the table.

Right after they ordered, Caleb's phone rang. He checked the caller ID and was surprised to see that it was a number he had just entered that afternoon: Floby's cell.

He answered quickly, then excused himself and went outside.

"Where are you?" Floby asked him.

"At Hunky Harry's," Caleb said.

"Well, I just thought that you might want to know what I found out right away," Floby told him. "I haven't even spoken with Jamison yet. He hasn't answered his page."

Caleb didn't reply to that. He didn't know Jamison well, and he had never met his wife. It wasn't his place to comment on what the lieutenant might or might not be doing that was keeping him from answering his phone.

"Thank you for calling me," he said. "I'd love to know what you've come up with."

"Here's the strange thing. I think this girl was buried—and then dug up and thrown into the water."

"What?" That was a twist on delayed immersion he'd certainly never thought of.

"She's been dead five or six months. If she'd been in the water all that time, she'd have been chewed to ribbons. You saw the guy who died in his car, so you know what the fish can do to soft tissue. This girl . . . her organs have decayed as if she's been dead for months, but there's just no way in hell she could have been in the water that long. Come by tomorrow, if you can. You need to see what I'm seeing to fully understand."

"Definitely. I'll be there first thing," Caleb said.

When he walked back inside, he could tell that the group had been talking about him again. Sarah had been right about the way they talked about people, even insiders, like Jamison. And they were probably worse when it came to outsiders.

"Anything new?" Will asked him as he took his seat again.

"No more bodies—I hope?" Renee asked.

"No, thankfully," he said simply, looking up as he saw their waitress coming over with the food. "That was fast."

The food was served. The fish was crispy and

delicious, and Caleb realized he hadn't known how hungry he was.

Renee suddenly put down her fork. "Maybe we should have had burgers," she said.

"Why?" Barry asked her. "You love the fish and chips here."

"No, I was just thinking that we're eating fish, and fish eat everything in the water."

They were all silent. She hadn't said what she was really thinking.

That fish ate corpses in the water.

"Okay, that's it, I'm done," Sarah said, and rose.

"Will we see you tomorrow?" Barry asked her.

She shook her head. "I've been given permission to take a leave of absence for a few days, and I have a few things I need to do, so I'm taking this chance to do them. Who knows, though? I may stop by and check in on you working stiffs—"

She broke off, looking stricken.

Will groaned. "We can't say anything these days, huh?" He stood up, too. "I'll get the check, so just wait for me. You're not walking home alone. And if anything more happens around here, you're not staying in that place alone, no matter what," he told her firmly.

"Thanks—Dad," she said. "But I'm all right, and I'm not a fool. And you can sit back down. Caleb is going to walk me home."

Will looked at Caleb, as if sizing him up for a moment. It was only natural, laudable even, that he should be worried. And when Will nodded approvingly, it felt good to see that although Will was the one who had called him a corpse magnet, the other man also seemed to trust him to take care of Sarah.

"All right," Will said. "But take care and try not to be your usual 'I can do anything myself, *by* myself,' self, okay? Please."

Sarah smiled and gave him a hug. "I promise. I will not go wandering alone in the dark, and I'll lock my door the second Caleb leaves. I'll *double* lock it. Trust me."

She and Caleb tossed some money on the table, then left. Out on the street, he looked at her and said, "I'm breathless with anticipation."

She laughed, and he was glad to see the humor in her eyes when she told him, "Sorry, but I'm not going to burst into your room looking for sex." After she spoke, she flushed slightly. "Sorry. Couldn't help myself. Anyway, there's a picture I need to show you. We can stand under that street lamp so you can see, and then I'll explain everything I discovered today while we walk back to my place."

She reached into her purse and handed him an old photograph in a frame.

It was amazing. He could have been looking at a picture of himself in costume.

"How did you do this?" he asked her.

"I didn't *do* it!" she protested indignantly. "It was at the museum. It's why Caroline and I thought we'd seen you before. It was part of a recent exhibit, so it must have stuck in our minds."

He stared at the photograph again. "This is the real thing?"

"Yes, and I can even explain it. I looked up your family tree."

"You did *what?*"

"I looked up your family tree. I'm sorry—I didn't mean to invade your privacy," she said.

"Sorry. I didn't mean to bark."

"Caleb, you have ancestors who used to live here. Did you know that?"

He shook his head. "My folks weren't the kind who were into figuring out their roots."

"Well, there are a lot of Web sites that do just that, and I printed off your family tree. I feel like such an idiot for bursting in on you this morning, and at least this explains why I was so . . . confused."

She was palpably sincere. Her eyes were silver in the moonlight, and he could smell the faint scent of her perfume. Somewhere in his core, he felt a stirring and a warmth. He'd wanted to touch her from the minute he'd seen her, but he'd never been more tempted than he was at that moment.

He needed to walk her home, see that she was safe.

He needed to keep his hands off her.

"Actually, you barging in that way was rather titillating," he said, unable to prevent a smile.

She laughed, her cheeks turning a becoming shade of rose, but she didn't look away. "Look, what I'm trying to explain to you is that I'm not a lunatic and I don't usually go banging on men's doors and yelling at them. I guess I did have a dream, but if you look at this, you can see why I thought what I did. I mean . . . this could be a picture of you."

"Point taken," he assured her, then shook his head sadly.

"What?"

"I'm afraid this means you're not going to barge in on me again."

"I upset Bertie. I think I'd better behave from now on," she said, turning away. "I need to explain things to her, and apologize."

"Show her the picture. She'll understand," he said.

She smiled and started walking. He stayed by her side, shoving his hands into his pockets to keep himself from reaching for her, determined not to act like a jackass and ruin this tenuous connection between them. The night was warm, but with a sea breeze that stirred her hair as they walked and carried a tantalizing whiff of her perfume to him. He found himself noticing everything about her. The silky sheen of her hair and the way that it swayed on her shoulders as she walked.

The way she walked.

The way she was built.

Her skin was smooth, and she was wearing a sleeveless knit dress that revealed a lot of that skin, and molded her curves so tightly that he had to swallow. Hard.

She had a great mouth, generous and well-defined. Beautiful lips. Perfect nose. He remembered how it had felt to have her underneath him that morning, the feel of her flesh against his.

He almost tripped over a cobblestone as they moved down Avila, ready to make the right that would lead them to St. George.

"Are you all right?" she asked.

"Yes, just clumsy," he assured her.

"It was strange that day, when I saw you just staring at the house," she said.

"It's a beautiful old house," he said.

"But it seemed as if you were drawn to it."

I'm drawn to its owner.

"I like historic architecture," he said lamely. They had reached her house, and stood staring up at it. The mansion had been magnificently constructed. That night, however, he felt as if the darkened windows were eyes, staring back at them. It was as if something brooding was living inside the house. He gave himself a mental shake; he wasn't prone to whimsy or flights of fantasy. It was a house.

A house and nothing more. But history happened in houses. Events occurred. The good, the bad and the very ugly.

Adam said there were two kinds of hauntings. Residual, the events of the past happening over and over again. And active, or intelligent, when spirits remained behind, chained by the trauma of their deaths. They could even learn to move objects and travel from place to place, which was why Abe Lincoln could be seen both striding the halls of the White House, or sitting in the seat where he'd been shot at Ford's Theatre.

He couldn't communicate with ghosts himself, but he worked with a number of intelligent and completely sane people who did speak with those long gone.

But this house . . .

It was as if the house itself wanted to tell him something.

He was suddenly anxious to get back inside.

But not tonight.

"Caleb?" Sarah said softly, studying him.

He turned to her. Her eyes were so wide and concerned.

Silver and beautiful.

"Let's get you safely inside, okay?" he suggested.

And maybe, just maybe, I can stay awhile, he thought.

9

She walked ahead of him to the carriage house, taking her keys from her purse. She opened the door, and he followed her inside, where she turned on a light. The room was neat and clean. He walked over to the bathroom and went inside, came back out and, shrugging sheepishly, ducked down and looked under the bed.

She turned on the television. She wanted the noise, the illusion of company, he realized.

"Great movie, *From Here to Eternity*," she commented.

"Yep."

He was still standing next to the bed.

"Would you like something to drink? I don't have a lot here—beer or white wine. Soda, coffee, tea."

He could tell that she didn't want him to leave. She was afraid, but she didn't want to admit it. "Sure. I'm not much for wine, so I'll have a beer."

"Have a seat. The sofa is comfortable," she told him, heading for the refrigerator and looking relieved.

He sat, and she brought over two beers and sat on the opposite end of the couch, facing him. Then she took a swig of her beer, smiling shyly.

Was it possible to envy a beer bottle because those lips had been around it? he wondered.

"So . . . how did you end up working with Adam Harrison?" she asked.

"Adam found me," Caleb said, then turned the subject to her. "How did *you* meet Adam? And by the way, I'm glad you did—you wouldn't trust me as far as you could throw me if it weren't for Adam."

She flushed and looked down for a moment. "Southerners," she said. "We're very hospitable, but that doesn't mean we actually trust outsiders."

"I'm a Southerner, too," he reminded her. "Born and bred in Virginia."

"That's awfully far north," she said. "That's where I met Adam, though. In Virginia. There was some trouble at a dig outside Fredericksburg—I was there taking notes and sketching finds. I met Adam when he came to see the director. Harrison Investigations had been hired to stop the weird things that were happening—tools disappearing, then reappearing, strange lights in the middle of the night, stuff like that. Even the newspapers had picked up on it and were joking that maybe the dig was haunted or cursed or something. Adam and his staff caught some college kids who had been creating all the trouble—no curses going on, just pranks. But my boss told me then that Harrison Investigations even gets called in by the government—quietly—to . . . look into weird events."

Caleb admitted, "It's true. He has an amazing network of people located all over the country. He brings the right person in on the right case every time."

"Does he ever find that . . . the rumors are true? That something . . . unreal is going on?"

"Some of the people who work for him seem to have an affinity for . . . I don't know, communicating with the . . . other side, I guess you'd call it. And yes, some of them do have what you might call ESP, but that just stands for extrasensory perception. Seeing is perception, touching . . . but scientists know the brain has much more capacity than the average person utilizes, and I think that's what ESP is, just utilizing those parts of the brain."

"What about you?"

"Me? I have a way of mentally rebuilding a crime scene. I'm not sure it's ESP, more just a different way to use logic by relying on my subconscious."

"Logic. I like logic. And the fact that we don't utilize all our mental capacities, that makes sense to me. The brain can take us by surprise, like my dream last night."

She was looking at him, smiling. Her lips were damp, her eyes soft and bright. And she was standing so close.

In the end, it must have been the perfume.

A sound escaped his lips, a groan, and he plucked the beer bottle out of her hand, set it on the side table alongside his own and pulled her into his arms. He met her eyes again. "I didn't exactly barge in," he said huskily, "but this bedroom will do just fine."

He waited, a heartbeat, a pulse, giving her the chance to pull away.

There were things he could say. Inane assurances that he wouldn't leave if she was afraid to be alone, even if they just sat and talked or watched TV, or just passed the time in silence.

People came together for lots of reasons, not all of them emotional. A lot of the time it was just basic biology, the laws of attraction. Whatever this was had begun to simmer the first time he had seen her, the first time he had heard her speak, the first time her eyes met his.

She reached up, her fingers molding his jaw, her eyes filled with curiosity and fascination. The stroke of her fingers against his flesh felt like flickers of fire, and her eyes went smoke-gray with pure sensuality, and he leaned forward, into her, hesitated, his mouth just a breath away. He watched her lips curve into a half smile as she waited. At last he kissed her and found her lips everything he'd imagined they would be. Holding her in his arms was like holding the essence of life and heat, and every drop of blood in him began to steam, slowly and mercilessly. Sensation rioted through him as their mouths met, the touch igniting an eruption of hunger and desire. He pulled her more firmly into his arms as their mouths parted, then met again, as her lips surrendered fully to his and their tongues began to parry in exquisite exploration. He felt the flesh of her neck and shoulders beneath his fingers, the teasing touch of her hair against his flesh. Her arms curled around his neck, and she seemed almost a part of him, as if she could never be close enough.

She pulled away and stood, looked at him for a long moment, then walked away to turn off the light.

The faint glow from the television bathed the room in a soft, velvet glow as she walked over to the bed and let her dress fall to the floor.

He stood, too, stripping his shirt over his head as he strode over to her, then took her back into his arms. The naked flesh of her breasts, firm against his chest, sent an infusion of fire streaking through him like lightning, straight to his loins. The scent of her perfume, the way it seemed to steam from her skin, was almost unbearable. He buried his face against her neck, kissed the delicate flesh, and fought for control. Their mouths met once again in a passionate kiss that went deep, that intimated all kinds of other things, and aroused and stoked the fire that was burning so high and fast between them. He trailed his fingers down her spine, cupped and cradled her buttocks, drew her closer still. Her fingers scratched a path down his back, pressing, teasing, arousing. Still fused together at the lips, they fell onto the bed, and, breathlessly, he rose above her.

There were a million things he could have said, but nothing rose to his lips.

Her words were all in her eyes. Silver smoke caught in shadow. Open, wide, inviting.

He wasn't prone to flights of fantasy, especially where romance was concerned, but . . . suddenly it seemed as if he had known her forever, loved her forever. Not just *wanted* her. Wanting was basic biology. Wanting could be eased by a stranger who would never be seen or even thought of again. This was something different—he almost pulled back to give himself time to understand this feeling of intense connection, of suddenly, unbelievably, realizing that he loved someone he barely knew, that he needed to be with her and protect her against all dangers. . . .

Even against herself.

But he didn't get a chance to dwell on the matter because she pulled him down to her, and then they were kissing in a frenzy, hot kisses, liquid and steaming and damp, and erotic beyond measure. He began to move against her, laving her breasts, adoring her flesh, breathing her in. Then he moved lower, fingers stroking down her thighs as he kissed her abdomen, her hips, the tip of his tongue a burning ember that sent her writhing against him, her fingers kneading his shoulders, and the softest, sweetest, most erotic sounds escaping her lips.

With no logic left, no thought, he made love to

her intimately with his touch and his tongue. She was transformed into a being of liquid, ever-changing sensuality beneath him, moving wildly, sending him into a spiral of desire. She rocked against him, arched and whispered, and drew him up until their mouths met again. He sank against her then, parting her thighs, sliding smoothly into her with a shudder of soaring sexual pleasure at being enclosed within her tight hot flesh. Her arms locked around him, followed by her thighs, and their mouths fused frenetically once more, as they began to move. . . .

He felt the climactic explosion of her body and allowed himself his own release, leaving him to shudder slowly as he sank back down to a place where he was aware of flesh and bone and the beating of their hearts once again. He rolled to his side, carrying her with him, gasping for one good breath and then holding her tightly as their heart-beats slowed.

He smoothed her hair, kissed the top of her head. The sensation that he had felt before, that he cared for her far too deeply, that he knew her laughter, knew her soul, swept over him. But it would be insane to say anything about how he felt. He would sound like an idiot if he suddenly whispered, "I love you."

So he fought the temptation and only said gently, "My God, I'm glad you barged in on me this morning. And that you found that photograph."

She went still for a moment, then rose, her hands on his chest and a smile on her lips as she replied, "Call it fate, because as much as I might have wanted it—" she blushed "—I'm not sure I would have dared to do anything about it. I'm not exactly accustomed to picking up men."

She eased back to his side, and he looked down at her, grinning. "No? I don't suppose you have to. I imagine men spend a great deal of time and effort wracking their brains trying to think of a way to bring you home."

She laughed. "Thank you. I think. I mean, that was a compliment, right?"

"Oh, yeah." He was silent for a minute, then said, "So tell me about your love life."

"Nonexistent," she told him. She was staring reflectively at the ceiling, and she looked at him. "I was engaged. He was in the service, and he was killed in the line of duty."

"I'm so sorry."

"He was a great guy. I still miss him."

"I'm sure you do," he said sincerely. *If you loved this guy, he had to be great*, Caleb added silently.

"It was three years ago now," she said.

He frowned. "You haven't . . . gone out with anyone since then? Even for dinner?"

"No. I haven't given up on life or anything. I just never met anyone I wanted to . . . I just never met anyone."

"Now I'm really flattered," he said, picking up her hand and kissing her fingertips. He loved her hands, he thought. Delicate, clean, manicured but not ostentatiously. They were well-tended but not fussed over. Like her hair. Clean and silky, but not cut in some hip, high-maintenance style, not highlighted, just . . .

Just beautiful.

She turned to him. "What about you?"

"I was engaged once, too."

"Oh . . . ?" she asked in a tone that said she wanted to know more.

"Nothing dramatic. We just went our separate ways. She didn't like my job or my hours. Or my occasional moodiness."

"Are you moody? You always seem to be watching. You listen to people. You see what's going on. You . . . you wear a mask," she told him. "You never seem to reveal how you're really feeling."

He stroked the skin of her face, amazed again at the breathtaking beauty of it. "It goes with the territory of what I do, I guess. And we broke up a long time ago."

"And since then? I would have thought that—well, quite frankly, I'd be surprised if women weren't throwing themselves at your feet."

"I suspect they can tell I wouldn't be interested. I haven't felt like this in ages. Maybe not even in this lifetime," he admitted.

She caught her breath, staring at him, but she didn't accuse him of overdoing the flattery—or of being insane.

"Hmm."

"Hmm, what?"

"This morning . . . well, the thought was in my mind. About tonight. Except I didn't plan on barging into your room again. But I *was* thinking—" she blushed "—about sex. With you."

"It was the boxers, right?" he said, and laughed.

"Actually, maybe," she replied, her own tone light. But her smoky silver eyes seemed to hold a serious message meant just for him, and she added, "I think this is more than sex. No pressure intended, plus I've been known to be wrong. On occasion."

"This is *much* more than sex," he agreed, then kissed her lips, lightly and tenderly. "Though the sex . . . was awfully damned amazing."

She chuckled, a deep and throaty sound that aroused him again all by itself.

"I hope I'm not looking at a one-hit wonder."

"Oh, Lord, is that a challenge?"

"I'm not sure," she said honestly and a little breathlessly. "It's been a very long time."

"In that case . . ."

And then he made love to her again.

And she made love to him.

As they strove together for the peak, the bizarre thought came to him that he was meant to be here.

With her. That he had somehow loved her, looked for her, forever.

Then the thought faded, and he lost himself again in pure, primal pleasure.

Afterward, when they were exhausted, sated, he stayed. He didn't suggest leaving, and she didn't say anything about it, either, just lay curled against him, quiet.

He reveled in her warmth, still amazed by the way he felt.

Finally, as the night deepened, they slept.

Sex.

It was good. No, it was wonderful. It changed the world. It was magic.

How the hell had she forgotten? How had she managed to stay dormant for so long, not just physically but emotionally?

She woke slowly, feeling ridiculously giddy, even though she knew she might be setting herself up for a long and painful fall.

They hadn't made any promises or anything. This wasn't the kind of slow, steadily building relationship she had known before. This was instant passion and need, and it might end up going nowhere.

Even so, it felt somehow right to have him sleeping at her side.

She stretched out an arm as she turned, seeking the warmth he had offered.

And the excitement.

But what she discovered was emptiness.

Then she heard him say "Hey," and she quickly sat up. He was already dressed, just slipping into his shoes.

"I have to get going." He walked back to the bed, leaned down and kissed her. He looked as good as ever by morning light. Damn good. Better than damn good. She felt elated after the night she'd shared with him and knew she should have been content with that, but she wasn't. She wanted more. It was as if she still hadn't learned enough about him, as if she hadn't touched him enough, melted deeply enough into his being.

She told herself that she was desperate and pathetic, and her inner voice warned her to act like a rational human being.

He had showered, and she couldn't believe the sound of the running water hadn't awakened her. His hair was damp, and he smelled clean, like soap and shampoo, and there was just a hint of five o'clock shadow on his face. She hoped she wasn't staring at him with too much hunger.

"Okay," she said, trying not to reveal how let down she felt.

He winced. "I have to go see Floby, and then some kids who were at that party on the beach when Winona Hart disappeared," he explained.

"Oh," she said, her tone changing to one of understanding. He wasn't trying to get away from her, he just had obligations he couldn't ignore.

"Be careful," he told her.

"I'm not a blonde," she pointed out.

"Neither was the woman I found yesterday. Anyway, I'll keep in touch during the day. Will I see you at Hunky Harry's tonight?" he asked.

"I'll head over when they kick me out of the library. And I'll wait for you. I mean, if that's what you're thinking."

"It's exactly what I'm thinking. Just keep your door locked and don't go anywhere alone—please. Especially after dark."

"Don't worry—I'll hang with the whole crew," she promised him.

"See you later," he said, but didn't make a move to leave, just stood there smiling at her.

"Okay." She looked at him curiously when he still didn't leave.

"You have to lock the door behind me," he reminded her.

"Oh, of course." She jumped up, feeling suddenly shy and dragging the covers along with her, and walked to the door with him. As he opened it, she was startled to hear a car coming up the driveway, wheels crunching on the stones. "Who is it?" she asked him.

"Nice-looking guy around our age—in a van with ladders on the side," he said. "Looks like the construction guy who found the bones," Caleb replied.

"Oh, good. They must have cleared him to start

working again," she said, pleased. "Tell him I'll be right out."

"All right."

He was studying her in the bright sun that poured in through the open door. She prayed that she didn't look like the complete mess she felt like, but she was certain that she did.

"You don't care if he sees me coming out?" he asked politely.

She shook her head, smiling.

He nodded, lowered his head, then looked at her again. "Lock the door."

He left, and she closed and locked the door. She knew now that no one had broken in the other night, but this wasn't the time to be taking any chances.

She spun around, still feeling ridiculously happy, as if she were walking on air, and headed for the shower. She was as quick as she could be, only towel-drying her hair before slipping into a pair of jeans and a T-shirt. She was anxious to see Gary.

But when she emerged, his van was already gone. Frowning, she pulled out her cell phone and called him.

"Hey, you," he said, answering after the first ring. "I was going to call you, but I wasn't sure you were up yet."

If there was any insinuation in his words, it certainly wasn't evident.

"No, no, I was awake. I was hoping you were working again."

"Nope, sorry. I just went in to pick up a few tools I'd left the other night. I'm assuming you'll know before I do when it's okay to start working on the house again."

"I'll get through to Tim sometime today and see what I can find out," she promised. "Thanks, Gary. Oh, we've all been hanging out at Hunky Harry's lately. Come by if you're at loose ends."

"Sure. Thanks," he said, and hung up.

It was still early, too early for the library to be open. She decided to take her book around the corner to one of the cafés on the plaza and combine coffee, a decadent pastry and some research.

Along the way, she picked up the newspaper.

Body Found on Anastasia Island, the headline read.

She scanned the story while she stood in line for coffee. So far, if the police knew anything other than the top-line details, they had managed to keep it from the press. The story did immediately dispel any notion that Winona Hart might have been found.

A woman's body was found on the beach yesterday afternoon on Anastasia Island, apparently having washed in from the sea. Preliminary reports suggest that the unknown brunette was approximately five feet tall. Age

243

and other identifying features are still to be determined. The coroner estimates that she has been dead at least six months. The police are asking for help from anyone who might know about a missing person who fits the description and timeline.

She felt ill, reading the article. It was quite possible that three women had been abducted and killed in less than a year. There were other possible explanations, of course. The cases might not be related at all. But Caleb seemed to think they were, and she was fairly certain—and not just because she was falling for the man—that he had an instinct about such things.

She heard a strange noise, a soft sob, and looked up. A woman was standing outside the window, wearing antebellum clothing, a corseted day dress with a wide skirt over a hoop petticoat, along with a bonnet. And she was staring directly at Sarah.

She couldn't have been the source of the sob, Sarah thought, because she wouldn't have been able to hear the sound through the glass.

"Miss?" The man in line behind her pointed to the counter, where a barista was available.

"Sorry, thank you," she said, stepping forward. When she looked back out the window a minute later, after giving her order, the woman was gone.

Sarah looked around the café, searching for her. Several of the tables were in use. Three couples, an elderly man, a woman with a name tag designating the tour company she worked for. She was reading the comics page and smiling.

None of them looked likely to have been crying.

She must have heard something else and mistaken it for a sob.

And a woman in nineteenth-century costume? They were so common here that the locals never even noticed them most of the time.

Dismissing what she had seen, she took her coffee and croissant, and headed for a table.

"Damnedest thing I've ever seen," Floby announced, drawing the sheet back from the corpse.

Dust to dust, ashes to ashes, Caleb thought. All things organic were meant to return to the earth. Including human bodies. Embalming was man's last desperate measure to stave off the inevitability of mortality. It was true that an embalmed body certainly appeared more lifelike than one left to decompose naturally, though Caleb had never seen a dead person who truly looked as he had in life, and in many cases the dead might have been better off left alone.

But what was truly horrific was what the combined forces of man and nature could do to human flesh.

This young woman seemed to have been consumed in more ways than fate should have allowed. First the land creatures—worms, flies and maggots—had gone to work on her, and then she had been left to the ravages of the water and the creatures that called it home.

Her face—with much of the jaw nothing but protruding bone—seemed to have frozen into a death mask, a caricature of an artist's rendering.

"How did she die, Floby? Have you figured that out yet?" Caleb asked. "She didn't fall off a boat, did she?"

Floby produced a magnifying glass from the table of tools at the side of the gurney. "My best guess is that she had her throat slit. If you look closely, you can see a cut, right there, at the jugular—or it might have been a series of puncture wounds. There's so much damage, I couldn't swear an oath in court and say exactly what weapon killed her." Floby paused and took a deep breath. "Basically, she was drained of blood."

"What?" Caleb asked, frowning.

"There was no blood left in her. That's why the body is preserved as much as it is. Usually, the drier a body, the more slowly decomposition occurs."

Caleb was silent. Drained of blood? That was definitely an unexpected twist. Were these women being abducted and murdered ritualistically?

"You said there might have been puncture wounds. You don't think someone is running around pretending to be a vampire, do you?"

246

"I'm the M.E.—you're the investigator," Floby said, shrugging. "But . . . honestly? I don't know. I was thinking maybe you should be looking for some modern-day Countess Bathory, wanting blood in large quantities to preserve youth or beauty. All I know is that the body is in perfect condition from the murderer's point of view. Any trace evidence—hairs, fibers—is long gone, and I can't get anything by scraping under the nails. Even if she scratched the killer and captured his DNA, there's nothing there anymore for me to find. Hell, so far, this is the perfect murder."

"Thanks, Floby. I appreciate you bringing me in on this."

Floby nodded. "Jamison doesn't want this information out yet."

"Then I won't say a word. But this has been a big help. You've confirmed that I've been heading in the right direction."

"Oh?"

"Both Jennie Lawson and Winona Hart wanted to do things that were truly creepy, to be genuinely scared. I think they looked for—and found—someone deeply into the occult in a really sick way."

"Mind if I suggest something?" Floby asked.

"What's that?"

"Whatever you're going to do, do it quickly. You've got to find this guy."

Caleb found himself looking down at what remained of the face of the dead woman.

"I can swear I'll do my best."

I hate her, Nellie Brennan had written in her diary. She is a monster, but no one else sees it. The fools keep coming to her. All because she gave Loretta Mason a potion, and then Loretta managed to get herself a husband. He has one eye and one leg, but since the war, any husband is better than no husband at all.

Reading in the General's Room, Sarah found herself fascinated by Nellie's stories. She might not have been the most beautiful girl in St. Augustine, but she was accomplished with her pen.

We came here during the war, when I was fourteen, and I know why. My father. He is a monster, too, of course. He told me we came to St. Augustine so he could find work—but it wasn't the truth at all. We came here because there was a terrible scandal about my father and Mrs. Pellingham back up North, where we used to live. The gossips said they had an affair, and then Mr. Pellingham found out about it. My father took me, and we headed south. But I know the truth because I came upon my father and that witch woman, Martha Tyler. She was telling him that he was indebted to her, that if it hadn't been for her, he would have been ruined by the Pellingham incident, so he had to do as she told him. He told her that if she didn't behave, he would sell her to a slaver, who would put her up for auction. That's all I heard before they must have realized they might be overheard and closed the door. Of a house that shouldn't be ours. Poor Mr. MacTavish, who was so dignified and kind, went broke and died while his son was away fighting. I think my father never paid him for our lodging, and that hastened his death. Before that, it was Mr. MacTavish, my father and myself—and often the young lady who was to marry Mr. MacTavish's son Cato came by to visit and play the piano. I remember when Cato MacTavish came home on leave. He was in butternut and gray, and he wore a plumed hat. I don't believe I've ever seen such a handsome man. I think he wanted his father to get us out of the house. I don't know what Eleanora said to him about my father, but Cato didn't like him. He was kind to me, though. But then the Yankees came and occupied the city, and Cato had to rejoin his unit, lest he be caught here and killed. Eleanora disappeared then, too. They say he killed her, but I don't believe it. He loved her so much. They were so happy together. But it's true that she disappeared, and other girls disappeared, too. But few people had time to pay attention. There was a war. Men were dying by the hundreds on a daily basis, and people had all they could do just to stay alive.

Sarah paused in her reading. What wonderful— if dark—insights into what life in St. Augustine had been like at the time. Was it skewed? Of course—everyone saw the world through their own eyes. But it was still wonderful information to add to her growing store.

She started reading again.

The authorities denied that the women were ever found, Nellie Brennan had written in her diary, but they were and are such liars. But I know the truth. Because I saw the body of Susan Madison.

10

Mindy Marshall was just getting out of a yoga class.

Caleb had found her schedule in the case file and headed to the gym, which was right on the plaza, to find her. He was waiting in the hallway, watching through the studio window as the class ended, and he knew who she was right away from her photograph.

Mindy was a pretty, slim brunette with large dark eyes, and she must have sensed that he was waiting for her, but she seemed in no hurry to come out and see what he wanted. Finally, though, as the students for the next class started arriving, with one sneaker still untied, she came out, and to her credit, she didn't try to evade him.

"Are you another cop?" she asked him, tying the second sneaker and looking up at him.

"No."

"But you're here for me, right?" she asked warily.

"Yes. My name is Caleb Anderson. I'm a private investigator, and I'd like to ask you a few questions."

"You must be here about Winona," she said miserably. "That body in the water . . . was it her?"

"It wasn't Winona," he said. "But the thing is, Mindy, something terrible does seem to be going on around here. I'm trying to find another young woman who disappeared about a year ago, as well as Winona. And the woman in the water . . . we need to find out what happened to her, too, and whether there's a connection. Can you think of anything from that night that might help me out?"

She shook her head, sad and confused. "We told the cops everything. . . ." She hesitated, looking around. "I know Nigel told you about the booze and pot—but just pot, nothing stronger. It was a big party. Winona was there, and then she wasn't. Where she went, if she left with somebody . . . I don't know how. If I did, I swear I would tell you. She was one of my best friends."

"Listen, there's a coffee shop right next door. Can I get you something? I can tell you what I know already, and you can tell me anything else you remember. Even something small could end up being a big help."

"Yeah, all right. They have herbal tea. The body is a shrine, you know."

He smiled at her. "Herbal tea—and beer and pot?"

"Hey, pot is an herb," she told him.

He laughed and led her next door. As soon as he opened the door for her, she headed straight for the counter and placed her order for an orange-infused chamomile tea, and then asked him if it would be all right if she got a cherry Danish, as well. He told her she was welcome to anything behind the counter and ordered coffee for himself.

The minute they were seated, she started wolfing down the Danish.

She worshipped the temple of her body in a strange way—a teenage way—he decided.

"So what else can I tell you?" she asked him, washing down the Danish with a big gulp of tea. "I have the feeling you know the story already."

"You, Winona and Nigel got there first. You were bringing the cooler and . . . other things."

She nodded. "Nigel drove. He has an old Xterra."

"You guys built a bonfire—and then a woman came out of the woods."

She finally smiled at him. "You're asking about the weird old hippie? I forgot all about her 'til Nigel reminded me."

"She was old?"

"Sure."

"How old? Fifty? Eighty?"

"No, no, not that old. I don't know. Thirties? Forties? She was wearing a long flowing skirt, a bandana and huge sunglasses. She looked like she walked out of that old comedy show. *Laugh-In.* That's the one."

Mindy took another bite of her Danish, then looked at him, frowning. "She was thin, too. I remember that. Trust me—Winona could have taken her. Besides, she was just a kook. She told us she was a medium and lived someplace where tons of mediums live, Castle-something."

"Cassadaga?" he asked.

"Yeah, that's it! Cassadaga. You know it?" she asked him.

"It's a spiritualist town. I think the people who live there are sincere, that they believe in their abilities to read palms and cards and even people."

"Whatever," Mindy said. "Well, Winona loved horror movies and ghost stories and stuff like that. She wanted someone to prove that stuff to her, though. Like, she thought most everyone was a fake. She wasn't rude to the woman, really, but she kind of suggested that *she* was a fake, too. Then the woman said something to her, right into her ear. . . ." She stopped speaking, frowning in concentration. "I couldn't hear what they said, and then Nigel asked me to watch the fire and I told him he was idiot, because the fire was fine. And by then Winona and the woman seemed to be getting along okay, and the woman left right afterwards. Oh! I remember one more thing about her. She was wearing these long black lace gloves."

"Gloves, huh?"

"Could that be important?"

"Maybe. Little details matter a lot. You're sure she said she was from Cassadaga?"

"Positive. Once you said it . . . yes, I'm positive. And I can prove it. I think. She gave Winona and me business cards. Except that . . ." She paused, her brow wrinkling. "I don't know what I did with mine."

Caleb's hand tightened around his coffee cup, and he tried not to swear, just kept his voice level and asked, "Do you remember her name?"

"Um . . . Betty? Wait, no, it was an M name. Missy? Mary? Oh, no, no! It was Martha." She flushed with pleasure. "Martha! That was it, I'm sure."

"Did Martha have a last name?"

"Well, of course."

He tried to remember that she was young.

"And do you remember her last name?" he asked.

"Um . . ."

"Do you remember what letter it started with?" he asked, trying to nudge her memory.

"No, but . . . it was a president's name," she told him. "I remember that, because last fall, Mr. Bayley, our history teacher, was upset because he said no one bothers to learn history anymore, not even the names of the presidents."

"Which president?" he asked, praying for patience.

"Oh, God, um . . ."

"Washington, Adams, Jefferson, Madison . . . Monroe?"

"No, no." She shook her head.

"Recent president? Old president?" He was trying to remember all the past presidents himself.

She shook her head. "He had some kind of a slogan, though. I remember we laughed about that."

"'Tippecanoe and Tyler, too'?"

"Oh, my God!" she exclaimed. "You know the slogan! That was it. Tyler."

"You're sure? Martha Tyler, and she was from Cassadaga?" he asked.

She nodded and he thanked her for her time, then rose to leave. He glanced at his watch. He wasn't sure how long it would take to drive to Cassadaga, but he was determined to get there as quickly as possible. First, however, he called information to find out if there was a listing there for Martha Tyler.

There was.

He punched the number into his cell and waited.

Martha Tyler answered on the third ring, and he noticed immediately that she had a pleasant voice, melodious, low and soothing. Perfect for a medium looking to get people to trust her.

He made an appointment to meet her in an hour and a half.

Sarah felt chilled as she sat and read in the General's Room, which had always seemed so comfortable and welcoming. But today it was as if a blanket of cold had settled over her, so chilling that she didn't want to keep reading—but she had to. Whatever the truth turned out to be, she had to know it.

They didn't know I was there—my father, or the Union officer who was the acting sheriff. It was Sergeant Lee who had brought her in; he had come up the side drive, in a small wagon. I heard them talking down in the library and I don't know why, but I crept down the stairs. When they went out to look at the body, I followed them, keeping my distance and lurking in the shadows.

Sergeant Lee pulled back a tarp, and I could tell he was angry. They were arguing—my father was angry, too. He didn't want anything to do with whoever—whatever—was under the tarp.

They kept arguing, and then Sergeant Lee covered the back of the wagon with the tarp again.

I hurried back inside the mudroom and hid behind a rack of coats. I suppose I was being an ostrich, thinking that I could hide there, for surely the men would see my feet.

But they didn't. They were still talking, but in hushed tones, and they were so intent on one another that they didn't even notice me. "I won't have it. I'm telling you, I won't have it," Sergeant Lee told my father. "It's bad enough that half the town is spying for the damn Rebs. That's why these girls are disappearing. They're running to the Rebs like a pack of harlots, hoping that any little bit of information will earn them a man. This is one incident. One incident."

"If the body is found, they'll just say that she was killed by the Reb who owns this place," my father argued. "It will be blamed on Cato MacTavish—he will be branded a murderer. The truth will come out."

Sergeant Lee stared at my father and said, "Really? Because this girl was seen after he skedaddled out of here to rejoin his regiment. So it would have been hard as hell for the bastard to kill her, since he was long gone."

My father swore and said he would open up the back door and they would haul the body in through the same door they used for household supplies.

My father said, "Don't you see MacTavish is still out there—somewhere."

Sargeant Lee snorted his disbelief, but said nothing.

As soon as they headed down the hall to open the door, I ran back outside. I couldn't help myself. I was horrified and frightened, but I had to see. I don't know why. Because I will never forget, and I will never be free from the nightmares that have haunted me in the weeks ever since that night.

I reached the wagon and hauled myself up to see inside the bed, and then I lifted the tarp.

She was dead, and I thought I was about to give myself away by screaming, but somehow I managed to keep quiet. I almost fell off the wagon, though, I was so stunned.

But I didn't. I had to see more of her. I was

both repelled and fascinated, as if I were caught in a terrible dream.

Her name was Susan Madison, and she was so beautiful—had been so beautiful. Her face was unmarred. In the moonlight, it looked as if she were a porcelain doll. But then I saw her throat. It was nearly nonexistent, and I thought instantly that there should be blood, with such a gaping hole. It looked almost as if an animal had ripped out her throat. And yet the face . . .

It was so perfect. White. Eerily white. A doll's face. She was a doll, beautiful—and empty.

I pulled the tarp farther back. And I saw what had been done to her.

I did fall from the wagon then, but somehow I kept myself from screaming, afraid that if they knew what I had seen, the same thing would happen to me.

Not only was her throat a red horror, but she was covered in dirt, as if she had come out of the ground. I could only think that her face was so perfect and white only because the sergeant had cleaned her up in an attempt to discern her identity. But it was more than the filthy condition of the body that was so disturbing. She looked . . . gnawed, as if consumed by wild beasts. She had no fingers on one hand, and a chunk of her midriff was entirely gone. Her legs had been worked upon as if they were turkey drumsticks.

I managed to get myself up. And still I never let

loose the scream that seemed to echo in my mind, terrified and shrill.

I lived in a mortuary. I had seen dead bodies before.

But never—never—anything like this.

I heard the door opening, and ran to hide in the bushes by the side of the house, my heart thundering. I was terrified.

I couldn't help feeling that I was in danger of ending up like that poor girl.

My father was still complaining to the sergeant for bringing the body to him.

"You can make her look beautiful. She deserves a proper funeral, and her family deserves to be able to mourn her."

"Sergeant Lee, you're mad! Why did you bring her here? Why didn't you leave her where you found her?" my father protested. "Better she had stayed in the dirt, stayed missing! What if someone insists on digging her up again? What if they discover our deception?"

"I chose not to leave her because—someone else would have discovered her. Stop worrying. No one will question her death. Doctor Howard, the old souse, has already signed a death certificate. She was struck by a carriage and left by the road. Don't you understand me? Her death must be seen as a tragic accident. The work of a coward who left a girl dead in the streets, rather than admit he had struck her. If the truth were to come out, the city would erupt. There would be slaughter of an entirely different kind if the populace were to discover that there is a killer in our midst—and we have not the slightest idea of who he is or what sickness drives him to his atrocities. You will do this, and you will do it right, or I will see to it that you are run out of this town. Get that witch of a housekeeper of yours to mix up a few potions so that she looks good. Start tonight. I must go and inform this poor girl's family."

My father was angry; furious. But Sergeant Lee was a powerful man. Watching them together, I felt ill. It was as if they knew things about each other that created a strange bond between them. They weren't friends, but there was a connection binding them. I waited in silence as they picked up the body, still wrapped in the tarp, and carried it to the back door. Still I didn't move. I didn't dare.

I stayed in the bushes.

I stayed there for a very long time.

At last, having no true concept of how much time had gone by, I slipped back into the house, only to find that she was there. Martha Tyler.

Martha always wore a bandana wrapped around her head as if it were a crown and she some kind of queen. One drop of African blood made a man or woman a slave, and Martha could have been a slave. But she wasn't, even though she came to us from the South and made no complaint when we brought her back there. I think she had been a slave, though, that she killed her master and escaped. But perhaps I only think that because I hate her. The girls in town who giggle and come to her for love potions don't know her the way I know her. They don't see her when she sits in front of a mirror, looking at her reflection. They don't hear her voice when she speaks to me, disdaining me.

They have never seen anything like the malicious evil in her eyes when I entered the house that night.

"Ah, little girl, little girl. Poor little ugly girl." She came to me and took me by the ear, hurting me, but when I would have cried out, she brought a finger to her lips. "Shh," she warned me, but she didn't let go. "Where have you been, little girl? You should not be nosy. Such bad things can happen to nosy little girls. There are panthers out there. And bears and alligators and snakes. Predators that own the night. They love to feed upon little girls, for no meat is so sweet as girl-flesh."

"Let me go," I pleaded, but I didn't cry out for my father. I knew he wouldn't have helped me. He had never loved me, because I wasn't a beautiful child.

He would have helped her feed me to the creatures of the night, the snakes and alligators and panthers.

She released me, laughing. "You had better

forget all that you've seen and heard, or else . . ."
She made a hissing sound through her teeth and
slashed a line across her throat with her finger.
"Nosy little girls go to feed the creatures in the
woods, and in the end, they are consumed by the
worms."

I raced past her, terrified.

I prayed for the day that she and my father
might die. I knew I would go to hell for such a
cruel thought, but I could not help it.

For I would prefer hell to this evil house, and
the company of my father and Martha Tyler.

"That poor girl," Sarah found herself saying
aloud. She quickly turned the page, but it was
blank. Mystified, she kept looking through the
journal.

The girl had never written in it again.

She stood up, stretching. Every muscle in her
body hurt; without even noticing, she had huddled
into a tight, defensive ball while reading. She
didn't feel the chill anymore, though. Instead she
felt angry that a father could be so cruel to his
daughter and allow his housekeeper to be even
worse. And yet, if perhaps that father had been a
serial killer, as the historical record seemed to
imply, perhaps she had been lucky simply to have
survived.

And yet, had she survived? Those blank pages
might be telling.

Vicky came into the room. "Well?"

"Fascinating—and awful. I think you have to read this yourself. It looks like there was a serial killer in the city during the Civil War."

"So the local hero *was* a killer?" Vicky asked. "Cato MacTavish was a war hero, but his fiancée did disappear mysteriously, and he was the last person known to have seen her. And there were other girls who went missing, too. In fact, there were rumors about Cato at the time, so it's no wonder he left town when he did."

"I don't think Cato MacTavish was the killer," Sarah told Vicky. "The timeline doesn't make sense, because girls kept disappearing while he was away fighting, and after he abandoned the house and disappeared. Oh, people said he was still around. But what—living in trees? You have to read the journal. Brennan's daughter says some pretty wild stuff about her father and a Sergeant Lee who was sheriff here during the war."

"Maybe you could do an article on it, Sarah. You have a master's in history, and you own the house the Brennans owned back then."

"Good idea. The whole thing is terrifying but fascinating."

"Cool," Vicky said, reaching for the journal. "Sorry, but I have to lock up now."

"No problem. Thanks, Vicky."

She had intended to head straight for Hunky Harry's when she finished at the library, but for some reason she found herself walking home first and staring up at her house.

So little had changed. The bushes where Nellie Brennan had hidden were still there. The driveway was much as it would have been all those years ago.

And that driveway was empty now, which meant no one was inside. It was just after five, though, so that didn't mean everyone was done and she could get started on her renovations again. She hesitated, then let herself into the carriage house and called Tim Jamison, as she'd promised Gary she would.

When he picked up, Tim sounded distracted. The police and M.E. were finished, he said, and there was no evidence of any more bodies, but she needed to call the professor from the university to make sure he was done, too. He gave her a number.

She called Dr. Manning, who was friendly and appreciative, expressing his gratitude that she had let the university handle the find. He assured her that they were currently looking into all the documents in the university collection, trying to solve the riddle of who had been responsible for walling up the bodies. As far as he was concerned, her house was her own again, though he hoped to stay in touch as more information came to light.

She agreed to meet him the following week for lunch, and assured him that the university was more than welcome to come back.

After she got off the phone, she went and stood staring up at the front of her house again.

Houses weren't evil.

Determinedly, she walked up to the porch, then let herself in. It was *her* house.

Her *dream* house.

Inside, she started turning on lights; it wasn't dark yet, but it was late enough in the afternoon that heavy shadows were starting to fill the place. She decided that she would call Gary Morton in the morning and get him to come back in and resume working. She could get her plans back on track.

She walked through the house and saw that, once again, everything had been left ship-shape. Except, of course, for the gaping hole in the wall. But that was all right. Dry wall was easy. Okay, not for her, maybe, but for Gary, dry wall was a piece of cake.

She went to the kitchen and reached into the refrigerator for a cold can of soda. She looked around the room, curious to see whether she would feel anything. Fear. Discomfort. Anything. She smiled after a minute. It was a house, made up of building materials and the imagination of an architect.

With her soda in hand, she walked up the stairs to her bedroom.

She was moving back in tonight. Taking possession again. This was her house. And everything would be okay, because . . .

Caleb would be staying there with her. At least, she was pretty sure he would be.

She jumped when she heard something, a bang from downstairs. She tensed, her heart thundering. What the hell?

Had the sound come from inside the house—or outside?

Another question: had she remembered to lock the door?

She looked around for her purse—and her cell phone—then realized she'd left them in the kitchen. She had a landline from the cable company, but she hadn't bothered to have them run it into her bedroom.

Of course, even if she had her phone, what was she going to do? Call the cops and tell them she'd heard a bang downstairs? And maybe it hadn't even come from downstairs. It could have come from the street.

She walked over to the wardrobe, determined not to be a total coward. She reached in, past her clothing, and found her old softball bat. It was good and sturdy—and she knew how to use it.

Cautiously, she started down the stairs. When she reached the main hall, she saw no one, and nothing seemed to be stirring in the house. She looked out the front window, then stepped out to the porch—relieved to find that she *had* remembered to lock the door. A couple of tourists waved to her, and she waved back. For a second she

267

thought they were going to ask about the house, even ask for a tour, but then they turned away and kept walking.

She went back into the house, feeling like an idiot. This was her home. She wanted to be comfortable in it. Deserved to be comfortable in it. She walked from parlor to parlor, through the library-to-be, the dining room and, finally, back to the kitchen.

The basement door was standing ajar. It hadn't been open before . . . had it? Could someone—maybe Gary—have come back for some reason?

"Hello?"

She walked over to the open door and looked warily down the stairs.

There was a light on down there, a lone naked bulb hanging from the ceiling. Over the years, the basement had been used to store bodies and as a hiding space for a totally different kind of spirit—booze during Prohibition. Now it was pretty much empty.

"Hello?" she said again, cursing the tremor in her voice.

She told herself that she wasn't actually going to go all the way down the stairs, just a few steps so she could look around. And if someone was there—someone who didn't belong—she would hightail it back up. She could just imagine Caroline reminding her that in bad horror films, only fools went down into dark basements alone.

She started down the steps, but all she could see were shadows cast by the stark light of the naked bulb.

Okay, that was it. She'd been determined not to be spooked out of her own house, but she wasn't about to be an idiot, either. Time to return to the kitchen, grab her purse and head over to Hunky Harry's. Later, with Caleb beside her, she would come back and try to figure out if anyone had even been there, or if it had just been the drafts common to an old house that had caught and opened the door.

If Caleb returned. It wasn't as if he'd promised her undying devotion or anything.

If he didn't . . . well, she had Will and her friends. She wasn't alone here.

She had descended four steps, her softball bat in hand, when she heard the door above her creaking.

She looked up just as it slammed shut.

At the same time, that single glowing lightbulb below her flickered and went out, turning the world around her to black.

11

The Cassadaga Spiritualist Camp Association had been founded in 1894 by a man named George Colby. It wasn't an actual camp, but spiritualist meetings had once been referred to as camps, and the term had persisted. There were only fifty-some homes in town, and at least half of them were inhabited by mediums.

Caleb had never been there, but he knew that Adam respected many of the inhabitants and had once explained to Caleb the way legit mediums, not the sideshow posers, operated. First, mediums weren't fortune tellers. The best readings didn't zero in on something that was about to happen but focused on what *was*, giving a person guidance to help forge his own future. And because mediums communicated with the dead, they didn't always have instant answers— even the dead had to think about a question sometimes.

Martha Tyler was not just a medium but an ordained minister of a religious group called The People Faith, and she saw people at her home for readings. Caleb found the house without difficulty, a charming whitewashed Victorian. As he shut his car door, he realized with an inner smile that he felt as if he were going home to Grandma's house—the porch boasted a swing, beautiful flowers in planters and vines twining through the railings, and two cushioned rocking chairs.

The sense of coming home to Grandma's house grew stronger as he walked up the steps toward the door and smelled fresh-baked chocolate chip cookies.

As he lifted his hand to knock on the wooden frame of the screen door, he found himself trying to picture the woman who lived here as a murderer who lured young women to their deaths.

"Hello? Mr. Anderson?" The voice from within didn't sound like a murderer, either.

The door swung open, and Martha Tyler smiled at him in welcome.

His immediate thought was that this couldn't be the same woman who had approached the kids on the beach.

Martha Tyler was tiny, no more than five feet. She was also eighty, if she was a day. She had brilliant, sparkling blue eyes and couldn't have weighed ninety pounds soaking wet. Despite that, she didn't look frail. Her hair was snow-white and smoothed back in a bob.

"Yes, I'm Caleb Anderson," he said, thinking that this was a complete waste of time. She clearly wasn't the woman he was looking for. "I'm awfully sorry," he began.

She cut him off pleasantly. "Come in, come in. You've come this far, young man. If you've changed your mind about a reading, that's just fine. Have some cookies and tea, anyway."

She drew him into the living room, and talk about Grandma's house . . .

As she steered him to a seat on a quilt-strewn sofa, he told her, "Ms. Tyler, I have to be honest with you. I'm a private investigator. I'm here because your name was given to me by a young woman when I was questioning her about the disappearance of another girl. I believe someone is impersonating you."

"Please, call me Martha," the woman said. "I can only imagine this has to do with all the terrible troubles going on up in St. Augustine?"

"Yes."

She was heading for the kitchen. "What is your pleasure, young man? Coffee, tea? I'm fond of tea myself, and I've just brewed a pot, but don't let that stop you from asking for something else."

"Tea is fine."

"It's my pleasure," she told him.

She disappeared into the kitchen but returned quickly with a tray holding two kinds of cookies—not just chocolate chip, but shortbread cookies, as well—and an old teapot with a cozy wrapped around it, along with cups and saucers. She set the tea tray down on the coffee table in front of the sofa, took a seat in a huge wingback chair and began to pour the tea.

"I do love tea," she told him. "Not just drinking

it but serving it. It's such a pleasant old custom. In our world today, everyone is moving at the speed of light. It's nice just to take time in the afternoon to sit down with a pot of brewed tea. Sugar? Milk?"

"No sugar, and just a drop of milk, please," he told her, leaning forward, anxious to waste as little time as possible.

And she seemed to be aware of it. Though her eyes were on the tea service, she was wearing a small, patient smile.

She handed him his cup and said, "So now you're worried that someone's using my name." She leaned back and sipped her tea. "You must have a cookie. I couldn't call myself a proper hostess if I let you out of here without tasting one of my fresh-baked cookies," she told him, her patient smile more obvious.

To his own surprise, he blushed. "I'm sorry. I don't intend to be rude, but several girls are missing, as you know, and yesterday we found a body. I'm not sure how much you know, though there's been a fair bit written in the papers and on the news."

"I read about it on the Internet first, actually," she told him, then added, when his eyes widened, "even we old folks have discovered the Internet, you know."

He blushed again and started to apologize, but she waved him to silence and went on.

"Let me tell me you what I know, and then you can tell me if you think I can help you," she said.

"I don't think this is a matter for a palm reading," he said.

"I didn't intend to read your palm. And I didn't suggest that my help would be of the spiritual kind. Don't you think it's time you stopped patronizing me?"

"I'm sorry," he assured her. "I don't know why I—"

He broke off, startled, when she took his teacup and set it down, then put her hands on his cheeks and looked into his eyes.

"You suffered an early trauma, and your dedication to what you do stems from that. I believe you have an exceptional soul, but not a trusting one, maybe because of everything you've seen. You like to go by the book—although I admit yours is a rather unorthodox book—because you're convinced that methodology can take you where you want to go. But there's more to you—others have seen it, but you don't accept it yourself. Yet." Then she sat back and was suddenly all business.

"All right, let's start with what's going on. Are you here because of Winona Hart or the woman whose body was found?" She must have seen something in his face, because she suddenly said, "You found the body, didn't you?"

He nodded. Unsure why he was so comfortable sharing with her, he admitted, "Yes, I found the body. I wasn't there looking for her—whoever she is. I came down here to look for a girl who disappeared a year ago. The police aren't officially connecting her disappearance to Winona Hart's—not yet, anyway—but I'm sure there's a link. Actually, I don't think the cops even believed they had a possible serial killer until I found the body yesterday."

She nodded knowingly. "Too often we don't see what we don't want to see, I'm afraid."

"Well, what I've discovered so far is that the two girls who are still missing were both fascinated by ghosts and the occult. They were both looking for more than the usual ghost stories. So far, I have no idea where Jennie Lawson, the girl I'm looking for, was when she went missing, but Winona Hart disappeared from a beach out on Anastasia Island. No one saw her leave. The police have pretty thoroughly investigated the other kids who were out there that night, and I don't believe any of them had anything to do with Winona's disappearance. The only possible suspect I've discovered so far is a woman calling herself Martha Tyler of Cassadaga who was talking to Winona earlier in the evening."

"And you don't believe I was out on that beach that night?"

He cast her an apologetic smile. "You don't look like a hippie in your thirties or forties."

"I'm ninety," she said, smiling. "My last birthday party was a hoot."

"I'm sure it was," Caleb said. "But this is serious. That woman was handing out your cards, with your address here in Cassadaga."

"Business cards are very easy to print. And I suppose it's still a point of amusement that there's a Martha Tyler in Cassadaga." When he looked at her curiously, Martha gave a decisive nod and explained. "My name is the same as that of a 'witch' who lived in St. Augustine over a hundred and fifty years ago. She didn't call herself a witch, of course. In fact, I don't think she called herself anything at all. Back when I was a little girl, kids up here in the north of the state had a nursery rhyme of sorts about her. 'Martha Tyler, Martha Tyler, trust me, child, there's no one viler. One, two, three, four, whatever you do, don't open her door or she'll see you buried far under the floor.' "

"That's quite a story. I appreciate you helping me," Caleb said, finishing his tea and dusting cookie crumbs from his fingers. "Thank you," he said, taking her hand to say goodbye.

She smiled, then surprised him by turning his hand over to look at his palm. "Looks like I'll be doing a palm reading after all," she said, laughing. Then she turned serious and looked closely at his hand. "You need to stop doubting yourself," she told him.

"I'm actually known as a pretty confident guy," he said lightly, but he didn't pull his hand away.

Her grasp was unexpectedly strong for a woman her age, he realized.

She looked up into his eyes and smiled. "It's the fear in you that's holding you back. No, no—don't get defensive," she said when he started to object. "You'd risk your life for someone else. What you're afraid of is risking your mind, but you shouldn't be. Let your imagination go. Don't demand a logical, provable explanation for everything. If you . . . just open your mind, you'll find the answers you need. Don't be afraid of being judged, don't be afraid of the opinions of others. Let yourself be you."

"Thank you. Good advice," he said.

"It's only good advice if you take it," she told him, then frowned suddenly, and her grip on his hand tightened. "Someone you care about is . . . in danger. She's very close to the situation. Too close. And you need to stay near her. Everything is connected. She's treading too close to the truth, and . . . you need her if you're to see this situation through."

He pulled his hand away, startled by the wave of electricity shooting between them as she spoke.

"Look, Martha, I'm not the doubter you seem to think I am. I work for a man named Adam Harrison, who—"

"Adam Harrison?" she said, clearly delighted. "I don't know him myself, but I have friends who speak very highly of him and the work he does."

"Good. Then you'll believe me when I say I know a number of people who . . . who believe they communicate with spirits, and I have to admit, they've solved some pretty impossible mysteries through whatever it is they do. So—"

"Her name is Sarah McKinley," Martha said.

"What? How . . . ?"

"The woman. And don't worry, it's just a simple deduction," Martha said. "In the nineteen hundreds Martha Tyler was the housekeeper at a mortuary. Sarah McKinley owns the old place now. I've seen it on the news—they found skeletons in the walls," she said. "You do know the young woman, right?"

"Yes."

"And you're close to her." It wasn't a question.

It was impossible to be closer, he thought, then wondered how Martha had known. Definitely more than simple deduction going on there.

He gave himself a mental shake. This was getting a little too weird.

"We've become pretty good friends," he said, wondering just how much this woman saw with her brilliant blue stare.

"The future is always and only what we make of it," Martha said. "So please open your heart and soul to everything that's possible—and even impossible. I believe that there's a deep evil sweeping over us right now. Be careful, very careful."

She stood, and he realized that she had said her

piece, had done what she could for him, and now she was done and ready for him to leave.

He rose, as well, both glad that he had come—it was interesting that this woman's name was the same as that of the long-ago witch but more crucial to know that she wasn't the woman who'd been on the beach that night—but also sorry he had come, because she had unnerved him by urging him to open his mind and explore his abilities further. And by making him afraid.

For Sarah.

She wasn't a blonde and that made her safe, she'd joked, but the woman whose body he had found on the beach had been a brunette.

This was not a killer—and now there was, beyond a doubt, a killer—who selected his victims by the color of their hair. He was selecting them by his—or her—ability to charm them into the woods or into a back alley . . . or off the side of the road.

He was selecting victims with an interest in the paranormal. Women who wanted to be afraid.

"Martha, it was a true pleasure to meet you," he said. "Thank you. And since I did make an appointment and take up your time, of course I'm happy to pay you whatever you normally charge for your time."

"That's very sweet of you," she said. "But I hope I've helped you with your investigation, and I can't charge you for that. I would feel guilty."

"Then I sincerely thank you again," he said.

She watched from the porch as he pulled away. Even as his car rounded the corner, he knew that she was still watching him.

And he couldn't forget the electric current he had felt when she held his hand. It was almost as if truths hidden in the shadows of his own soul had come surging forward, drawn by her words, her power.

Open your mind, she had said.

He really didn't want to.

And he didn't want to feel so . . . *unnerved* by this encounter. At least it hadn't been a total dead end, even though she clearly wasn't the woman he was looking for, a woman who had somehow known that this Martha Tyler existed—and probably also about the odd coincidence that the name of a modern-day Cassadaga medium was the same as a so-called witch who had lived almost a century and a half ago.

As he drove, he realized that he needed to call Jamison; he had promised to keep the lieutenant up-to-date on what was going on with his investigation, which was only fair, since the police had given him every bit of assistance possible.

But when he picked up his cell phone, he felt a strange chill shoot along his spine.

Sarah.

Sarah was in danger. He was sure of it.

He punched in Sarah's number, glad that he'd thought to copy it from her cell that morning, but she didn't answer, and the chill came back, more powerful than before.

Martha Tyler's words haunted him.

Someone you care about is in danger.

He told himself it was probably nothing, but he couldn't help it. He needed to make sure she was all right. She'd been at the library, but the library would be closed by now. So where was she, and why wasn't she answering her phone?

Was it possible to care so much about someone when they weren't even in your speed dial yet?

Maybe she had already gone to Hunky Harry's, and she couldn't hear the phone over the noise in the bar. Maybe she'd forgotten to plug in her phone, and her battery had died.

There were a dozen perfectly logical—and perfectly safe—maybes, and he told himself he was being ridiculous to panic because of the words of a medium he'd never even met before today.

He called Tim Jamison, who was out of the office on personal time, though he could be paged if there was an emergency. Caleb passed and tried Will.

But Will hadn't heard from Sarah yet, and since he and Caroline were already at Hunky Harry's, that put paid to one possible explanation of her whereabouts.

"Will, can you try to find her?" Caleb asked.

"Sure, but where are you?"

"On the way back, but still a ways away."

"Where have you been?"

"I'll explain later. I'm just uncomfortable, not knowing where she is."

"Does she usually give you her schedule?" Will asked.

Caleb almost smiled at Will's protective alpha male persona, then said seriously, "Will, I can't reach her, and I'm worried."

"Any particular reason?" Will asked.

"Just everything that's been going on lately," Caleb said.

"Right. We'll head right out and check the library on the way over to her house, then head back here," Will said. "And don't worry. We're on it."

Caleb pushed down hard on the gas pedal, hoping that Adam Harrison had some influence with the Florida Highway Patrol, because otherwise he would be looking at one mean speeding ticket if he got pulled over.

At first, Sarah just stood dead still in the dark.

She told herself that she was merely stunned by the sudden turn of events, but that she certainly wasn't frightened.

The wind had closed the door.

Lightbulbs blew all the time.

But as she turned and strained to see in the dark, she couldn't help wondering how the hell wind was blowing in the kitchen. And why would the light have gone out at the precise moment when the door slammed shut?

She forced herself to think logically.

There was nothing to be afraid of; she was in her own basement. Yes, there was something about the darkness that had always scared humankind, a fear of the unknown. But that didn't mean that fear had any basis in reality.

She climbed the steps to the door and turned the knob. Or tried to.

Panic did set in then. How could the door be locked? That was certainly well beyond the power of the wind. She pushed against the door, then beat her fists against the unyielding wood. "Hey!" she yelled.

Stupid, stupid, stupid! If someone was in her house, she really shouldn't be yelling.

She turned around again, desperately trying to see in the darkness, and told herself to get a grip. She had her softball bat. She was only frightened because it was human instinct to be frightened. What she needed to be was angry—angry with herself. Sensible people who discovered skeletons in their houses stayed away. They sent workers in to return things to normal before they thought about making the place their home again. Especially when they owned a perfectly good carriage house.

She groaned, then was surprised to see that a dim light seemed to be seeping into the basement from . . . somewhere.

She started down the stairs again, intently holding onto the softball bat with both hands, ready to swing.

And then, to her horror, she tripped.

Swearing, she dropped the bat as she reached out in the darkness, trying to find the rail, but it was as if it slipped out from under her hands. She went tumbling down the wooden stairs, continuing to curse herself all the while.

With a thud, she landed at the bottom of the steps, the baseball bat landing at her side.

Stunned and winded, she lay on the cold stone floor of the basement, seeing the light disappear and feeling the darkness press against her like a heavy cloud.

"She's definitely not in the library—the place is locked up tighter than a drum," Caroline told Will.

They had walked around the building, but the front gates were locked, as was the fence to the backyard.

"I could scale the fence," Will said.

"Or we could call Vicky," Caroline suggested, punching in the number as she spoke.

Vicky answered and told Caroline that Sarah had left the library some time ago, long before she herself had locked up for the night.

"Okay, so she's not here," Caroline said. "There are a couple of ways to get to Hunky

Harry's. I'll take the main streets, and you go around the plaza."

As she started to walk away, Will shouted, "No!" and hurried to catch up with her.

"What's the matter?" Caroline asked him.

He took her arm. "I don't know, exactly, but Caleb sounded anxious. It's not late, and there are a lot of people walking around, but . . . I don't want you going off alone."

"You're scaring me, Will," Caroline said.

"What's going on *is* pretty scary."

"It is, isn't it?" Caroline asked. "Just a few days ago, I wasn't afraid at all. I knew Winona Hart had gone missing, but it seemed like an isolated incident, nothing to do with me, and I wasn't scared. Now . . . now we've connected that other girl, Jennie, with Winona. And then Caleb found that body on the beach. . . ." Her voice trailed off. "Will, I'm frightened, really frightened. We have to find Sarah. Now."

He took her hand and started walking.

"This isn't the way to Hunky Harry's," she said.

"I know," he told her, his grip firm on her as he started moving more quickly.

Sarah lay on the floor for several long moments, feeling a dozen pains streak through her. She groaned aloud as she finally tried to move.

She flexed her muscles, moved her arms and legs. Luckily she didn't seem to have broken anything. She carefully got to her feet and realized she hadn't even sprained an ankle. She wasn't injured, just sore.

And still in a very bad place.

Note to self, she thought dryly. *Find cell phone and attach to body.*

She thought she heard movement nearby, and she spun around, lightning bolts of terror streaking through her once again.

Hello? a voice breathed somewhere in her head.

She gripped her softball bat and inched forward into the dark. She couldn't see a thing, even though she was young and had very good vision.

If she couldn't see and someone else *was* in the basement with her, at least that person couldn't see, either, she told herself.

She held very still. Nothing happened.

She continued to wait, holding her breath, for what seemed like forever.

As she waited, she realized that those fractured particles of light seemed to be seeping back into the basement. From where?

As she stood there, she suddenly felt a strange warmth settling over her.

Something—some*one*—touched her shoulder. She wanted to scream, but she was frozen with fear.

She insisted to herself that whatever it was, it wasn't real.

And yet . . .

He was there. A man. Indistinct. Just a product of her imagination, she told herself. She couldn't possibly be looking at Civil War soldier Cato MacTavish in his cavalry uniform. She couldn't possibly be feeling his hand on her shoulder as he put his finger to his lips, warning her to silence.

He couldn't be real. She had hit her head in the fall, and now she was seeing things. Or maybe her mind had gone because she was so terrified.

He led her forward, still cautioning her to silence, and, inexplicably, she let him. She followed him through the basement to a far corner where a number of old wooden crates had been piled haphazardly.

She could have sworn she saw him reach out as if to move one of them.

She moved it herself and saw that, behind it, the rest of the crates had been stacked into a series of steps.

Keeping her bat firmly grasped in her hand, she crawled up onto the first crate. She could have sworn that Cato gave her a boost.

She crawled up on the next crate, and her excitement grew. There was more light here, though it was still pale and dim.

She turned when she felt herself being assisted up onto the next crate, and for a moment she saw him.

Really saw him.

As if he were a man of solid flesh and blood and bone.

The sweeping Southern hat, with its huge plume. The handsome dress cavalry jacket. The eyes that were so like Caleb's.

He moved an arm, impatiently, as a whisper seemed to sound in the air. *Go. Go quickly.*

She moved on to the next crate.

And then she discovered the source of the light.

Just as he was about to turn the corner to St. George Street, Will suddenly drew back.

"What?" Caroline demanded.

"Look," he whispered. "But carefully."

They were behind a string of bushes alongside one of one of the smaller of the old mansions, which had an overgrown lot on the far side of it.

A car was parked in front of the lot. Caroline didn't recognize it, and she didn't understand why Will was staring at it, and why he was hiding behind the bushes now when he had been so intent earlier on hurrying to Sarah's house.

"Will? What's going on?"

"Shhh. That's Tim Jamison's car."

"So? He's a cop. He can park anywhere he wants. Maybe he's investigating something," Caroline said, perplexed.

"Caroline, he's not investigating anything, he's just sitting in his car," Will said. "And he's not alone."

Caroline peeked around the bushes. There were two people in the car. Tim Jamison.

And . . .

The other person had long flowing hair. And a feminine profile. And as she watched, the two of them leaned in toward each other and met in a passionate kiss.

Caroline let out a loud gasp. Will clasped a hand over her mouth and drew her back into the bushes.

She shook free of his grasp and whispered, "Stop it. If Tim wants to have an affair, that's his own business. We're on our way to Sarah's, so come on. I don't care if they're going at it like rabbits in there. We have to get to Sarah's."

As they were whispering in the bushes, she was suddenly aware of headlights as an old Volkswagen Bug pulled up next to them.

"Hey!" Renee Otten stuck her head out the passenger window. "Why are you two hiding in the bushes?" she asked, and giggled. "Get a room."

Down the street, the engine of Tim Jamison's car revved, and the car drove off down the street.

"We're on our way to Sarah's. She's not answering her phone," Will said.

"Then quit wasting time skulking around and hop in," Barry offered, leaning past Renee.

"It's just around the corner—we'll meet you there," Will said, then gripped Caroline's hand and started walking quickly again. Will glanced up at the house by the vacant lot and remembered the last time he and Sarah had been at this very house. They had been wary, and suspicious, seeing the lieutenant's car.

"What?" Caroline asked.

"Do you know who lives here?"

"No. Do you?"

"Sure do. That would be Mr. Terrence Griffin the Third."

Caleb made it back in record time. Luckily—or possibly dangerously—most people on the highway were doing at least ninety, which made it less obvious that he was pushing the speedometer toward one hundred.

He was impatient at every red light he hit as he entered the city.

As he neared the streets of Old Town, he decided to pass on checking out Hunky Harry's or even trying to call Will again.

He headed straight for Sarah's house on St. George.

There were no cars in the drive, so he swung in off the street practically without braking. As he threw the car into Park, he saw a Bug coming around the corner. It jerked to a halt on the street just as he jumped out of his car.

"Hey!" Will called to him, walking up with Caroline just as Barry and Renee hopped out of their car.

"You haven't found her?" Caleb asked.

"No, we keep calling and calling, but . . . nothing," Caroline said, trying again as she spoke.

Caleb headed for the porch and raced up the steps. As he got to the door, he heard Sarah's cell phone ringing—inside.

"Sarah!"

He tried the door. It was open, and he cursed under his breath as he rushed inside.

"Sarah!" he shouted again, anxiety rising in his tone as he followed the sound of the ringing.

Her purse was on the kitchen counter, her cell phone inside it.

The others were right behind him. "Sarah!" Will shouted. He turned and headed for the stairs, then ran up them two at a time. Caroline hurried into one parlor, Renee and Barry into the other.

Caleb saw the door to the basement standing ajar. Had Sarah gone down there, hoping to find a hidden clue? He threw it open and looked down into the darkness. "Sarah!"

"What?"

He was startled when he heard her voice behind him and spun around.

She was leaning against the door frame between the kitchen and the hall.

And she was covered in mud and spiderwebs.

12

Caleb was stunned at the sight of her, but he didn't have a chance to speak, because just then Will came tearing back down the stairs and rushed into the room.

"Sarah! Where the hell have you—" He broke off and stopped dead, just two feet away from her. He'd been about to hug her in his relief, but suddenly he seemed to notice that she was covered in filth, and it gave him pause.

"Sarah?" Caroline said, crashing into Will.

Sarah offered them all a weak smile. "Hi, guys."

Caleb had managed to tamp down his own sense of sheer panic by then and stepped back to lean against the refrigerator. "What happened to you?" he asked finally.

Renee and Barry appeared just then and stopped in silence, Renee's mouth agape.

"I somehow managed to lock myself in the basement. I know, it's idiotic," Sarah said.

"And you just got out now?" Caleb asked. "People have been call—"

"*How* did you get out?" Renee asked, cutting across him.

"There's a screen window, just at ground level," Sarah said. "I never knew about it—there's a big hibiscus growing right in front of it. There's dirt all piled up in front of it, too—I don't think anyone has noticed it for years."

"Did you just get out?" Caleb asked again.

She turned her silver gaze to him and smiled, a bit embarrassed. "Yes."

"Sarah," he told her, "the door to the basement wasn't locked. It was open when I got in here. And so was your front door."

"Oh, Lord, I could have sworn I locked it," she said.

He saw that she was trembling, even though she was trying to be cool and slough off the experience as if it had been nothing.

But he could tell that she was badly shaken.

"Oh, my God, we were so worried. We've been calling you and calling you," Caroline said.

"I'm sorry, but I'm also very grateful that you were so concerned," Sarah said.

"Well, a lot of scary shit has been going down, and when you didn't answer, we got worried," Barry said.

"I know, and thanks again for worrying about me," Sarah said again, then looked at herself and grimaced. "I think I need to take a shower."

"I don't think you should be staying in this house," Renee said. "It's creepy."

"Oh, Renee," Barry protested. "The house isn't creepy."

"She was locked in the basement, wasn't she?" Renee said defensively.

"Apparently I only thought I was locked in the basement," Sarah said. "You said that the door was open, right, Caleb?"

"Yes," he said, still leaning against the refrigerator, watching her. He could see that she didn't want anyone to see just how badly shaken she was. He wondered if she was going to tell him the truth about what happened.

"But . . . even if you only thought you were locked in, it's the house that did it to you," Renee said, shivering. "Oh, Sarah. You really have to sell this place. There are other houses you can buy. And you'll be much happier. They won't come with bones in the wall."

"It's not like I knew this one came with bones in the wall when I bought it. Anyway, I'm a historian, remember? I thrive on this stuff. And right now I'm going to take a shower, because I'm starving and I want to go to dinner, but I don't want anyone waiting on me. You all go and get some appetizers or something. Please."

"I don't think we should leave you alone," Will said.

"She won't be alone. I'll wait for her," Caleb said. "Why don't the rest of you go on? We'll be right behind you."

"Okay," Caroline said slowly. "If you're sure, Sarah? Because we can wait."

"I'm sure. Please. I'll move faster if you aren't all waiting for me, honestly."

Will gave her a careful kiss on the forehead—despite the muck and spiderwebs, and then the others all headed for the door, but not before Renee looked back one last time and shook her head. "You need to get out of this house. I mean, think about all those horror movies and how everyone watching sits there and thinks, 'You stupid idiot! Get out of the house.'"

And then they left, with Renee closing the front door in her wake.

Silence descended. A silence Caleb broke when he asked, "What really happened?"

"I told you what happened," Sarah said. "Except that . . ." Her voice trailed off and she shrugged. "I tried the door. I could swear it was locked."

"What were you doing in the basement in the first place?" he demanded.

"I . . . I thought that someone was in the house, maybe Gary. The basement door was open, and I saw a light on down there, and thought—"

"Was Gary's truck in the yard?" Caleb asked her.

"No."

"But you decided he might be down there anyway?"

"I thought I'd heard something, but I guess the sound came from the street. Anyway, the whole thing is pretty ridiculous when you think about it. The lightbulb blew and I thought I was locked in, but then I saw light coming from a corner of the basement and realized that by climbing up on some old crates I could reach the screen. And it's so old . . . I just pushed my way through. I didn't realize the basement was so dirty. It's probably a good thing the bulb burned out. . . . I didn't see all the spiders."

He didn't believe her. Or rather, he was sure there was more. But he knew that pushing her at this moment wouldn't get him anywhere.

Quickly changing the subject, she said suddenly, "You won't believe how much I found out today. I was reading a journal written by Nellie Brennan. She thought her father was a monster, and there *was* a murderer killing women here during the Civil War. A lot of people believed it was your ancestor, Cato MacTavish, but I think that was because the Yankees had control of the town and he was a Reb, so they wanted to believe he'd done it. I found another memoir that mentioned Brennan and this place, and she thought Brennan was nasty, too—him and his housekeeper, Martha Tyler. She was supposedly some kind of a witch. Here's the thing—life hasn't changed much. We still believe rumors with no logic, when we want to."

"Martha Tyler *is* a medium," Caleb told her.

"What?"

"Before she disappeared, Winona Hart spoke to a woman at the beach who claimed to be a medium from Cassadaga named Martha Tyler. So I found a Martha Tyler in Cassadaga, and went out to see her," Caleb said.

"And?"

"The real Martha Tyler is a charming old woman who probably weighs eighty pounds on a fat day," he said. "But she knew about the housekeeper here, because people teased her about her name when she first moved to Cassadaga," he said, then looked thoughtful for a moment. "You know, I don't really believe a house can have a personality," he said, "but maybe it's not such a great idea for you to stay here."

She shook her head adamantly. "No. I think it's important for me to stay here. I think we're closer to the past here, that we may find a clue here—or even more fully realize something we already know here."

She stared at him determinedly. He stared back at her.

"I own the place, and I'm staying," she said firmly.

He let out a sigh of exasperation.

"What?" she asked.

"Well, I'm sure as hell not letting you stay alone," he told her.

She smiled, still looking somewhat tremulous. "I was kind of hoping you'd say that," she told him.

"All you ever had to do was ask," he said.

"Okay, then," she said awkwardly. "I'm asking. And now I'm going to shower and change, so we can go to dinner and . . ."

"And what?" he asked.

"Come back, and talk," she finished lamely.

He was tempted to tell her that he wanted to do a lot more than talk.

Except she hadn't told him the truth yet—not the whole truth. There was more to her story, and he wanted to hear it—needed to hear it—before he got in any deeper with her.

"I'll be back down in ten minutes," she promised, and headed for the stairs.

He ached to follow her, but he managed to wait until she reached the top of the stairs before he followed.

People were waiting for them, he reminded himself.

Too bad. They would have to wait.

The bathroom door was ajar.

Maybe she had hoped that he would come.

He joined her in the shower just after she'd sluiced away the spiderwebs and the mud.

She had just poured shampoo on her hair, and he took over, massaging her scalp and working up a lather. She leaned back against him, and when he felt her trembling, he took her into his arms.

"Sarah . . ."

"I don't want to talk about it anymore," she said. "Just hold me. Please?"

He held her. Water beat out a rhythm around them, steam rose, and he held her. Then he moved, and the friction of their bodies against each other created a new kind of comfort. She was slick and vibrant, electric in his arms. He felt as if heat infused him. Thunder echoed in his head and in his loins. She pressed her lips against his neck, his chest. He slid his hands down the length of her spine, then lifted her, and the water continued its cascade of liquid fire as they made love, her back against the tile.

Eventually, pent-up emotion overrode everything physical, and they rose to a volatile crescendo together, climaxing in one another's arms. He could have stayed that way forever, but she smiled a real smile at last, then kissed his lips, but lightly. "People are waiting for us, and I still need to finish washing my hair."

"I can help you."

"Out! Or we'll never make it to dinner," she said.

Regretfully, he set her down on the floor of the old tub and left. He toweled off, found his clothing and dressed, then headed back downstairs.

He cursed himself as he reached the bottom of the stairs. They had forgotten to lock the front door. He locked it then, as pointless as it seemed, and as he waited for her, he walked around the lower level, checking every window to make sure it was locked.

He went to the top of the basement stairs and looked down into the darkness. There was a switch near the door, and he flipped it. Nothing happened. He dug through the cabinets until he found a flashlight and, turning it on, he went down.

The basement was empty other than the crates Sarah had mentioned, which had been stacked into something resembling stairs. He trained the light on the torn screen through which she had escaped.

Anyone could have entered the house at any time through that window, he thought—especially with that makeshift stairway saving them from the long drop to the floor. He needed to make sure no one could use that window moving forward. He would have to board it up or put bars across it—or get Sarah's friend Gary to do it.

He trained the light around until he found the fuse box. He walked over and opened it, and saw faded cursive writing labeling the different fuses to indicate which sections of the house they were linked to. He found the fuse for the basement. It had been switched to "off."

He turned it back on, then rearranged the crates, wedging them tightly into the window opening.

It wasn't a perfect job, just a jerry-rigged solution until something more permanent could be done, but it made him feel better.

Then he went back up to the kitchen and made certain the basement door was closed and locked behind him. For good measure, he went to the dining room and got a chair, then wedged it under the doorknob. If anyone managed to get in while they were gone, he would know.

He had just finished when Sarah came back down the stairs. "All set?" she asked.

"Not really. Hang on one minute."

He went back upstairs and went through every room, checking every window. Houses weren't evil—but they could definitely be used for evil purposes. He made absolutely sure that the upstairs was empty and locked, then took another cursory run through the ground floor.

"What are you doing?" Sarah asked him.

"Making certain we're alone," he said.

She grinned. "A little late, don't you think?"

"Better late than never," he said lightly. "Besides, at some point, we'll actually need to sleep, and I don't want to worry about anyone getting in."

They left the house, and he watched as she locked the front door. They were halfway down the front walk when she said, "You went out to see Floby about the dead woman on the beach, didn't you?"

"Yes."

"And?"

"We'll talk later. Right now I'm starving, so let's get going."

"You know," Caroline said, sitting back and pushing her plate away, "I like Hunky Harry's, but we could expand our horizons. Eat somewhere else."

"But it's such a nice central place to meet," Renee said.

"Yes, but we could meet here, maybe have a drink, then wander on to another restaurant," Barry pointed out.

"We could," Will said. "But why?"

Sarah was happy to see that the conversation was light and trivial. Caleb was an investigator, but there was nothing the rest of them could do about the ongoing disappearances other than try to stay safe.

Except for her. She had discovered so much today. And while she hadn't been ready to talk to Caleb about her experience earlier—she was still sorting it out in her own mind, now—she found herself anxious to talk to him. Alone.

She picked up her rum runner and sipped quickly. She was frightened suddenly by the intensity of the relationship they had developed so quickly. If she had any sense, she would step back.

She would take a vacation to the Bahamas or Paris.

She would do anything but be here. And yet, everything she'd said about her house was true; she had never felt more . . . *needed*.

Had her mind created an illusion to help her figure out a way to escape? Or had she really been helped out of the basement by a ghost? Maybe she had seen that window at some time and not really noticed it. Maybe she had imagined the ghost because she was desperate and afraid. Had it been her way of dealing with panic?

But she had to face it, the entire thing had been . . . weird. First the noise. Then the basement door closing just as the light went out . . .

There hadn't been anyone else in the house—or had there? Tim Jamison had a key. Gary had a key. And Dr. Manning must have been given a key, too.

There were definitely too many keys to her house in other people's hands.

"Looks like Tim Jamison has gotten smart enough to stop coming here," Renee said, leaning in close to be heard over the music and surrounding conversations.

"I should hope so," Barry said indignantly. "He should be spending every second looking for the murderer."

"No one can work all the time," Caleb remarked.

True enough, Sarah thought, and yet it often seemed that *he* was always working. He was watching everything around him all the time.

When he was with her . . .

No, she wasn't going there. He sure as hell wasn't with her because of the case, so she wasn't even going to think in that direction, wasn't going to question everything that was going on between them.

"There's been no word on Winona Hart, right?" Barry asked.

"No, I'm afraid not," Caleb said.

"What about the woman you found on the beach?" Renee asked, her eyes wide.

"They don't even know her identity yet," Caleb says. "It takes time. Forensic science is pretty amazing, but it doesn't always produce instantaneous results."

Caroline shivered. "I think it's scary, so . . ." She paused and looked around. "How come nobody looks panicked?"

"That's true," Will said. "I hope people are being careful, though. Three women missing or dead, all in one year."

"It's possible that the woman Caleb is looking for and Winona Hart will still show up," Renee offered hopefully.

"It's possible," Caleb agreed. As he spoke, he reached into his pocket and pulled out his cell phone. He glanced at the caller ID and excused himself, saying, "I'm going to take this where I can hear. I'll be right back."

When he was gone, Barry said, "Business?"

"I guess," Sarah said.

Renee looked across the table at her. "We need another round. Poor Sarah! You must have been scared to death in that basement."

Will, at her side, pulled her close in a hug, then knuckled the top of her head. "My cousin can handle anything."

"But that house! I'd be terrified if I were locked in a basement. And then to find out the door was really unlocked all the time. Here's what I think, and I can't help it. The house locked you in. Then, just to make you look like an idiot, it opened the door again."

Will burst out laughing. "Oh, Renee! Come on."

"I'd be creeped out," she said. "You wouldn't catch me living there."

"The house is just a house. Those bones were old, but there's a real killer out there now," Will said.

Barry rolled his eyes. "I think we're obsessing on this more than the cops are. So let's forget all about it and dance," he said, nodding toward the dance floor. When no one moved, he said, "Renee?"

"Sure," she said, and shrugged unenthusiastically.

As she and Barry walked out to the dance floor, Will leaned closer to Sarah and spoke directly to her, his eyes intense. "Sarah, maybe you *should* come stay with me. Or maybe I should get someone to cover for me at work and take you to . . . I don't know. New York City. The Bahamas. Anywhere else, just for a while."

Ignoring the fact that only a few minutes ago she'd contemplated running away to the Bahamas herself, she said, "I'm okay. Really. Anyway . . ." She blushed, then went on. "Caleb's staying with me."

"And I'm supposed to find that reassuring? We don't know enough about that guy yet," Will said.

She smiled. She loved her cousin and was grateful for his protective nature, but she knew in her heart that this time there was no need for it. "I know everything I need to know," she said. "I met Adam Harrison in Virginia, and anyone working for him is by definition aboveboard. And just so you know, *I* know everything I need to about Caleb."

"Oh, really?" Caroline said, shifting around to her other side. "What do you really know? That he looks good in boxers. Or naked? You can't let yourself be blinded by the physical thing, Sarah. I know I wanted you to start dating again, and I even kind of pushed you two together, but . . ."

"Would you two have some faith in me?" Sarah demanded. "I'm fine, and so is Caleb. I'm worried about *you*, Caroline. Will, you need to stay close to her. She's a beautiful blonde, and both the missing women were—*are*—blondes, too."

She stopped speaking when she saw Caleb returning to the table. Whatever he had heard during his phone call had made him thoughtful. He sat down, then said, "I think I need to call it a night. Sarah, you ready?" he asked.

"Yeah, I'm all set," she said, then frowned. Barry was coming back, weaving between tables, and he was alone. "Where's Renee?"

"With friends," he said, sliding into his chair, sounding disgusted.

"We all have friends," Will offered.

"She left me in the middle of the dance floor," Barry said.

"We were going to take off," Sarah told him. "But if you need me to stay . . . Are you all right?"

He looked startled; then he smiled. "Of course I'm all right. I'm a big boy. I'll be fine. *We'll* be fine. I'm just aggravated, not suicidal. Go ahead. We'll see you tomorrow."

"We'll hang out for a few more minutes," Caroline said, looking at Will. "That way you won't have to sit here alone."

Barry smiled again, shaking his head. "You're all free to go. Honestly. I *have* been in a bar by myself before."

Sarah took him at his word and gave him a kiss on the cheek, then told him to tell Renee goodnight when she returned.

Will and Caroline left with them, but at the plaza, they split up to walk their separate ways.

Caleb glanced at her. "You're sure you want to stay in the house? The carriage house is just fine, you know."

"I want to stay in the house," she told him firmly.

"What really happened today?" he asked her.

"I honestly don't know. I thought I saw him again—your ancestor," she admitted, glancing at him sideways.

He frowned. "Please tell me that my ancestor didn't lock you in the basement."

"No, he helped me out of it. Or I hallucinated he

helped me out of it, because thinking he was really there . . . that's ridiculous."

"The front door was unlocked when I got there—and so was the basement door," Caleb said.

"Do you think someone might have been trying to scare me, locking me down there?" she asked, perplexed. "Tomorrow I need to get all my keys back."

"It's not just a matter of getting your keys back," he said. "Tomorrow, you're getting a locksmith out there to change the locks."

She nodded. "That's not a bad idea," she admitted, then asked, "Who was that on the phone?"

"Floby," he told her.

"Floby?" she echoed, surprised. "What's up?"

"He found traces of a hallucinogen in the dead woman's system."

"She was on LSD?"

"He's not sure what. He doesn't have all the results in yet. I'll head over to see him in the morning," Caleb said, his tone thoughtful.

"I found out something interesting recently, too," Sarah said. "This same scenario occurred before—years ago, during the Civil War. A bunch of women disappeared, and people assumed they'd been murdered, though only a few bodies were ever found. And I read two memoirs that talked about it—one written by a woman who moved down here after the Yankees occupied the city in 1862, the other one a journal kept by Nellie Brennan, the daughter of Leo Brennan, the man who forced MacTavish out and kept running the mortuary business. The first woman saw the body of a dead girl in a coffin. She said that the corpse was so white it was as if all her blood had been drained. Brennan caught her and a friend staring at the girl, and threatened them with a shotgun the next time they ventured onto his property. Nellie said that her father was furious when a Sergeant Lee brought a corpse to the house. She snuck out and looked at it, and it sounded as if that woman had been drained of blood, too, though maybe that was because her whole body looked as if wild animals had been feeding on it. The sergeant wanted her father to cover up the fact that the woman had been murdered. In both cases, the cause of death was listed as being run down by a carriage."

"Really? Is there a way I can read those memoirs?" Caleb asked her.

"I still have the first one, but the other is one of the library's newest acquisitions, so they won't let it out. But you can go to the library and read it."

"Maybe," he said contemplatively. "There are certainly correlations between the past and the present that are . . . extraordinary," he said. "You know about the historical Martha Tyler, right?"

"If what Nellie wrote was true, she was horrible. She threatened Nellie. She told her that she could wind up like the dead woman."

"And a woman who called herself Martha Tyler but wasn't the real woman by that name was at the beach when Winona Hart disappeared," Caleb said.

He looked as if he was going to say more. When he didn't, Sarah demanded, "What? Caleb, I'm a part of this. If someone is repeating the past and these disappearances have something to do with my house, then I'm in it as deep as you can get. You have to tell me what you know."

He paused, then studied her. "She was drained of blood," he said at last. "The woman I found on the beach—she'd been drained of blood."

Sarah paled, then pulled herself together and said, "We need to see Mr. Griffin again. His daughter disappeared, too. It was years later, but maybe history just keeps in repeating itself. He wants to help, and it's possible he knows something, that his memory will trigger something. . . . Maybe we can even help him by finding out what happened to his daughter."

They had reached the house and paused to look up at the facade. They had left the lights on, and now the place looked beautiful and inviting.

"You're sure you want to sleep here?" he asked.

"You do have a gun, right?" she asked him.

"Yes."

"Then yes, I want to sleep here. I'm not afraid of ghosts, and I have you to protect me from the living."

They went in, careful to make sure that the door was locked behind them. Caleb wasn't content with the fact that he'd secured the house earlier. He went back through and checked everything again, including the chair by the basement door, which was still securely in place.

When he was done, she looked at him teasingly, then raced up the stairs. He followed, and after that they gave themselves up to learning about each other, just exploring, savoring their freedom to discover. Clothing went flying, and there was laughter and breathlessness. . . .

It was explosive; it was sweet; it was magic.

Touching his flesh, feeling the flex and fire of his muscles, Sarah thought it was like falling in love again, something she had almost forgotten, almost given up on.

They were fervent, urgent, but not frantic. There was something about being together. . . . What they shared wasn't superficial, not something destined to end quickly, and they both felt confident about that.

When Sarah slept, she did so feeling more secure than she had in all her life. She didn't fear the darkness, didn't fear ghosts, and in his arms, she also had no fear of the living.

She was awakened suddenly by his abrupt movement. She blinked, then jackknifed into a sitting position, wondering what had happened, fear seeping into her blood.

"Caleb, what is it?" she whispered.

He was sitting up himself, staring toward the foot of the bed.

Suddenly he rose, as if he hadn't heard her.

As if she didn't exist at all.

13

"Caleb?"

He heard Sarah call his name, but it seemed to come from a distant place, or maybe he was only hearing it in his mind.

He opened his eyes . . .

And saw himself.

No, not himself. His double. That other Caleb was standing at the foot of the bed, his hair longer than Caleb's own, and he was wearing a gaudily plumed hat. He had a moustache and goatee, and long sideburns. He was handsomely dressed in Victorian attire, silk waistcoat, tailored overcoat and white shirt.

And his expression was grave.

Help me.

Caleb stared, sure that he was dreaming, yet he couldn't shake the dream.

Help me, please. And help yourself. I know what happened to her, and who did it. I loved her, and it wasn't me.

As he continued to stare, the apparition beckoned to him.

Please.

Caleb rose slowly, still staring at the man who was—and yet was not—himself.

Cato MacTavish. He was staring at Cato MacTavish.

At last, certain that he had Caleb's attention, Cato turned and walked from the room.

Unable to help himself, Caleb followed.

They left the bedroom and walked along the hallway to the small, narrow staircase that led up to the attic.

There were two small eyebrow windows, and the pale pastel light of the early dawn was just beginning to seep in. The light fell over old trunks, broken chairs and several dressmakers' dummies, headless sentinels guarding the attic realm. Motes of dust danced in the pastel light.

Cato MacTavish paused in the center of the room, surrounded by the past, and looked at Caleb with great sadness.

I have looked forever, he said. *And finally I have found her.*

He moved to stand by a huge wooden steamer trunk with tarnished metal strapping.

Brighter light flooded the room as the sun continued its inevitable rise, and Cato began to fade. Caleb realized he was standing naked and alone in the dusty attic in the coming light of day.

"Caleb!"

He started and turned, feeling the warmth of Sarah's delicate touch on his arm. She was staring at him with deep concern shining from her enormous silver eyes.

She was so enticing, her hair a wild mane around her head, her skin so soft, the silk wrap she had grabbed to follow him seductively draping the curves of her body. The sight of her, the feel of her, triggered something within him.

"Caleb?" she repeated.

He looked at the trunk and gave himself a mental shake, pulling himself free from the mists of sleep and dreams.

"The trunk," he said hoarsely, pointing.

He knew he was awake at last, but memory of the dream was vivid. He walked closer and saw that the trunk was padlocked, preventing him from opening it. He looked around and saw that someone had stowed a set of dumbbells in a corner—years ago, judging by the coating of dust, and yet not so many years as the trunk had been there. He strode across the room, oblivious to his own nakedness, and picked up one of the dumb-bells.

"Caleb?" Sarah said, louder now, firmly. "What are you doing?"

Without answering, he smashed the lock and lifted the lid of the trunk, revealing a trove of loosely piled Victorian clothing. He drew out hose, capes, petticoats, stays, throwing things aside . . . until at last he found what he was seeking.

Bones.

Bones nestled in decaying silk and satin. Wisps of hair still clinging to a skull with leathery skin still covering the bone. Dried and mummified flesh adding substance to the bones. She was real, and yet she appeared to be nothing but a decorative prop for a macabre haunted house.

"Oh, my God . . ." Sarah breathed from behind him.

"It's Eleanora," Caleb said with grim certainty.

"How do you know?" she whispered.

"There's a locket around her neck—with a likeness of Cato," he said. "Cato didn't do it. He loved her."

"What?" Sarah asked, shaking her head in concern and stepping back, as if she were afraid to touch him. "I don't understand." She studied him for a moment, and then realization lit her eyes. "You saw him, didn't you? I didn't dream him. He's a ghost," she whispered.

"I had a dream," he said, but even as he spoke, he wasn't sure he believed his own words. And if not, what *did* he believe?

What had he seen, and how had he ended up in the attic?

"It was a dream," he insisted. "We were talking about the past and what happened here, and I had a dream that led me here, that's all," he said. "Call Jamison. And then you might as well call that professor—Dr. Manning. I need to shower and dress—we both do. She's been in that trunk for over a hundred and fifty years. Another hour isn't going to make any difference. In fact, I don't want to call anyone yet. I'm going to go see Floby anyway, and then I'll bring him back here and we can figure out how to proceed and whether this has anything to do with everything else going on."

"Caleb, it all *has* to be connected," Sarah said. "Whatever you say, I know we both saw a ghost. And he's not trying to haunt anyone or hurt them—he's trying to help. People accused Cato of having killed Eleanora and the others, and he left because he couldn't prove the truth."

He set his hands on her shoulders and wondered why he of all people—a man who worked for Adam Harrison and spent his time investigating the incursions of the paranormal into the real world—couldn't admit to having seen a ghost.

Sarah was still staring at him as if he had changed in some fundamental way. She looked wary. She looked . . .

Afraid.

He winced and tightened his grip on her shoulders. "All right, here's what I think. Something terrible happened here years ago. Maybe that housekeeper, Martha Tyler, conned people into believing she had some kind of power, like the tricks Marie LeVeau used in New Orleans. She would *listen*. She would get people to tell her things they didn't even know they were telling her. That way, she could tell one heartbroken woman that there was nothing she could do to help, then tell another that she could help her win the man of her dreams. She would have mixed her potions and convinced people of their efficacy, and maybe she even had a certain power of her own. But, she couldn't have been working alone."

"Brennan," Sarah said. "Brennan was working with her. She worked for him, not Cato—he was the one who brought her here. He got here ahead of the Union occupation, and old Mr. MacTavish needed money, so he took him in as a boarder. And then Brennan talked MacTavish into using the house as a funeral parlor. MacTavish would have been willing to do anything to survive the war and save the house so his son could inherit the old mansion when he returned. But MacTavish died, and when Cato finally came back from the war, Brennan was already established in his house. There were all kinds of ways for the carpetbaggers to keep a man from reclaiming his property. And with Eleanora missing, and then the other women, the accusations would have started—fed by Brennan, no doubt—and eventually Cato MacTavish must have had enough, and he left. Brennan was a nasty man—his own daughter wrote about how much she hated him. She stopped writing, though, and I don't know what happened to her, but a son inherited this place. I don't know where he came from. Maybe he was born later, or maybe he was fighting with the Union army when his father and sister moved down here." She paused, staring first at him, then sadly down at the trunk and its pathetic contents. "If this is Eleanora, how did the line go on? How can you be his descendent?" she asked.

"Either she had a child before she died and someone managed to hide the fact and get the child out of the city—or he went on to find a wife when he left St. Augustine," Caleb said. "You were the one who discovered the connection—what did the records say?"

"They didn't say anything. There was no mention of a wife, just the reference to his son being named Magnus. And then his son's family and so on."

"Where and when did Cato die?"

"In Virginia, in 1901."

"So why is he back here?" Caleb asked.

"Aha!" Sarah said.

"Stop it. Please. If we tell Jamison that a ghost is leading us around—and I'm not admitting *or* denying that fact—I guarantee you, he and everyone else will call us crazy," Caleb said.

They stared at one another for a long moment.

Then she smiled slowly. "You wear dust well," she assured him.

He grinned and pulled her close, his expression grave as he said, "Thank you for the compliment, but I have to go see Floby and then bring him out here. Let's get showered and dressed before we do anything else."

"Sounds like a plan," she told him.

319

A few minutes later they stepped into the shower together. Sarah looked at him and said, "You know, our world is going to go crazy again when the media finds out that we've discovered another corpse in this house."

"I know," he said.

"We might want to spend a little more time . . . just us, before everything goes to hell," she said somberly.

He nodded and pulled her into a tight embrace.

Water. Heat. Steam. Slick bodies in close proximity, and a feeling that every second now was unique . . . precious.

Eventually they stepped out of the shower and got dressed.

Eleanora and Cato had been in love, their relationship cruelly ended, Caleb thought. And now, together, he and Sarah were going to exonerate Cato and put Eleanora to rest at last.

It wasn't until Caleb called Will and asked him to come over to Sarah's, then headed out of the house, that he realized he might have discovered the remains of his own great-great-great—however many greats—grandmother. It was a poignant thought, and surprisingly painful.

"I've gotten back some of the tissue samples," Floby said from behind the desk in his office.

"Right. You said the victim had taken some kind of a hallucinogenic drug?"

"Nature's own," Floby said. "Yaupon holly—and poppy seeds."

"Poppy seeds? You mean opium?"

"More or less. An extract from the seeds."

"And yaupon holly?" Caleb was thoughtful for a minute. "Isn't that one of the ingredients in the black drink a number of Native Americans—including the Seminoles—use in their rituals?"

"Exactly," Floby told him.

"So was she high enough that she was hallucinating?" Caleb said.

"Given how she ended up, let's hope she was very high and seeing beautiful sights," Floby told him.

Caleb nodded. "Okay, now I need you to come with me back to Sarah's place. I want you to see something before we call anyone else in."

"Oh, God. You've found another body," Floby said, staring at him.

"A woman. In a trunk in the attic," Caleb admitted.

Floby shook his head. "What is it with you and corpses?" he asked. "I just wish you could find Winona Hart—alive."

"I wish that, too," Caleb assured him.

"Have you called Jamison?" Floby asked.

"Not yet. I will." Caleb hesitated. "There's some mummified tissue on this body. I'm hoping you can figure out if there were any drugs—like the black drink—in her system when she died . . . if

321

you can figure out how she died, before we get the zoo back in.

"I think there's some kind of connection between what went on back then and what's going on now, and I can't wait for the historians and the anthropologists to do whatever it is they do. I need to know now." He hesitated. "And I also want you to do a test for me—on the side, without telling anyone."

"Oh?"

"A DNA test."

"I'll need someone to compare her DNA to."

"You have someone. Me."

Will sat in the kitchen, shaking his head over a cup of coffee, not looking at Sarah. She had brought him up-to-date on all the reading she had done, and the details of Caleb's investigation.

"The man's a corpse magnet," he said.

"Stop it! He's an investigator, Will—corpses are a part of his work," Sarah said and stood up, suddenly impatient. She was glad that her cousin was with her. Not that she was afraid to be alone, she told herself, but things had been so strange lately that she was glad of the company. With nothing to worry about on the safety front, she was free to focus on the one thing that seemed impossible to believe and yet had to be true.

She'd thought about it a lot, and as crazy as it seemed, as much as it went against the grain of everything she'd always believed, she'd come to the conclusion that Cato MacTavish was a ghost. He might have been buried in Virginia, but he was here now, because girls were disappearing again, and he wanted it to stop. He didn't want to see a repeat of what had happened before.

"This place is creepy, Sarah," Will was saying now. "I mean, sure, it could be a beautiful bed-and-breakfast. For ghouls," he said. "And I don't like just how much *you* seem to be getting involved in everything that's going on. Okay, the bones in your house weren't your fault. But since Mr. Corpse Magnet is trying to find whoever killed that woman on the beach—and maybe those other two girls, as well—I don't think you should be hanging around with him so much. I mean, I like him, I honestly do. But I'm worried sick about you. What if he finds out something . . . and people decide you know it, too? You could be in danger, Sarah."

"Stop it," she warned him. "You're with me now, right? So I'm safe."

He groaned and leaned his head on the table. "It's barely eight in the morning, and I don't have to work until this afternoon."

"Quit whining."

"I'm tired."

"I'm sorry." Then she brightened and said, "Let's go pay a social call."

He stared at her as if she had lost her mind.

"I want to see Mr. Griffin."

"Why?"

"His daughter disappeared—in or around this house."

"Do you think she's the corpse in the attic? And why the hell haven't you called the cops yet?"

"No, she isn't the corpse in the attic."

"How do you know?"

"The clothing is Victorian, certainly not from the 1920s. And we haven't called anyone in yet because we want to hold off—just a bit—on causing another frenzy. Please, Will, you have to pay attention to me and help me out with this. Do it my way. Caleb is going to bring Floby here to see the body, and I want to talk to Mr. Griffin."

"What about Caleb? Shouldn't you wait 'til he gets here?"

"I'll just send him a text message, in case he gets back before we do. We're just going around the corner."

"All right," Will said with a sigh. "Let's go."

Floby sat in the car, staring straight ahead. "You certainly do have a knack for finding bodies."

Caleb groaned aloud. "We were diving—*hoping* to find a body—when I found the guy in his car. Wrong body, but a mystery solved." He fell silent for a moment. They had assumed that his first discovery had nothing to do with the missing girls. Had they been wrong?

Frederick J. Russell, banker. That was who he'd turned out to be.

"Floby, you finished the autopsy on Frederick Russell, right?" he asked.

"Of course."

"And what did you find?"

"He drowned."

"Had he been drinking?"

"No."

"So how did he wind up in the water?"

"I assume he was speeding."

"Did he have a lot of speeding tickets?"

"How should I know? I'm the M.E., not a traffic cop," Floby said. "I give the police my findings, and they take it from there." Floby looked at him. "You can't think Russell was involved with the missing girls, do you? At the very least, the man was in the water before Winona Hart disappeared."

"It's just the timing of his death that intrigues me," Caleb said. "And the fact that we found him while we were looking for Winona. I'm not saying there was a connection, I'm just curious. For the moment."

"Interesting. All right, you've got Frederick Russell and the unidentified woman from the beach. Then there are two missing girls, and a houseful of bones. And we need to discover what—if anything—some or all of them, have in common. We know the unidentified woman had an opiate mixed with a hallucinogenic in her system.

325

Russell was clean. Jennie Lawson? She's a total mystery, other than that she and Winona look like twins. Then we have rumors about murders and disappearances from the Civil War era, bodies in the walls, and now a body in a trunk. Are we actually trying to connect everything?"

"We? You just said you were an M.E., not a cop," Caleb reminded him.

"An intrigued M.E.," Floby admitted. "Does Jamison know you're trying to put all these pieces together?" he asked.

"Not yet, but he will. I just haven't had a chance to talk to him about it yet."

Cary Hagan opened the door to their knock, looking gorgeous even in workout clothing, the kind of fancy sweats you saw on models in pricey catalogues. The kind of clothes most people would never actually wear to work out in. But Cary was wearing them—to spend her time with a man who was a hundred years old.

"Hi, how are you guys?" Cary asked, as if it were the most natural thing in the world that the two of them had come by first thing in the morning. "Mr. Griffin will be thrilled to have company."

Will was staring at Cary the way a dog stared at a juicy bone. Sarah didn't doubt that her cousin really cared about Caroline, and she was sure it would be hard for any male *not* to be entirely charmed by Cary Hagan, but she had the sudden fear that he might actually start drooling. He looked positively hypnotized.

Sarah nudged him in the ribs. "Um, sorry. We're fine. How are you—and Mr. Griffin?"

Cary just laughed. "We're both fine, too. Come on in. He's in the parlor, reading."

Mr. Griffin's house was built along the same lines as Sarah's, and Cary led them into the parlor on the left.

Mr. Griffin, resting in an armchair, an afghan over his knees, looked up when they entered. He barely glanced at Will before fixing his gaze on Sarah.

"You've come to see me. Thank you. Have you learned any more about what I told you?" he asked her anxiously.

Cary, who probably heard him talk about the past all the time and was glad they were there to listen, said, "I don't know about you all, but I need some coffee, and I'm getting Mr. Griffin's favorite tea all set up. I'll be right back." With a smile, she was out the door.

As soon as she was gone, Mr. Griffin looked at Will suspiciously and spoke to Sarah as if Will couldn't hear. "Who is he?" he asked her.

"This is my cousin, Will Perkins. He's one of my best friends."

Mr. Griffin smiled, seemingly satisfied.

"Mr. Griffin," Sarah said, "we've discovered that a number of women disappeared here in town during the Civil War, and at least some of them seem to have been linked to my house. You said your daughter disappeared in 1928, and that she was on her way to my house when it happened. I was hoping you could tell me a little more about what was going on then, if maybe other girls went missing then, too, if maybe what's happening now is repeating a pattern that's played out at least twice before."

He looked at her thoughtfully. "When I heard about the skeletons in the wall, I was hoping you would find Clara," he said softly. "Then I was hoping you wouldn't." He looked away for a minute. "They said that the housekeeper kept a book, the witch Martha Tyler."

"I was asking about your daughter, Mr. Griffin," she said gently. "Not the Civil War."

"I know exactly what you asked me, young lady, and I'm trying to answer!" he snapped.

"I'm sorry," she said quickly.

Mr. Griffin rolled his eyes impatiently. "Here's what I'm trying to explain," he said. "Soon after Cato MacTavish left St. Augustine, there was a tragedy at the house. Brennan's daughter, Nellie, fell from her bedroom window and died on the stone walkway in front of the house. And soon after that, the townspeople marched on the place. You won't find this written in any book—it's a story my father told me. They dragged the housekeeper out of the house, and they took her out to the unhallowed ground behind the cemetery wall, where they hanged her. Before she died, she cursed the house. She said that others would find her 'book.' And when they did, she would come back, and all the beautiful young girls would die. I didn't believe any of it. I thought it was nothing but fodder for the tourists. But there was a different Brennan—old man Brennan's grandson, the son of the son who'd been fighting up north during the war—who was running the old mortuary then. He had a daughter, and she had friends, including my Clara. Two of them supposedly ran off with boys their folks wouldn't approve of, while my Clara just went out to visit her one day and never came home." He looked toward the door, as if assuring himself that no one else was there—including Cary—then leaned closer and whispered heatedly, "The housekeeper's book exists, and someone has it, and that's why girls are disappearing again. Find whoever has the book, and you'll solve the murders."

Cary Hagan came back in then, walking as smoothly and gracefully as a southern breeze, her smile as brilliant as the sun. She was carrying a silver tray with a coffee service, a cup of tea and a plate of fresh baked muffins. "Here we are. Mr. Griffin, I have your tea right here. Oh . . . ! I should have asked. Would either of you prefer tea?" she asked Sarah and Will.

"Coffee is great, thank you," Sarah said.

"Anything you have is just fine for me," Will told her.

Sarah wanted to smack him. He was fawning again.

As Cary started serving, Mr. Griffin pointed to a painting on the wall. "That's the old Castillo, done at the turn of century. Beautiful, isn't it?" he asked. He clearly wasn't going to say anything more about the murders. Will might be too smitten to see it, but Sarah was very aware that Mr. Griffin didn't want to speak in front of his own nurse.

As soon as she politely could, Sarah made their excuses and dragged Will out.

"What's the matter with you?" she asked the minute they were back on the sidewalk. "Don't you see? Mr. Griffin doesn't trust Cary."

"Oh, come on," he protested, looking back toward the house. "You're just jealous because she's so gorgeous, so you don't want to trust her."

"Will! I am not jealous. I'm . . . suspicious."

"You're being ridiculous, Sarah. Some sicko is doing this. How can you possibly think that it's Cary Hagan?"

She shook her head and started walking more quickly.

"It's pretty obvious that she's having an affair with Tim Jamison," Will said, hurrying to catch up with her. "So what do you think? She ditches

Mr. Griffin, lures young women with some kind of drugs, kills them, bathes in their blood or whatever—and then sleeps with the cop in charge of the case?"

"Look, I didn't say she was guilty of anything, I just said that she was suspicious," Sarah told him. Her cell phone started ringing and she quickly pulled it out of her pocket, expecting it to be Caleb calling to say that he and Floby were at her house.

But it wasn't Caleb. It was Caroline.

"Sarah, can you get over to the museum quickly? Please?"

"Okay," Sarah said slowly, wondering why Caroline sounded so upset. Caroline wasn't a fool; if there were a real emergency, she would have called 911. "Why?" Sarah asked.

"Just hurry, please," Caroline said. "Oh, Sarah, it's so awful!"

"What's so awful?" Sarah asked.

Will was staring at her tensely. "Awful?" he echoed. "What's so awful?"

Sarah frowned and waved a hand in the air, trying to shush him until she understood herself.

"Last night . . . last night Barry and Renee got into a fight. Barry left, Renee decided to go bar-hopping and . . . oh, Sarah! She was attacked."

Floby looked at the body in the trunk and shook his head sadly. "Poor woman."

"Well?"

331

"Well what? She's practically mummified," Floby said. "What do you want from me? Time of death?"

"Any opinions?" Caleb asked.

"Not at this moment," Floby said slowly. "I'll tell you, though, I would love to do the autopsy on this one. For the body to be as well-preserved as this one is . . . I'm thinking that she might have been drained of blood, like our Jane Doe from the beach." He sighed. "Thing is, Caleb, this is another case for the university guys."

"It's a body found in a suspicious context in a private residence, Floby. You have every right to handle it."

Floby didn't answer as he knelt down by the trunk, opening his pathology kit. "First I'll take a tissue sample—we should be able to get DNA, and that's what interests you most, right?"

"It interests me, yes. Stopping the killing interests me more."

"It would be impossible for this woman's killer to be killing anyone else now," Floby pointed out.

"I need to know how she died," Caleb said. "I want to know about drugs in her system."

Floby groaned. "I'll do my best."

"So call for a meat wagon to come get the corpse."

"I can't do that without calling the cops, and you know it," Floby told him.

"I'll call Jamison myself," Caleb said. "This is important."

Caleb reached for his phone, but as he did so, it began to ring. Sarah.

"Caleb—" she began, but her next words beeped out by his call waiting.

It was Jamison on the other line.

"Sarah, hold on."

"Wait! I need to tell—"

He'd already switched over. "I need to know every little thing you've discovered since you've been here, and I need to know it now," Tim Jamison said with no preamble. "Because Renee Otten was attacked last night."

14

Sarah had always loved what she did, and she loved where she did it.

But today she was ready to scream, because all she could think about was Renee. On top of that, one boy of about ten was fascinated with the legend of Osceola, and he was driving her crazy.

"How *much* of his head was cut off?" the boy asked. "The whole thing? I heard that he runs around St. Augustine at night looking for his head."

The kid next to him stuck out his arms in a Frankenstein's monster pose and started to chant, "I want my head. I want my head."

The parents merely smiled benignly at their charming children.

"Excuse me, please," Sarah said, glaring at Caroline across the room. "Miss Roth will help you with your questions."

And then she escaped quickly to the employee lounge, where she dug through her purse, anxious to find her phone.

They hadn't kept Renee in the hospital; she hadn't wanted to stay, and the blow she'd taken on the head hadn't caused a concussion, so it hadn't been deemed serious enough for them to force her to stay.

Barry had, predictably, been feeling both upset

and guilty, so he had taken the day off to be with her.

And now everything seemed to be going to hell, Sarah thought. She'd managed to get in one quick conversation with Caleb after he'd left her on hold for what had seemed like an hour. Despite her hope that everything could be kept low-key, he'd had no choice but to involve the police. Floby had claimed the body for an initial autopsy, but after that, the state would certainly be trying to take charge.

"But Floby *is* the state," she said.

"Yes, but . . . there are all kinds of legalities when such an old corpse is discovered. Listen, I'll talk to you later. I have to go talk with Jamison right now," he'd told her.

And so, with a corpse in her house and Caleb with the cops, and Renee in a state and Barry with her, she'd been left with no choice but to offer visitors a plastic smile and do her best to be cordial.

But those two boys had about done her in.

She looked at her watch, praying that the day was nearing an end and disappointed that it wasn't, and was about to put through a call to Caleb when Caroline came in, bringing Cary Hagan in with her.

Sarah closed her phone, surprised.

Cary must have seen the look in her eyes, because she hurried to speak. "I'm sorry, but I heard about Renee, and I just wanted to tell you how sorry I am. I never should have let her leave like that."

Sarah shook her head blankly. "I'm sorry. I don't know what you're talking about."

"I feel responsible for what happened to Renee. She was with me last night," Cary explained.

"Oh?" Sarah said, still confused.

"Renee ran into me at a bar over on South Castillo. She was angry with Barry, and she was downing bourbon and soda really quick. She seemed all right, though—just upset with Barry for not understanding that she likes to dance, and it doesn't have anything to do with flirting. And then she got a call before she left, so I was sure she was meeting up with Barry again. . . . But with everything going on, I never should have let her leave alone, no matter what, and I just wanted to apologize and say how glad I am that she's going to be okay."

Sarah nodded and smiled. "Thank you. We're grateful that she's all right, too."

"And, please, come by the house more often. You made Mr. Griffin's day. Most of the time he just sits around, thinking about the past. The man doesn't have a single physical ailment other than old age, but he needs to start living in the present. He was so much happier after you came by," Cary said, offering her a brilliant smile.

"I'm glad to hear it. I'll make a point of dropping in on him more often, then."

"Wonderful. So . . . I'll see y'all," Cary said, and with a cheery wave, she was gone.

"What the hell was that all about—really?" Caroline asked.

"She wanted to apologize?" Sarah suggested. "Either that, or she's just trying to be friendly."

"Then she should stop sleeping with married men," Caroline said with a sniff, before changing the subject. "Hey, my folks will be back in an hour or two, and then you'll be able to leave. Take tomorrow off to make up for today, why don't you? Barry will be coming back in, and Renee said she'd rather be working than sitting around being afraid."

"Well, good for her, I guess. But it's still terrifying to think of her being attacked that way."

"I talked to her, and she said she felt kind of dizzy when she left the bar and knew she probably shouldn't have been walking alone, and then suddenly she didn't realize quite where she was. That was when she saw lights. She can remember the lights. Then . . . nothing. She was conked on the head and woke up in the hospital sometime around two a.m. Apparently someone saw her lying there and got her to the hospital, then took off."

"Was her purse stolen? What do you think her attacker wanted?"

"No, and I don't know," Caroline said.

"Why just hit someone on the head if you're not

337

going to steal something from them—or worse?" Sarah asked. "It doesn't make any sense."

"I know, but look, I have to get back out there. Hang in with me just another hour or so, please?"

"Don't worry. I'll hang in as long as you need me."

"Thanks," Caroline said. "We need to stick together these days." She shivered, then hurried out of the room.

Caleb felt as if he'd been sitting in Jamison's office—wasting time—for an eternity. Jamison was aggravated with him, he knew, complaining that Caleb hadn't kept him fully informed about his follow-up investigation into the woman who'd been on the beach the night of the party.

Now, however, Caleb had been over everything he'd discovered, and Tim Jamison was still hostile. "You had a clue—and you went out without telling me?" Jamison demanded.

"Look, it was a worthless trip. The Martha Tyler in Cassadaga is elderly and petite, and she wasn't running around on the beach the night the Hart girl disappeared."

"She's a medium," Jamison said. "She didn't tell you where to find the killer?" he asked sarcastically.

"No, she didn't," Caleb said and leaned forward. "Look, it's very possible you have a living witness—Renee Otten. Why aren't we with her now, pressuring her to tell you what she knows?"

"I've already questioned her," Jamison said.

Caleb hesitated. He wanted to remind Jamison that the police had also questioned the kids from the beach and hadn't come up with Martha Tyler's name, but that wouldn't help their working relationship—quite the opposite, so he refrained.

"I'd like to speak with her myself."

Jamison shook his head. "She got hit on the head while she was walking home drunk. The girl's an idiot. Who takes off alone knowing that a killer is loose in the city? Whoever attacked her, it wasn't our killer or she'd be missing and probably dead right now."

"Unless someone came up and interrupted the killer before he could carry her off."

"What do you think we are—backwoods yokels?" Jamison asked. "We've released her picture, and the media are asking for help, anonymous tips included, from anyone who might have seen something."

"Even so, do you mind if I question her myself?"

"If she'll see you, you have my blessing. But I want to know everything—and I do mean everything—you find out. Which reminds me, why were you so insistent on Floby taking the newest body from the Grant house?" Jamison sounded seriously aggravated. He'd been looking worn-out before; today he really looked like hell. His suit was wrinkled, and his shoes were muddy. He leaned back in his chair, popping an antacid. "Well?" he persisted.

"I think that corpse is an ancestor of mine," Caleb said.

Jamison frowned. "Excuse me?"

"Sarah McKinley did some research, and she found a direct link from Cato MacTavish to me. If I'm right and that corpse is Cato's fiancée Eleanora, there's a possibility she's my whatever-number-of-greats grandmother."

Jamison shook his head. "Look, Eleanora Stewart died or disappeared halfway through the war, and the odds are that your ancestor did her in. Meanwhile, I have two women still missing, another one dead on the beach, and you're trying to catch a killer from the 1800s. Are you here on a case, or are you just looking for your roots?"

"I didn't know a damned thing about the Grant house before I got here," Caleb said, trying to control his temper. Jamison was being a jerk, but he was still the lead homicide investigator and someone Caleb needed on his side.

Adam Harrison had a way of staying calm under duress that Caleb envied. Adam said it had nothing to do with being the better man; it was just a good way of making the other guy realize he was being a jerk. Caleb tried it now, sitting back and letting Jamison take the lead.

"You've talked with Floby, so you know about the drugs in our corpse's system, right?" Jamison asked.

"An opium derivative and yaupon holly," Caleb said.

"Yaupon holly, a key ingredient of the so-called 'black drink,'" Jamison said. "There actually might be someone out there trying to relive the past. Maybe trying to get revenge for the way his people were treated way back when."

Caleb groaned aloud. "Come on, Jamison. You're a trained cop. Are you really trying to convince me that a modern-day Seminole is imitating his ancestors and murdering women because of some centuries-old vendetta? That's absurd."

"You're the one suggesting that we've had a killer hanging around for more than a hundred and fifty years. Now *that's* absurd."

"I never said that. I'm saying we have a killer who is either imitating the past or honestly believes in black magic. I think you have a couple, a man and a woman, who are doing the killing, but for exactly what reason, I don't know, though the body on the beach was drained of blood, and that may have something to do with it. It's a theory of mine, that there are two people involved. One to do the luring, maybe. The logistics involved, toting, carrying, and all in the dark—I'd say two people. One with the real power of persuasion. One easily led. I'll tell you one thing for sure, this is someone who knows the area, who knows the history—and the legends."

Jamison stood up. "I'm going to follow the

Seminole lead—and the yaupon holly. I also have men in the streets watching every ghost tour, history tour and haunted happening out there. I don't think Miss Otten will speak with you—she seems to be afraid of you. But knock yourself out. Do whatever you want short of trespassing, harassing or making a public nuisance out of yourself."

"I think you're on the wrong track, and I think you're wasting time—time we don't have. Renee was attacked last night, and that means the killer is stepping up the pace. We need to find out who it is quickly, before someone else goes missing or dies."

Without a word, Jamison walked to the door to his office and held it open, waiting. As he left, Caleb noticed again that Jamison's shoes were covered with mud.

As soon as Sarah was able to leave the museum, she headed over to Renee Otten's place.

Renee had rented a small free-standing town-home just outside the historic section of the city. She had decorated it pleasantly with a mixture of modern furniture and period pieces, old throws, tapestry pillows, framed prints and bric-a-brac.

Barry opened the door for Sarah, and she looked past him to see Renee sitting on the sofa, propped up on a pillow, with a tray holding the remnants of tea and toast.

Sarah turned to Barry and asked, "She doing all right?"

Barry nodded, then spoke, his voice low. "She got lucky. Insanely lucky. She drank too much, she was mad at me . . . thank God some Good Samaritan came along and got her to the hospital. She'll be happy to see you." Then he frowned suddenly and asked, "What are *you* doing out on your own?"

She was surprised by the question. Yes, the world was getting scary, but it was broad daylight. She smiled, though, glad that he was concerned. "It's the middle of the afternoon! And I told Caroline exactly where I was going, and I'll give her a buzz to let her know I got here. Will had to work this afternoon, but they'll both be over later."

"I just don't want anything to happen to anyone else. I just can't help thinking this was my fault," Barry said miserably.

Sarah touched his face. "Stop that. It's *not* your fault."

"Yes, it is. With everything going on around here, I should have followed her all over town whether she was mad at me or not," Barry said.

"Hey!" Renee called. "I can hear you, you know."

Sarah smiled reassuringly at Barry, then walked into the other room, and leaned down to give Renee a hug and a kiss on the cheek.

Despite the bandage on her forehead, Renee looked better than Barry.

Sarah took the chair across the coffee table from her and said, "What the hell happened? Cary Hagan came by the museum to say she was sorry—she thinks it's *her* fault."

Renee had the grace to look guilty. "It was my fault and no one else's. I had a few drinks with Cary—I remember that—and then, after I left the bar, I remember feeling really woozy."

"Alcohol will do that in large quantities," Barry said.

"Very funny. I was walking down the street, and . . . I know this sounds crazy, but I saw lights. And then I woke up in the hospital. I'm really lucky. I don't even have a concussion," Renee said.

"Are you sure you were attacked?" Sarah asked. "I mean . . . it sounds as if you might have just passed out. The bandage is on your forehead. Maybe you just crashed forward."

"The doctor said she was struck with a heavy object—like a big flashlight," Barry said. "That's why they called the cops. Tim Jamison took the case, and then he called me right after he got there."

"I know this will sound crazy, and I admit I was loaded, but . . ." Renee hesitated, staring at Sarah.

"Tell her," Barry said.

"Tell me what?"

"All right, I didn't say this to the police, because they just would've said I was crazy, but . . .

344

someone was there. A car pulled up. I remember hearing it, but I didn't see anyone get out. And then, I could swear I saw Caleb Anderson all dressed up in some kind of costume, heading straight for me. And that's all I remember," Renee said miserably.

Sarah was silent, stunned. Had Renee also seen the ghost of Cato MacTavish?

"Caleb was with me," she said.

Barry cleared his throat. "You're not just saying that, right?" he asked her.

"No, I swear to you, he was with me. But, Renee, you should have told the police the truth."

"I wanted to talk to you first," Renee said. "I mean, you're seeing him and all, so I . . ." She trailed off.

But Sarah was barely listening. Caleb had been with her all through the night, until he had awakened to follow a ghost—Cato's ghost—up to her attic.

What the hell had Cato been up to last night? And if he was innocent, as he claimed and her reading seemed to prove, why would he have harmed Renee? Or had he been the one to save her by scaring the killer away?

"It's frightening, whatever you saw," Sarah said. "No matter what, you can't be alone anymore. Promise?"

"I promise," Renee assured her, then said, "You need to be careful, too, you know. I don't care what anyone says, I think someone locked you in your basement. Maybe they just wanted to scare you—or maybe you weren't supposed to get out."

Before he could leave the station and head for Renee's place, Caleb heard his name called.

"Mr. Anderson?"

He stopped and turned, and saw a uniformed officer standing nearby, a young man with dark close-cropped hair, dark eyes, bronze skin and square cheekbones.

Native American?

Caleb strode toward him.

The man spoke quickly. "Officer Jim Tiger," he offered, shaking Caleb's hand. "Can you meet me around the corner at the Coquina Café? I can't talk here," he said.

"I'll see you there," Caleb said.

By the time Caleb had ordered two cups of coffee, Officer Tiger arrived. He accepted one of the cups, saying, "Thanks. The stuff at the station tastes like dishwater. Come on out the back. There's a terrace, and no one will see us there."

As Caleb followed him out, Tiger kept speaking. "Look, I'm not trying to be disloyal or anything, but I'm worried about Jamison. The mayor is down his throat, so he's getting desperate. And the thing is . . . he hasn't been himself lately. If you ask me, he's grasping at straws. I don't think we should have called the Frederick

Russell case an accidental death as quickly as we did. And now he's accusing you of chasing old legends, while he thinks we have a vengeful Indian on the warpath."

"Are you a Seminole?"

"Miccosukee, from way down south. We're a separate tribe, but back in the day, we were all lumped together as Seminole. We have a black drink ceremony, too, though, and that's what's getting to me here. Jamison is way off base on this. He's ranting on about the fact that the woman you found on the beach had been drugged. And because of the yaupon holly in her blood, he's decided it's a vendetta. That's just crazy." He hesitated for a second. "Look, I love my job. I love St. Augustine. I even think the world of Jamison—most of the time. But he's taking the wrong road on this one. I just . . . well, I'm just hoping you'll keep looking in a different direction, because I'm telling you, this has nothing to do with the Seminole. Trust me," he said, "we were warriors once, and we fought desperately to stay alive and stay here, where we'd had our home forever. But we didn't drain anyone's blood, and we didn't run around drugging people."

"Thanks for coming to me with this," Caleb told him. "Is there anything else I might not know?"

"Yaupon holly. It's not a sedative. In fact, it tends to make a person more alert. It *can* cause delusions in sufficient quantity." He laughed. "The black drink is like . . . like a night out with your frat brothers. You go a little crazy, but you don't start killing people and draining their blood."

"But if you drugged someone with enough of it, could you convince them that something was happening—when it wasn't?" Caleb asked.

"Oh, hell, yeah. I convinced myself once that I was a flying eagle. I jumped off a bridge and nearly broke a leg," Jim Tiger told him.

"Thanks. This has been very helpful." They shook hands.

After they parted ways, Caleb decided that before going to see Renee, he would make a side trip to the hospital.

"You're not going back to your house, are you?" Renee demanded when Sarah rose to leave.

"No, not right now. And don't worry. I won't be alone," Sarah assured her.

"You should stay right here," Renee insisted.

"I'll be all right. I'm going to take a tour, actually," Sarah said, surprising herself, wondering when she had made that decision.

She wasn't ready to go back to the house, though. That much she knew. Renee's words were haunting her. *Maybe you weren't supposed to get out. . . .*

She felt shaken, disturbed that Renee, too, had seen Cato's ghost.

On top of that, the events in the diaries were

plaguing her, and she wanted to get an overview, one untainted by her own take on both history and recent events.

What better way than by taking a tour?

And she certainly wouldn't be alone.

"All right then, but be careful," Barry said.

Sarah said her goodbyes and left Renee's apartment, then hurried down to the Castillo. Once there, she bought a ticket for one of the popular tram tours, then called Caroline to tell her what she was doing, since they'd agreed that keeping tabs on each other was the safest practice.

The tour director was a guy named Gil Vinici, who she knew from school. He saw her as he was collecting the tickets and arched a brow. "What the hell are you doing here, Sarah? Should I bring you up front and let you do the talking?"

She laughed. "No thanks, I feel the need to hear a different voice."

He grew serious. "I heard about the house. Are you selling it?"

"No way."

"Why would you, come to think of it. This is St. Augustine. Someone probably died in every historic house in town," he said. "So . . . want to come sit up front with me, anyway?"

"Sure, thanks."

She leaned back once the tour started and enjoyed hearing him speak. Gil was good. It wasn't a ghost tour, but he had a few grisly stories to tell, even so, like the one about the time that the garroting of a prisoner on the plaza had failed, so the prisoner had gone free. They went by the spectacular hotels built by Henry Flagler, and Gil talked about how Flagler's second wife, Ida Alice, had attempted to kill him. He'd managed to obtain a divorce instead. Gil was informative and amusing, but he wasn't saying anything that spurred any new thoughts in Sarah's mind.

At one of the cemetery stops, Gil explained that there had been many more gravestones at one time, but now the road extended over many of those graves, and corpses were often found whenever the foundation was dug for a new building.

He let his tour group off to take pictures and turned to Sarah. "I guess your house isn't all that unusual, come to think of it." He cleared his throat. "I, uh, do go by there and talk about the bones in the walls, you know."

She smiled. "It's all right. I would, too."

"Hey, how's your friend? I saw the article about her in the paper today. The police are asking for help in finding out who attacked her. They seem to think maybe it's linked to Winona Hart's disappearance, and maybe even that dead woman they found on the beach."

"I don't know," Sarah said.

"I hope they catch whoever it is," Gil said. "As you can see, business is suffering."

There weren't as many people on the tour as she

would have expected, Sarah had to admit. As they sat there, a woman came up to Gil.

"There are a couple of broken headstones over there," she said. "On the other side of the wall. Why did they leave some of the graves outside the wall when they built it?"

"Actually, those graves were intentionally dug beyond the wall. This part of the cemetery was consecrated. It's hallowed ground. On the other side of the wall, the not-so-holy were set to rest. Suicides, murderers . . . They didn't always get markers. Oh, and that little area over there, where you see the oaks and cypress, and all that moss? That's where a witch was supposedly hanged. Some people claim to get all kinds of strange vibes from over there."

Sarah suddenly jumped down from her seat.

"Hey, what's up? Where are you going?" he asked her.

"Oh, just looking around. Don't leave without me," she teased.

Sarah walked along the wall and found a place where she could get across, then walked over to the copse where the cypress and oaks seemed to hug one another in the shadows, the dripping moss like extended arms.

She looked at the earth beside the wall on that side.

It was disturbed, as if it had been dug up. She drew out her phone. It didn't take great pictures, but they might be good enough.

351

At the hospital, Caleb waited patiently for the orderly who had first seen Renee to get a minute to talk to him. Luckily he didn't have to wait long, since nothing much was going on in the emergency room. Someone was waiting with a sprained ankle, someone else had gotten cut up on a coquina shell and a girl sat in one corner, sneezing.

The orderly was a young man named Rick Diehl, and he seemed happy to talk to Caleb once he had seen his credentials. "I told the cops everything I could think of, which isn't much," he admitted.

"You found her—just outside the emergency doors?" Caleb asked.

Rick nodded. "She was just over there," he said, pointing. "I saw her lying there all crumpled up, and I went running out there. Two of the nurses and the doctor on duty followed me, so we got her inside real quick. There was a lot of blood on her forehead—looked like she'd been whacked with something."

"Did you hear a car out there before you saw her?" Caleb asked him.

"No, sorry."

"Are there security cameras out there?" Caleb asked.

"Yeah—but it's a funny thing. The camera covers the area up to that trash can there. She was left just on the other side of it. Anyway, if there really is a serial killer out there and that's who attacked her, she's lucky as hell to be alive."

Caleb thanked him, and managed to talk to the doctor who had treated Renee, a harried man in his forties named Martin Thayer. Since he was just getting off work, he gave Caleb a few minutes as they walked to his car.

"Lucky girl," Thayer said, casting a glance Caleb's way. "What with everything that's going on around here." He shook his head. "I saw Winona Hart in the E.R. just a few days before she went missing. Nice girl. Cute. A real flirt, but nice."

"What was wrong with her?" Caleb asked.

"She had a burn on her hand. She told me it was from incense. But she was with a friend, and they both kept giggling and whispering and looking through this book they had. I think she was playing around with some kind of spell book."

"You saw the book?" Caleb asked, suddenly excited. "What did it look like? Was it old?"

"No, no, just a paperback. I wasn't really looking. I just took care of her hand and told her to quit playing with fire. She was silly—she was young. But she was a sweet kid."

"What about Renee Otten? What was up with her?"

"We checked her alcohol level, that was for damned sure. She came to pretty fast. She was dazed, kind of panicky. Tim Jamison was here in seconds—I swear, it really was just seconds—after we called, and he was pretty brisk with her, mad as all hell that she'd been out running around alone."

"Do you know if she was on drugs? Maybe opiates, or strange herbs?" Caleb asked.

"We didn't do extensive drug testing, We were more interested in getting an X-ray of her skull. The cops didn't ask me for anything else."

"Jamison was here, and he didn't ask you to do any drug testing?" Caleb said.

"We still have the blood." The doctor looked at him. "But I'll need authorization to do anything with it," he said.

"Don't worry," Caleb told him. "I'll put in a phone call. Your superiors won't give you an argument."

"Me? Nope, not me. I'm on my way home," Doctor Thayer said. But he was already wearing a sinking expression, as if he'd just been dragged off the beach. "All right, I'll go back in and get things started. I won't wait for the results, though. They'll call me, and I'll call you."

"Fair enough," Caleb said.

He left Thayer and put through a call to Adam, bringing him up-to-date and asking him to pull strings and get the tests authorized. He warned Adam that Jamison was behaving strangely, and that he wasn't Jamison's favorite person at the moment.

Adam assured him that he would make sure that

Caleb didn't have any trouble with the authorities. "How's Sarah doing?" Adam asked.

"She's fine. She's great," Caleb said. "That's right—you two know each other."

"Whatever you do, let her talk . . . draw her out. I think that young woman has capabilities we haven't seen yet," Adam said. "And to think—I sent you down there on behalf of the Lawsons, and you've discovered your past."

"Yeah, great. There's supposedly a ghost running around town looking just like me."

"And you've seen this ghost?" Adam asked, amused.

"I've . . . had a dream," Caleb said stubbornly.

"Dreams are the mind's way of accessing the levels we don't use when we're awake, maybe even a means of communication. Don't close your mind to anything, Caleb."

"Trust me, Adam, I never have. Now, hang up on me and get hold of the powers that be—I need to know if that girl was drugged last night or not."

Adam promised, "Will do," and hung up.

Caleb was finally about to head over to see Renee Otten when his cell phone rang. He didn't recognize the number but decided to answer anyway.

It was a husky female voice. "Mr. Anderson?"

"Yes?"

"Martha Tyler gave me your number."

For a moment, he was blank. Martha Tyler, the

witch who had lived and died a hundred and fifty years ago?

Of course not, he realized almost instantaneously. Martha Tyler, the medium.

"Who are you?" he asked.

"Ginger Russell. Mrs. Frederick Russell. You found my husband's body at the bottom of the bay. Please, I need to speak with you."

"I'm very sorry for your loss, but I'm afraid I'm fairly busy—"

"Please, Mr. Anderson, you don't understand. My husband's death was no accident. He was murdered."

15

The disturbed earth bothered her, but Sarah wasn't sure why or where to go with her feelings of unease. She could just imagine calling the police to tell them that she might have found a body. When they asked her where and she said "The cemetery," they would laugh her into the next county.

She tried calling Caleb, but he told her that he was meeting with Frederick Russell's widow and would have to call her back. Before hanging up, he asked her if she was still at work, and she glanced around the street, nearly empty now that the tour was over. She told him no, but not to worry, she was fine, then blurted out, "I'm at church. Lots of people around."

Once the lie was out and she'd hung up, it actually seemed like a good idea.

Okay, so there weren't *lots* of people.

She was still certain she was safe in church. And there were things she could do there. Useful things.

Sarah used the fact that she was a local and owned a piece of local history to get permission to look into the church records. The Cathedral of the Basilica, dating from 1565, was the oldest house of worship in the city and had the oldest records in the United States, since the parish had been founded immediately upon the Spaniards' arrival. But the English tended to be Anglican or Episcopalian. Trinity was founded later, in 1821, but, still, it would offer wonderful records.

Though she hadn't come across any reference to religion as far as the MacTavishes or the Brennans went, she was pretty sure that they would have been Episcopalian, since the majority of Americans at the time had been Episcopalians.

Mrs. Hopkins, the secretary in charge of the records room, had been good friends with Sarah's mother and was glad to see Sarah. She commiserated with her about the strange events taking place in their beloved city—and in Sarah's beloved house.

There were several documents Sarah was actively looking for, particularly a death certificate for Nellie Brennan and a birth certificate for Magnus MacTavish, who might have been born there, out of wedlock, since Eleanora and Cato had never married—or might have been born in Virginia to some other woman entirely.

At last she found one of the pieces of information she had been seeking, buried in a long list of births and deaths in an old parish record book.

Nellie Brennan had died on May 16th, 1866. She had been seventeen years old. The old cursive script wasn't easy to decipher, but there was a notation that she had died from a fall, just as Mr. Griffin had said.

Had Brennan killed his own daughter?

Sarah was afraid he had. Nellie had seen too much. She had known what he was doing, something Sarah was certain she knew, too.

He'd been abducting and killing young women, draining their blood for some awful, probably ritualistic, reason. He had most likely killed Eleanora Stewart first—and stuffed her body in a trunk in the attic, then moved on to other victims, some of whom had probably ended up behind the walls of the house.

His accomplice had been the witch Martha Tyler, who had helped him lure the girls with promises of love potions, then met her end at the hands of a lynch mob and died cursing the Grant house.

But she'd had a book. A book of magic, a book of spells. Spells that required human blood.

Sarah was about to give up the search when she found another entry that looked as if it could well be the other one she'd been most eager to find.

Baptized 1862, male child, Mag S, child of E.S.

Was that it? The record of Magnus Anderson? Born under his mother's name, Stewart? *S*—for Stewart?

The full names—even the child's first name—weren't written out, as if whoever had made the entries knew the truth and wished to hide it, presumably to protect Eleanora's reputation.

She carefully closed the record book and

replaced it on the shelf. The past was falling into place, and nothing she'd found out contradicted her belief that the current atrocities were related to those of the past. But where did they go from there?

She hesitated, not knowing what to do. The afternoon was waning, and it would grow dark soon, so she tried calling Caleb. No answer.

She decided to try Floby, who might have found out something about the body in the attic.

He did answer her call, then groaned when she identified herself.

"Please don't tell me that you've found another body in your house," he said fervently.

"No, but . . . I think I might have found . . . well, I've found a bunch of dirt that's been recently dug up."

"In your yard?"

"No."

"Where?"

"The cemetery."

"The cemetery? Is this some kind of a joke?" he demanded.

"No. Please, Floby . . . can you come out and see what I'm talking about?"

"For God's sake, why?"

"Floby—what if someone was buried there and then dug up? Would you be able to tell?"

"In a cemetery?"

"It's actually outside the cemetery proper, in

unhallowed ground. The thing is . . ." She paused, then drew a deep breath and went on.

"I think the woman Caleb found on the beach might have been buried there, then dug up and thrown in the ocean later."

"All right." He sighed. "Actually, it's already been a theory of mine that she was buried—then dug up and dumped. It's past quitting time anyway, and I won't have the results I want until tomorrow, at least. You shouldn't go wandering around by yourself, though, seeing as it's almost dark. I'll come get you, so just stay put, you hear?"

"Thank you, Floby. I'm right on the plaza, so I'll wait for you in the café near the Casa Monica Hotel, okay?"

"I'll find you."

Frederick Russell's widow, Ginger, was a perfectly named slim redhead. She had pretty features, though looking drawn now, from the sadness that seemed to weigh her down.

She'd suggested they meet in the parlor of an Old Town hotel, now charmingly set for evening tea.

"I'm very sorry for your loss," Caleb said as he took a seat across from her. "But I'm not sure how I can help you. I found your husband's body, but I don't know anything about him or how he came to be there. You said he was murdered, but . . ."

"First you should know that Ricky—sorry, that's

what I called him—didn't speed, and he knew these roads like the back of his hand. He was one of the most responsible people I've ever met. He didn't drink, and he didn't do drugs. There's no way his death was an accident."

"Perhaps there was something wrong with his car," Caleb suggested.

She shook her head, smiling sadly. "No way. He kept it in perfect repair." She took a deep breath, visibly steeling herself. "I've asked around, and I know who you are and why you're here. I'm just curious if you're aware that my husband and the girl you came down here looking for disappeared at pretty much the same time?"

"I knew it had to be around the same time, yes, given when you'd reported him missing. But with the amount of time your husband was in the water, they couldn't establish an exact time of death," Caleb said.

"The night he disappeared, I was talking to Frederick on the phone when he suddenly said something like, 'What the hell . . . ?' And he wasn't in his car then, he was walking in Old Town. He was meeting a client for dinner. I think he saw something, something that bothered him, and went to see what was going on. You had to have known my husband—he would never have passed up a chance to help someone. And that's the last that was seen or heard of him," she said. "But I think—no, I'm sure—that when he went to help, something happened, that he got involved in something he couldn't handle and was killed for it. The police didn't believe me then, and I doubt they'd believe me now, but I'm sure of it."

Caleb glanced at his phone, which he'd set on the table, and realized he'd missed a call.

From Sarah.

He rose. "Mrs. Russell, thank you for calling me. I swear to you, I'll do my absolute best to find out what happened to your husband, and whether his death is related to the disappearances of these girls."

She offered him her sad smile again. "I know you will. Martha Tyler told me there's something special about you. That you would help me."

"That was very kind of her. I'll keep in touch," he promised.

He walked out onto Charlotte Street and pulled out his phone, trying to reach Sarah. He felt his heart slamming as the phone rang.

But then she answered. "Caleb?"

"I'm here."

"I was just trying to reach you. I need you to meet me as soon as you can."

"In church?"

A long moment of silence followed, and his eyes narrowed in suspicion as he waited for her answer, and then he cursed silently when she finally replied.

"No. The cemetery."

• • •

Old Town was usually one of the safest areas of St. Augustine. There were always people about: a dozen different tours going on, locals and tourists filling the bars and restaurants, even people just out walking their dogs.

But that night, when they turned off the main street and headed toward the cemetery, there seemed to be no one around. No one but her—and Floby.

A slight breeze had risen, drifting through the moss that hung from the oaks and cypresses along the way. In the dark, the old cemetery felt lonely and forlorn.

Even Floby seemed creepy in the darkness.

Sarah glanced over at him. His hair was disheveled, and he was bent over staring avidly at the ground.

Like a mad scientist.

Like a man who believed that the blood of virgins would restore his vigor and his youth.

She mocked herself for her fear; she doubted that any of the recent victims had been virgins, and she herself certainly wasn't. Apparently it wasn't virgin blood that was needed, just the blood of the young.

"Where exactly are we going?" he asked, his glasses slipping down on his nose so he had to look over the top of the wire frames at her.

"The copse—where Martha Tyler was lynched,"

364

Sarah said. "But we can wait, if you want. Caleb is on his way." She had stopped as she spoke, but he had kept on walking. Now he turned around, and for a moment the glare of his flashlight blinded her. She felt a sudden and terrible fear that he was suddenly going to grab her and start laughing maniacally.

"Sarah!"

It was Caleb's voice, and she spun around, shaking. He was striding down the street toward them, his steps brisk. "What the hell are you doing out here alone?" he demanded.

"I'm not alone—I'm with Floby," Sarah said. She realized she was shaking—which was absurd, of course. She'd known Floby forever. He wasn't a sadistic killer.

"I'm over here," Floby said, waving his light.

Caleb stared at Sarah. "What are we doing here?"

"Caleb, you said that the Jane Doe found on the beach had been moved—that she hadn't been in the water all that time, that she'd been buried somewhere first. When I came out here today—"

"You came to the cemetery alone?" he interrupted.

"No. I came with a tour group," she said impatiently. "There's a patch of land in the back—it's where the so-called sinners were buried, back in the day. And it's where Martha Tyler was lynched. Someone has been digging back there recently. I

365

wanted to see if someone was . . . buried there now. Or if someone *had* been buried there. Can you tell?"

Floby sighed. "We can take soil samples and find out if any organic material decomposed in the soil, but it's not going to be easy to discover if a body was there, and if so, how recently." He turned to Caleb.

"You have a gun, right?"

"I do."

"And you know how to use it, right?"

"I do."

"Good, because it's dark back there and you never know who might be around," Floby said.

With Floby's light leading the way, they started along the wall.

When they reached the area of disturbed earth, Floby said, "Maybe we should call Jamison."

Caleb stared at the ground, then hunkered down and felt the dirt. "No," he said. "Let's see what we can find first."

He stood up and turned around, looking for something with which to dig. Floby reached into his lab coat and produced a small trowel and several glass bottles. He began to take samples from random spots and depths. "Come help," he told Sarah, and she hurried over to take the sample bottles from him after he filled them.

Caleb came back over with a thick oak branch and started digging. After a while, sweaty and muddy, he leaned on the branch and said, "We could use a real shovel." Then he shoved the branch into the dirt one more time, shaking his head. "We'll have to bring in the cops, but it does look like a good place to dig."

Sarah stared at the point where the branch was sticking into the dirt, and her words caught in her throat.

Fingers—delicate, long fingers—were protruding from the earth, as if a hand were raised in supplication, begging for pity, pleading for help.

She pointed, unable to speak.

"Oh, lordy," Floby said.

Caleb took out his phone and called the police.

Caleb found it difficult standing there next to Jamison while the floodlights lit the small field behind the cemetery. Jamison was quiet, his jaw locked, as they watched the girl being unearthed, and everyone went quiet when Floby carefully dusted the dirt from her face.

It was Winona Hart.

Jamison got on the phone immediately, as a van came to take Winona Hart's corpse back to the morgue in a body bag. Once she was gone, the digging continued, going on all through the night as they kept coming across bones.

Old bones.

It had been decades—at least a hundred years—since the so-called undesirables had been interred on the "unholy" side of the wall, and now they were digging up nothing but the sad and lonely remnants of lives long gone and never appreciated.

"I'm still trying to figure out how you knew to look here," Jamison told Caleb, his tone suspicious, his eyes narrowed.

"It wasn't Caleb, it was me," Sarah informed him. "I heard how this is where the housekeeper from the Grant place was lynched, and when I came out here on a tour today, I started looking around, and I saw how the dirt looked disturbed. Then I remembered that the Jane Doe had been buried before being thrown in the water. I didn't know we'd find Winona Hart, but I thought we might find proof that Jane Doe had been buried here and then dug up."

"I find it more than interesting that you keep finding dead people," Jamison said to Caleb.

Caleb tried to think about everything Adam had ever tried to teach him about keeping his cool. "You know, the night Winona Hart disappeared—"

"You had just gotten to town," Jamison said. "You were with us on the dive the next day. So you were here when she disappeared."

"And you had mud all over your shoes earlier today, before you ever came out here tonight, didn't you?" Caleb countered.

Jamison swore. "I'm a homicide lieutenant, and I know my business. Get out of here—get out of here *now*, before I arrest you."

Furious, Sarah spun around to leave the cemetery. Caleb followed her quickly.

"Hey, Anderson!" Jamison called after them.

In unison, Caleb and Sarah stopped and turned back. They might have been onstage, caught in the unforgiving glare of the floodlights. Everyone working the crime scene stopped awkwardly to watch.

"Don't even think about going anywhere," Jamison said loudly. "I spoke to Renee Otten again today. She thinks she saw you on the street, right before she was attacked."

Caleb stepped forward angrily, but Sarah grabbed his arm to stop him. "Tim, that's impossible, and I told her so. Caleb was with me. We left the bar, walked back to my house and went to bed. We didn't leave until this morning."

"Are you sure he didn't duck out in the middle of the night, Sarah? While you were asleep, maybe?" Jamison asked.

"Of course I'm sure," Sarah said indignantly.

Caleb got hold of his temper at last. "I know exactly where I was, lieutenant. My conscience is completely clear—on every level. Can you say the same?"

Then he took Sarah's arm, and they left together.

It was growing late, so they considered and rejected the idea of stopping at Hunky Harry's, and went straight to the house. Caleb felt more tense than ever before in his life. Sarah went upstairs to take a shower, and when she came down, he was pacing like a caged tiger, furious that Jamison was trying to direct suspicion toward him.

"Get the mud off—you'll feel better," she told him.

He nodded and headed up the stairs. The water was steaming hot, and as he stood beneath it, eventually some of the tension began to ease.

When he went back downstairs, Sarah was busy in the kitchen.

"Omelets," she said.

"That sounds wonderful," he told her, then sat at the counter, grabbed a scratch pad and started making notes as he talked his way through everything they knew so far. "Killed, that we know about—Frederick Russell, banker. His wife claims he went to help someone and got himself murdered, and that he would never have driven off a curve. Jane Doe—we still don't know her story. Winona Hart, found this evening buried in unhallowed ground, near where a witch was hanged."

Sarah came over to stand by him. "Don't forget the past. We know that a girl named Susan Madison was murdered—and that Nellie Brennan saw the corpse. Also, I looked it up in the records today and found out that Nellie herself died from a fall from her bedroom window, not long after she saw the corpse. At least one other girl's corpse turned up, too—and don't forget Eleanora. And then there are the bones in my walls. Maybe they're connected somehow, too. Plus there are several references to Martha Tyler's book of spells. Our killer has to be someone who knows all the stories—who's maybe even found the book—and is trying to replicate history."

She hesitated, then asked, "What was going on tonight between you and Jamison? Why were you talking about mud?"

"When I went to see him at the station today, he had mud all over his shoes. Mud—like the dirt we dug up tonight, outside the cemetery."

"Oh, my God, you can't think that Tim Jamison . . ." Sarah's voice trailed off, but her horror was written all over her face.

"He's a local. He knows the area, the tides, how to fool forensics—and all the stories. And even some of the other cops are starting to talk," Caleb told her.

"Plus he's seeing Cary Hagan," Sarah said thoughtfully.

"Either that—or he wants people to think he's seeing her, setting up an alibi. Better to be an adulterer than a murderer," Caleb said.

"As soon as we're done with dinner, I want to pay a visit to your friend Renee. And then you and I are going bar-hopping."

Barry opened the door when they arrived at Renee's. It was as if he were her guard, making sure that only the worthy were allowed to see the wizard.

"Sarah," he said warmly. "And Caleb," he added, trying to sound polite.

"Hey, Barry," Caleb said smoothly.

Sarah was impressed with the casual ease Caleb maintained when he greeted Barry, knowing what Renee had said.

Without making a big deal of it, Caleb stepped past Barry and went over to Renee, who was sitting up on the sofa and seemed to be just fine. But she looked at Caleb guardedly as he sat down across from her.

"What's going on at the cemetery?" Renee demanded, as Barry sat down beside her. "And don't tell us that you don't know. We saw the two of you in the background on the news report."

"They've found Winona Hart," Caleb said.

"Dead?" Renee asked, wide-eyed.

"I'm afraid so," Caleb said.

"Oh, God." Renee shrank back, as if she could become one with the sofa. "*You* found her, didn't you?" she accused Caleb.

"Actually, I did," Sarah said, sitting down in an empty chair next to Caleb.

Renee's double take was almost humorous. "How? You just decided to go digging in the cemetery?"

"I went on a tour," Sarah told her.

"*You* went on a tour?" Barry said incredulously.

"I needed a fresh perspective," she said, and shrugged.

Caleb was still studying Renee.

"Renee, are you sure that you were attacked last night? That you didn't simply fall? Just how loaded were you?" he asked.

Renee flushed. "Loaded enough to black out, all right? So no, I'm not sure of anything. They said at the hospital that I had been attacked, so I figured . . ."

"And you told the police you saw . . . *me* before whatever happened, happened?" he pressed.

She flushed again. "I saw someone who looked like you, only in costume, coming toward me. I do remember that. I'm not imagining it."

"Okay, and while you were out last night, who else did you see?" Caleb asked.

She stared back at him, her face wrinkled in puzzlement. "I saw all of you, obviously—Caroline, Will, the two of you, Barry. And then, later on, at the Dirty Duck—or maybe it was when I got to the Mainmast, I don't know—I saw . . . I saw all kinds of people. Gary and the guys from his crew were there, a group of tourists who had been over to Cassadaga, some kids who looked too young to be there, if you ask me—"

"You saw Cary Hagan, too, didn't you?" Sarah interrupted. "She came to see me at the museum to apologize for letting you leave on your own."

"Yeah, I saw Cary. She can sure drink. I think

that's where I messed up. I was trying to keep up with her, and she can drink anyone under the table," Renee said.

"What about Tim Jamison?" Caleb asked. "Did you see him anywhere when you were out?"

Renee squinted in thought, then shook her head. "No, I don't think so."

"Okay, Renee, this is really important, so please, think hard. Do you remember any details at all of what happened after you left the Dirty Duck?" Caleb asked her.

She let out a sigh. "Just what I've told people already. I saw lights—they must have been from a car, I guess. And then I saw a guy in Civil War clothes and . . . thought it was you. I didn't tell Jamison at first—only Sarah, when she came to see me. But she said it couldn't have been you, so . . . I don't know. It was *someone*, though, and he must have looked kind of like you. And then someone hit me, or maybe I did just pass out, only everybody is suspicious because . . . there's a killer out there. I just don't *know!*" she practically wailed.

"Hey, hey, it's okay," Barry said reassuringly, putting an arm around her.

"It's all right. We're leaving. Get some rest, Renee. And thanks," Caleb told her.

Sarah gave her a goodbye kiss on the cheek, and then Barry saw them out, locking the door behind them.

"I want to check out the bars she mentioned and see if anyone remembers what she was up to last night," Caleb said.

"Then let's go."

Sarah was surprised to discover that Caleb was carrying a picture of Frederick Russell on him, along with shots of Jennie Lawson, Renee, Winona Hart and Tim Jamison, the latter out of uniform.

They hit paydirt almost immediately with one of the bartenders at the Dirty Duck, who came over and looked at the pictures, then focused on those of Frederick Russell and Jennie Lawson. "Those others are locals, and I see them all the time. But these two . . . I kind of think I do remember them. . . . This is the guy who was just found in the car in the bay, right? I think they were both in here about a year ago."

"Together?" Caleb asked.

"No. No, the guy was alone—we got talking about our favorite local restaurants. And the girl . . . she came in alone, too, I think, but she was the friendly type, talked to a lot of people. She looked pretty blitzed when she left, too. This guy, he left right after her, said he was going to get her into a cab."

Caleb thanked him, and they moved on to the Mainmast, but they didn't find out anything else of interest, so they headed back to the house. He was quiet as they walked.

"Well?" Sarah asked softly at last.

He studied her, touched her hair gently. "You're not afraid of me, are you?" he asked, his expression intent.

She shook her head.

"Are you afraid of . . . my ancestor's ghost?"

She shook her head again, and smiled. "No, though for the first time in my life I believe there really is a ghost. He's trying to help us. He *did* help us. He wanted us to find Eleanora and made sure we did."

He nodded. "Okay, so let's look at what we know. Martha Tyler—the original Martha Tyler—had a book, and she and Brennan used it as part of their MO when they were killing girls back in the day. Now someone's found that book, and they're using it and killing people, too—killing them just like Martha and Brennan did. I'd lay money that Jennie Lawson is dead. She was drinking at the Dirty Duck, and someone spiked her drink. She looked so blitzed because she'd been drugged. Frederick Russell tried to help her and was killed for his pains. I'm assuming they drugged him, too, and decided to make his death appear to be an accident, in case he was ever found. Six months later, the killer took Jane Doe, but for some reason, he, she or they dug up her body, then threw it in the bay. My guess is they intended to do the same with Winona Hart's body, except that you found it first. Last night, one of two things happened. Either Renee just got shit-faced and fell, and some Good

Samaritan found her and dropped her off at the hospital, or else someone drugged her but didn't get a chance to snatch her because that Good Samaritan—who for all we know was Cato's ghost—came by and messed up the killer's plans."

"So how do we figure out which it was?"

"That part will be easy," Caleb said.

"Oh?"

"The doctors are testing Renee's blood for drugs—including yaupon holly, which undoubtedly would have been in Martha's black drink and which our current killer seems to be relying on, too. As soon as they have answers, we'll have answers. At least on that score."

"What do we do until then?" Sarah asked.

"Well, it's nearly one a.m., and not only don't I believe your house is evil, I think your bedroom is quite extraordinary."

"So we're going to sleep?" she asked teasingly.

"Well, yes, eventually."

"And until then?"

He drew her close as they walked. "I have few ideas," he promised.

16

Sarah woke early, feeling as if she had enjoyed the sweetest night of sleep imaginable.

If ghosts had been prowling the house that night, they were kindly spirits, tiptoeing past and happy to let the house's owner savor a night in her lover's arms.

When she opened her eyes, Caleb was already up, showered and dressed, and looking down at her intently.

"What's up?" she asked him.

"I have several things I need to do this morning," he told her. "So why don't you get up and get dressed, and then I'll drop you at the museum and get started."

"If you need to go now, it's okay. You don't have to wait for me. It's broad daylight."

He shook his head. "I don't trust anyone or anything right now. The victims were really all just *young* women. Please, Sarah? At first, I thought it was a serial killer who chose a *type*, but now we know the victims are young woman, not necessarily a physical type."

"All right," she told him.

"Then . . . hop to it," he said, grinning.

Something trembled deep in her belly. It was crazy, but despite everything going on, she was falling head over heels for him. A killer was stalking the city and she should be afraid, but she wasn't. She was, despite everything, almost unbearably happy to be falling in love.

She hurried into the shower, then dressed quickly and found him downstairs. He'd made coffee, and she drank a cup quickly before being ushered out the door.

"Sarah!" Caroline said happily when she let herself into the employee lounge. "You decided to work today after all, huh? Great. Now the whole gang's here."

Renee and Barry walked in just then, already in costume. Renee had arranged a lock of hair to cover the bandage on her forehead, and Barry looked elegant. Not like Cato, but with his costume and from a distance . . .

He might have been a ghost.

"It's going to be a great day," Caroline said cheerfully. "And tomorrow, *I'm* taking a day off."

Caleb headed to the morgue first.

Floby was elbow-deep in an autopsy when he arrived, but an assistant led Caleb back. "I haven't been barred by Jamison yet?" he asked.

"No. I think he would have liked to, but apparently, he doesn't dare. Your boss has some serious pull." Floby was in scrubs, standing behind a stainless steel gurney that bore the remnants of Winona Hart.

Caleb tried not to look, but it was impossible.

Her body had been washed, and her pale features had somehow escaped being eaten by insects and worms. Floby had already opened the rib cage, revealing her organs.

"Can you tell me anything about how she died?" Caleb asked.

"I've taken tissue and blood samples, but no, I can't tell you much yet. I've just begun my exam. However . . ."

"However?"

"I got some info back from the lab. Your DNA is a matchup to the lady in the trunk."

Caleb wasn't surprised by the news, though he was blindsided by the pang that shot through his heart. Eleanora had died so long ago. An unwed mother during the Civil War, she had somehow managed to hide her child, allowing Cato to claim him on his return, then escape with his son, even though he'd had to abandon all hope of ever again seeing the woman he had loved, or even learning her fate.

"Was she drugged?"

"Patience, buddy. Some tests take longer than others. Don't you want to ask me about this young lady?"

"Well?"

"Totally drained of blood," Floby said.

Caleb's next stop was the hospital, where he talked to Doctor Thayer, who apologized because he hadn't received results back yet, either.

Next Caleb went to the police station, where he was told that Tim Jamison was out in the field.

He tried the lieutenant's cell phone, but Jamison wasn't picking up—at least not for him. After that Caleb headed for the cemetery, but though there was a highly visible police presence, Jamison wasn't there, either.

He left, finding his way along the narrow streets, and suddenly saw Jamison's car, minus Jamison, parked in front of an empty lot.

An empty lot filled with mud. Did they come there just to park, believing they were away from prying eyes?

Caleb was convinced that Jamison was having an affair with the very beautiful and more than a little suspicious Cary Hagan, but did that make him a murderer?

Caleb drove back around to the plaza and parked, ready to hit the pavement again, now that he was certain that the present-day victims were being scoped out and then abducted from local bars,

"Gary just called and said he can't get into your house," Caroline said, catching Sarah just as she was about to begin a tour.

"Damn! I changed the locks and forgot to give him a key," Sarah said, feeling like an idiot.

"What do you want me to do? Tell him to crawl in through the basement window?" Caroline asked, laughing.

"No, just tell him I'll head over at lunch and open the door for him. I can leave in about half an hour."

Caroline shrugged. "Why don't you just call him yourself? I can cover you here. And you can't leave until someone can go with you. I won't have you going over there alone, not after what happened before."

"Thank you for worrying, even though there's no need," Sarah said. Smiling, she headed back to the employee lounge, found her phone and called Gary, promising to get there as soon as she could find an escort.

"As far behind as we already are, another half hour or so won't make any difference," he said, sounding resigned. "Just as long as there are no more bones in the walls."

"They say they found them all," Sarah reassured him. "So I'll see you as soon as I can get away."

Renee came in just as she was finishing her conversation. "I'll walk you over there now, if you want to go," she offered."I probably shouldn't be here today, anyway. I'm still a little woozy."

"All right. I'll just let Caroline know we're leaving," Sarah said. "A couple of interns from the college are here today to help out, so it's not like she and Barry will have to handle everything on their own."

A few minutes later, as they walked down the street—still in costume, which drew waves from the tourists—Sarah saw that Renee was frowning and asked her what was wrong.

"I really wish I could remember what had happened," Renee said. She glanced at Sarah. "I'm so sorry for making trouble. I don't know why I was so certain the guy in costume was Caleb. When I think about it now . . ."

"Don't worry about it."

"But I told Lieutenant Jamison I thought it was him. Won't that cause a lot of trouble for him?"

"It's all right. Really. Here we are. And there's Gary, waiting on the porch."

"Don't you two look gorgeous," Gary said as they reached him. "Renee, I heard what happened. You doing okay?"

"I'm fine, Gary, thanks. Thirsty, though. You have any diet sodas, Sarah?"

"Yeah, give me a sec and I'll get you one."

As Sarah walked into the house, heading straight for the kitchen, her cell phone rang. She rummaged in her purse—a big leather thing that looked ridiculous in comparison to her costume—and saw that it was Caroline.

"Hey," she said. "Is everything all right?"

"Yeah—great, actually. I left the college kids helping Barry and started crawling around in the archives, and I found some stuff on your house. I even found a picture of the witchy housekeeper. Stay there, and I'll bring them over to you. Wait— you're not alone, right?"

"No. Gary and Renee are here."

"Where's your hunk of heaven?"

Sarah laughed. "Caleb? Investigating."

"Okay, I'll be right there," Caroline said and hung up.

Before Sarah could collect the sodas, her phone rang again. This time it was Caleb.

"What's going on?" she asked him.

"I've been to see Floby, and he's still waiting on results. But my DNA is a match for Eleanora's."

"Oh, Caleb, it's what we thought," she said. "Are you all right? They're your ancestors. Maybe we can arrange to have her buried with Cato. It shouldn't be that hard to find out where he's buried."

"That's a nice thought, but it's not why I called you."

"Oh?"

"I just got a call back on the testing I asked for on Renee's blood."

"And?" she asked.

"She had yaupon holly in her bloodstream."

"So she *was* an intended victim!" Sarah said. Before he could answer, she heard a noise from the front of the house, then a worrisome silence.

She didn't want to worry Caleb, but she needed to see what was going on. "Oh, hell, it's getting busy around here," she said. "I'd better go."

She set her phone down and raced to the front of the house.

"Renee? Gary?"

"In here—ladies parlor!" Renee called.

Sarah started to head in that direction, then heard the front doorknob turning. A moment later, Caroline, in costume, walked in, looking very excited. She had a big bag over her shoulder, and a large cup of take-out coffee in each hand. "I've brought the stuff—let's go look at it."

"Great. Renee and Gary are in the parlor, so—"

"Good, they can look, too. Only I don't have coffee for them."

"Someone can have mine," Sarah offered.

"No, I know how you love your coffee, and I got extra sugar in it—it's marked on the cup—just the way you like it. I'll give mine to Gary, if you don't mind making some tea. Renee prefers tea, anyway," Caroline said.

Sarah shrugged. "No prob. I'll put the kettle on and be right there."

Caleb walked into a bar on a side street just off Castillo. As his eyes adjusted to the light, he realized that Cary Hagan was sitting at the bar.

And she was wiping tears from her cheeks.

"Cary?" he said cautiously, approaching her. "Can I . . . do anything?"

She flashed him an angry glare. "Don't you think you've done enough?"

"I'm sorry?"

"You should be. I've just been fired."

He sat down on the stool next to her and asked, genuinely puzzled,

"How is it my fault that you were fired?"

"Tim broke up with me, and then Mr. Griffin fired me, all because of you."

"I've never even spoken with Mr. Griffin," he told her, noticing the empty glasses in front of her and deciding to cut her some slack.

"But you've made Tim's life hell, making him look incompetent because *you*, Mr. Hotshot, are always the one to make the breakthrough. He called and told me all about it this morning. And then he said how you practically accused him of being the killer just because he had mud on his shoes. And then . . . Then he broke up with me, because he said being with me so much was getting in the way of his career, plus people were starting to talk about us and his wife was starting to suspect. So I left and went to find him and try to get him to change his mind, but he wouldn't listen, and when I got back to the house, an ambulance was there, because Mr. Griffin had fallen out of his chair—and he fired me!"

"Cary, I'm sorry, but I don't see how I'm responsible because you decided to date a married man, not to mention you're the one who left your patient alone so you could try to get your lover back," Caleb pointed out calmly.

"Well, I'm ready to blow this town anyway," she said, shaking her head. "Everyone pretends to be nice, and then they turn around and talk about you behind your back. And to think I was sorry about that Renee Otten the other night. Well, I'm not sorry now. She got what she deserved."

"How do you see that?" Caleb asked.

"She talked about Tim and me, just like the rest of them," Cary said. "I saw the way they all looked at us in Hunky Harry's. Well, I've seen a few things, too, let me tell you."

"Like what?" Caleb asked.

"For one thing, I can tell you that Miss Goody Two-shoes is nothing but a lying, slutty little bitch."

"Who are you talking about?" Caleb asked her.

"Oh, my God! Do you think this was really written by her—by Martha Tyler?" Sarah demanded.

Caroline had brought a book she'd found in the archives. It wasn't a spell book but a grim record of the mortuary's activities. It listed the dead and which room they were in, and, often, how they had died. Caroline had found a picture of the house-keeper, as well. The woman had been stunning, with proud, strong features and large dark eyes that would have been able to seduce any man whose heart was beating. She had worn the plain clothing of a servant as if she were a queen and they were robes of the finest satin.

"Of course it was written by her," Caroline said, excited. "And isn't the picture amazing?"

Absently, Sarah took another swallow of her coffee and stared at the picture. All of a sudden, it seemed to move.

"Look at her dancing," Caroline said.

She *was* dancing, Sarah thought, and beckoning to her.

"Sarah? Sarah, are you all right?" Renee asked, as if from a great distance.

No, she wasn't all right, Sarah thought, but she couldn't seem to get the words out. Everything in the room was moving, and her limbs were growing heavy, her vision narrowing, as she slid to the floor.

All she could see was Caroline, smiling.

"Sarah?" Renee was leaning over her, looking worried. Sarah tried to answer Renee, and then she tried—and failed—to warn her when, to her absolute disbelief, she saw Gary pick up the fireplace poker and slam it against Renee's head.

Renee fell to the ground with a startled expression and her lips forming a silent *O*.

Gary? Gary was the killer?

And not just Gary.

Caroline. Her best friend, now completely insane. Standing there and smiling benignly as she said, "I found all this history, Sarah. No one ever thought I was as good a historian as you are, but I am, and I proved it when I found all these documents—documents *you* missed—in this house. It should have been my house, you know. And one

388

day, it will be. I found Martha Tyler's book—not this book, her spell book—and she said if we drink the blood of the young and healthy, we can live forever. Oh, Sarah, I really am sorry. I didn't want to hurt you, and we tried to scare you off, but you wouldn't go away. And you and Caleb are so ridiculously good at finding bodies and figuring out the truth." She sighed sadly and went on. "Now, when he comes looking for you—and we both know he will, especially because sooner or later he'll check your phone and see the text message I left you saying I found a reference to the old Rebel cemetery when I was going through the archives—he'll die, too. But we'll make sure he looks guilty of killing you and Renee first, and if we're lucky, maybe he'll take the fall for Winona, too."

"It's still daylight, what do we do now?" Gary asked.

"We take them out to your truck in burlap bags, and then we dump them. We'll have to use another cemetery, though, which sucks. I really liked using Martha's final resting place, but we can use that old one out by the highway. Now get moving," Caroline snapped. "We have to move quickly. And we've got to be on our game tonight. It has to look as if I barely escaped Caleb before I managed to kill him. You have the knife—and a gun, right?"

Gary nodded, and then they left the room, presumably in search of burlap bags and God only knew what else.

Paralyzed as she lay on the floor, Sarah tried desperately to think of a way out, a way to at least leave a clue for anyone who came looking for her. A way to warn Caleb and save his life, even if it were at the expense of her own.

She couldn't move or speak, but she could still see.

And what she saw was a man in nineteenth-century clothes.

It was Cato, and when he hunkered down next to her and swept his plumed hat from his head, he looked at her with deep sorrow in his eyes.

Help me, Sarah thought.

The floor was still coated in plaster dust. If she could just move a finger, she could write a message, but though she tried, her muscles remained stubbornly paralyzed.

Help me, she pleaded to the apparition again.

Somehow he understood, and though it seemed to be difficult for him, he reached for her hand and started to write. She tried to think, but the world was beginning to fade. She heard Gary and Caroline come back in, saw them reenter the room carrying huge burlap bags that had once held cement. She could still see the ghost as he followed while she was dragged across the floor.

No, stay here, she ordered him silently. *You have to lead Caleb to me.*

But she knew he was still with her, even as she was tied into the bag and tossed into the back of Gary's work truck.

"There's only one word for that woman, no matter how sweet as pie she acts!" Cary exploded. "She was at the bar that night, too, sneaking around and watching her friend."

"Cary . . . are you saying that Caroline Roth was at the bar the night Renee Otten was attacked?"

"She was lurking in the back, but yeah, I saw her. Just like I've seen her with that guy who's fixing up Sarah's house," Cary said.

He was off his bar stool before she'd even finished speaking.

He called the museum as he ran, but the college kid who answered told him that the only docent there was Barry Travis.

He tried Sarah's home phone and got the machine, then her cell, which only rang and rang before going to voice mail.

He forgot all about his car and ran all the way to her house. The door was open when he tried the knob, sending a chill coursing through him. "Sarah!"

There was no answer. He checked out the downstairs, and when he reached the kitchen, he saw her purse and phone lying in the counter. He ran down into the basement, but it was empty, then raced up the stairs and through the bedrooms.

He tried the attic.

He hurtled down the stairs again, then stopped short, staring, sure he was dreaming.

But he wasn't.

A host of people were standing in the foyer as if they'd been waiting for him forever, their clothing elegant and their eyes sad.

One woman stepped forward. She was extremely beautiful, with translucent blue eyes, and she looked at him sympathetically as she reached for him. And even though he could see through her, he felt her gentle touch on his face as she directed his attention to the ladies' parlor.

He walked closer and saw drag marks through the plaster dust.

And then . . .

He leaned down . . . and examined a series of smudges, realizing that they spelled out words.

rebel cemetery gun kill you

He stood and raced for his car, his phone already to his ear.

Sarah slowly came to. She was lying in a cemetery, and as soon as she looked around, she knew which one. It was a very old one and had served the out-lying farms. Rebel soldiers were buried here, along with Spanish homesteaders and British immigrants. There was even a mound marking the final resting place of some of the Yankees who had died at the battle of Olustee.

She was lying on an old stone sarcophagus, and

she was vaguely aware of voices droning in the background. She tested her muscles and realized that she could move—just a little bit, but at least she was no longer totally paralyzed.

She managed to turn her head toward the voices and blinked, sure she must be hallucinating, then realizing that this was all too real. She saw two figures in hooded capes, one holding a massive bowl, the other a huge curved knife with elaborate engraving along the blade.

The words . . . they were chanting were a mixture of English, French and something else she didn't recognize. Maybe Spanish. Maybe Creole.

"For blood is life!" one of them cried as they lifted the bowl and knife toward the sky.

Where was Renee? she wondered. Had they already killed her?

Suddenly one of the figures moved closer and loomed over her. From the size, she realized it was Gary.

"Let's do it," Caroline said impatiently.

"No. Not yet. I want to play with her," Gary said, tossing back his hood as he leaned down, staring at Sarah in fascination. He smiled cruelly. "Her eyes are open. She sees me. Or maybe a dragon. Or a monster. Maybe a giant wolf."

"Gary, get away from her."

Gary flashed Caroline an angry look. "I get to play with the girls first, because I am the god. That's what it says in the book."

"Not her," Caroline insisted.

"Especially her," Gary said. "I love her. I've always loved her. But she never loved me. Never."

"Get away from her, Gary. We have to hurry. What's the matter with you? She has to die, and we have to be ready when Caleb gets here—we have to kill him and then mess me up so it looks like he tried to kill me, too. Get smart, Gary, come on," Caroline urged.

"Shut up! Give me a minute."

He touched Sarah's face, and she tried not to twitch. She couldn't let him know that she was starting to be able to move, because she needed the element of surprise.

She might have only one chance of saving herself.

Caleb drew his car up in the shelter of the trees outside the cemetery wall and killed the motor. He got out and scaled the wall, dropping silently to the ground and moving carefully between the old headstones until he could see them.

Gary was bending down over a weathered sarcophagus, with a knife in his hand as he stared intently at Sarah.

Or Sarah's body.

No.

Caroline was standing beneath a tree.

Where was Renee?

He looked around and he saw a burlap bag bulging with . . .

Renee's body. Dead or alive.

He held still for a long moment, watching, judging his distance. Wondering how far behind him the police cars were.

Then, to his amazement, he saw . . . himself. No, not himself. Cato. Running toward Gary and Caroline.

"It's him!" Caroline shrieked. "Shoot him, Gary! Shoot him!"

Gary straightened, dropping the knife as he pulled a gun from under his robe and started to fire. His aim was good.

But there was no way to shoot a ghost.

Caleb counted the shots, then leapt to his feet when he reached six and made a beeline toward the action. Gary took aim again. At him.

He drew his own weapon as Caroline let out a shriek of pure fury and went racing toward Sarah, grabbing the knife off the ground as she ran.

Caleb's shot took Gary down. He had aimed to kill. And he did.

But now Caroline was on top of Sarah, knife raised. Suddenly Sarah lashed out with her legs, catching Caroline in the chest.

Caroline flew backward, slammed into a tall headstone, then fell forward again.

Right on the knife she had meant to use on Sarah.

A blood sacrifice.

• • •

It was days before everything began to untangle and the full truth came out. The police reached the cemetery moments after Caroline's death, leading to hours of interrogation for Sarah and Caleb, while Renee, who this time didn't regain consciousness for hours, made her second trip to the hospital in twenty-four hours.

At the station, Jamison had the grace to apologize and then fell silent. Then there was the process of trying to understand what had triggered Caroline's insanity, even as Sarah, stunned, grieved for the loss of her best friend, a friend she now realized she had never really known.

As they put the pieces together, Caroline's MO began to emerge. She had lived with her parents, so every night, after Will saw her home, she had turned around and gone back out to meet Gary. It would always be impossible to know for sure, but apparently they'd started dabbling in black magic years earlier. At first it had been a lark, a fun way to scare themselves, but somewhere along the way they'd started to take it seriously, and their murderous rampage had begun.

And while there was no way to prove it—and in fact, Sarah would never even consider trying, since she had no desire to be branded insane—Sarah suspected that maybe the insanity that drove them had been a result of the original Martha Tyler's curse. How else to explain not only their actions but those of the forever unidentified killer who had murdered Mr. Griffin's daughter and the other missing girls back in the 1920s?

The house was gone over with a fine-tooth comb, and Jennie Lawson's body was found buried beneath the stack of crates in the basement. And because Caroline had been so determined to emulate Martha Tyler, she had left behind a book of her own, which her parents found in her bedroom.

She and Gary had killed Frederick Russell when he had found them trying to stuff a drugged Jennie Lawson into Greg's truck, then come up with the idea of sending both him and his car to the bottom of the bay.

Given the DNA match, Caleb was able to claim the body of Eleanora Stewart.

Will was stunned. He had never suspected that Caroline had a secret life, and he seemed ready to wallow in his misery for the foreseeable future. But then Cary offered her shoulder, and Sarah didn't think it would take long for them to do more than commiserate together.

Ten days after the events in the cemetery, Sarah and Caleb headed to Virginia, where they traced the grave of Cato MacTavish and saw Eleanora laid to rest next to him.

Sarah was never entirely sure that she wasn't dreaming, but she could have sworn she saw the two of them together.

Not at the cemetery.

But when she woke in the middle of the night.

They were standing at the foot of the bed, arm in arm, looking down at her and Caleb with approving smiles.

Caleb moved slightly, reaching to take her into his arms.

Then they faded gently away, and Sarah had the feeling that she would never see them again but that there would be others like them in her future.

Caleb edged closer to her, his body like a sleek spoon against her.

"My love," he murmured.

She closed her eyes, filled with the sense that so long as she was in his arms, she was exactly where she was supposed to be. She didn't know what the future would hold, if they would set up house-keeping in Virginia or move back to St. Augustine, or go somewhere else entirely, and she realized with complete serenity that it didn't matter.

Whatever they did now, they would do together, and that was all that mattered.

Center Point Publishing
600 Brooks Road ● PO Box 1
Thorndike ME 04986-0001 USA

(207) 568-3717

US & Canada:
1 800 929-9108
www.centerpointlargeprint.com

B

Graham, Heather.

Unhallowed ground